THE FIRST BAYONET
Steven Hildreth, Jr.

ISBN: 1478380640
ISBN-13: 978-1478380641

The Ben Williams Series by Steven Hildreth, Jr.

The First Bayonet
The Sovereigns

For Zayne

"A revolution is an idea which has found its bayonets."
-Napoleon Bonaparte

THE FIRST BAYONET

CHAPTER ONE

Heliopolis, Cairo, Egypt
15 July 2006
09:30 hours Eastern European Time (07:30 hours Zulu)

THE TEMPERATURE WAS EIGHTY degrees and rising. That would persuade some people back home to forego the cup of coffee in lieu of an energy drink, but Ben Williams was set in his ways. He'd had a hot cup of joe every morning for the past twenty-nine years, long before the age of Red Bull and Monster. Williams did not have anything against those drinks—in fact, he loved Red Bull—but his strict rule was that between sundown and noon, it was coffee time. His first two cups accompanied some *eish masri* bread with a sweet *kessiah* pudding, and he began his third with his second cigarette of the day. It was a meager meal, but it would get him through the day.

Williams pulled on the cigarette, flicked the excess ash, and took another sip of coffee. Dressed in a khaki polo shirt, loose-fitting jeans, and beat-up New Balance sneakers, he looked like any other Western tourist, and the Canon digital camera slung around his neck added to the perception. He almost blended in, which was as good as he could get with his six-foot-five and two hundred and fifty pound frame. That was where his demeanor played a crucial role: his face was impassive, his head pointed no place in particular, his posture relaxed. Black aviator shades covered his hardened brown eyes, which went a long way in hiding what he really was. With a thick beard, he would have been able to better blend in with the populace, but being clean shaven accentuated his non-Arab features.

After one last drag, he snubbed the cigarette in the ash tray and finished his coffee. He checked the watch on his left wrist: *09:35*. Williams dug into his pocket for his billfold, left a Canadian twenty dollar bill on the table, and stood. He stretched, worked some of the kinks out of his arms and neck, then walked to the gate and made his way down the street. As he walked, Williams kept his hands in his pockets and kept silent. Across the street, a family of four stopped next to a building to consult a map.

Williams contemplated the scene. During his reconnaissance, he had been thinking like a shooter, not a tourist. He had walked the quarter several times over the past few days and memorized his travel routes. The subterfuge factor that a map could provide had eluded him until that moment. Williams suppressed a grimace and let out a long exhale past his pursed lips.

Shit, he cursed internally. *Oh, well, fuck it.*

Cars raced past on the street to his right as he continued along his way. Williams resisted the temptation to light another cigarette. He was on a tight schedule and he had to be in position, or else the play would not work. Behind his shades, his eyes moved left to right, up and down, and checked everybody's hands. The likelihood that he had been compromised was slim, but the government was not known for its tolerance or trust of the people. Unlike back home, the only thing Cairo law enforcement needed for an arrest was an excuse, regardless of how flimsy. There were no boundaries the police could not cross, so long as it was done in the name of homeland defense and the subject did not have enough money to bribe their way out, in that order.

Williams reached the intersection of Ibrahim al-Lakani and al-Ahram. After a pause, he received the signal to walk, and he crossed al-Ahram. He waited at the other corner, tapping his foot incessantly. Williams checked his watch again—*09:38*. The window was still open, but it was waning quickly. Finally, the pedestrian signal gave him the affirmative, and he briskly crossed and continued on al-Ahram.

As he walked down Al-Ahram, Williams paused for a second, glanced at the building to his left, and snapped a photograph. He did this three more times as he followed al-Ahram all the way until it curved to the front of the building and merged with al-Nadi. He checked his watch one more time—*09:44*.

Perfect timing.

Williams brought the camera to his right eye, aimed at the edifice, and snapped a picture. He looked at the preview screen and smiled at the picture quality. Next, he shifted his focus to the armed guards patrolling the premises, their MISR-90 Kalashnikov knockoffs held at the low ready. He took a picture of their patrol from afar, then zoomed in and snapped a picture of each individual soldier as they made their way around the building. Williams's last photograph was of the two soldiers posted by the door, their expressions stoic.

Good shots, Williams thought. *Maybe I'll sell these to* Time *when I'm done.*

Next, Williams took a photo of the view in front of him. He then faced outward and started snapping photos of the adjacent building, focusing on the rooftops and upper floors. Satisfied, Williams continued down al-Nadi and stopped when he was roughly symmetrical to his previous position. He repeated the routine: the buildings, the guard patterns, the soldiers, and the adjacent buildings. With the front covered, Williams retraced his steps towards al-Ahram.

* * *

FROM THE LOWEST LEVEL rent-a-cops to the Secret Service presidential detail, working the camera room was the bane of every security guard's existence. It required long hours of staring at television screens and staying awake. That did not sound like much to the average person, but those who had done it could attest its monotony. As the low man on the totem, Corporal Dhakir Mukhtar was saddled with camera duty while the more experienced soldiers—all sergeants—guarded the complex in preparation of their principal's arrival.

When Mukhtar had volunteered for the Republican Guard, he had been promised advanced training and postings that would pave the way for career advancement. He had proven himself as a mechanized soldier in the 9th Armoured Division's 314th Brigade, and had come highly recommended to the Republican Guard. Upon completion of his requisite training,

Mukhtar had been given a promotion from private to corporal, and within six months, he had been assigned to the big detail. Being a corporal in the company of sergeants made him the whipping boy for the less-than-desirable details. His situation rapidly approached the point where he considered completing his term of service and getting as far away from the army as possible.

Despite his sinking morale, Mukhtar brought a level of professionalism to his job rarely seen in men who shared his twenty-one years of age. He never read a book or watched television during his six-hour shifts, and he certainly did not fall asleep. Mukhtar would bring a bag of pistachios, a couple bottles of water, and watch each screen intently for even the slightest threat. He always sat up straight to prevent complacency and to be afforded a greater view of the camera feeds.

Something on one of the front cameras caught the thin young corporal's attention, and he leaned forward for a better look. His eyes narrowed as he took in the image: a man, dressed in civilian clothing, snapping photos of the building. That, in and of itself, was normal. It *was* a historical building, and it was just the kind of thing a tourist would love to show to their friends back home. After a few shots, the man would turn around and snap a few more pictures. The man moved to the right side of the front gate and repeated the process. After a moment, he began making his way back down al-Nadi, where he had first appeared.

A map was posted on the wall, adjacent the right side of the television monitors. Mukhtar spun to face it and placed his index finger on the red pin that marked the complex. He moved his finger to the front gate, then moved it in the direction that the man had faced. Several buildings in that direction afforded the proper distance and elevation necessary to hit a target inside the compound. Mukhtar traced his finger to the east and saw more of the same. He looked at the screen once more and barely caught the man as he disappeared around the corner and back onto al-Ahram.

Mukhtar reached for the radio on his duty belt and brought it to his lips. "Sergeant Arfan, this is Corporal Mukhtar."

Sergeant Arfan, the senior non-commissioned officer on duty, came back a moment later. "What is it, Corporal?"

"I've got a suspicious looking man photographing the premises," Mukhtar said calmly. "He took an interest in both the complex and the surrounding buildings."

"Could just be a tourist," Arfan replied.

"If he was just focused on the building, maybe," Mukhtar said. "Looks to me like he's scoping out angles for sniper hides."

The line was silent for a moment. "How do you know you're not just imagining this?"

"Sergeant, with respect," Mukhtar said, his tone tactful yet firm, "are you sure you want to risk being wrong today?"

After another long pause, Arfan finally came back with, "All right. I'm close to where he's headed. Moving to intercept."

"Roger that." Mukhtar clipped the radio to his belt, locked his eyes on the screen, and folded his arms.

What are you up to, you bastard?

* * *

WILLIAMS MADE GOOD TIME back to the compound's rear side, where security was heavier. Once the rear was within view, he brought his camera up and started taking photos. The guards there were even more vigilant than their counterparts in the front, as if they expected something or someone important. He got the shots he was looking for, then did a one-eighty and started to scope the background. The trajectories and distances came to him slowly. Williams would have more time to work out the finer points once he got into position.

He lowered the camera and turned to walk to the opposite side when three men sporting woodland camouflage and MISR-90s moved in his direction. Their faces revealed their intent, but Williams moved forward and continued to thumb through his pictures. He literally bumped into the front man, a bearded gentleman whose muscles bulged from beneath his fatigues. At the last second, Williams pulled his camera back and out of the soldiers' reach.

"What are you doing here, sir?" the front man asked. He was a sergeant by the look of his rank.

Williams pointed to his camera and looked the soldier in the eye. "I-I'm taking photos. Who are you?"

"And what are you taking photos of?"

"Who are you?" Williams repeated, with a hint of

indignation.

"What are you taking photographs of, sir?" The sergeant took a step forward. "I won't ask again."

"I will *not* be bullied by you jackbooted government types!" Williams declared. His voice rose in crescendo. "I am a Canadian citizen and you have no right—"

The sergeant grabbed the camera and yanked it towards himself. Williams maintained his grip. His left hand balled into a fist and struck the sergeant in the solar plexus, which knocked the wind out of him. Williams then cocked back and threw a giant haymaker that went clear over the sergeant's head and left his ribs and back open. The sergeant's escorts took advantage of this and drove their rifle stocks into Williams's back. He relinquished the camera as he fell to the ground. Once he hit the sidewalk, Williams huddled into a ball to protect his vital organs while the three guards kicked him furiously and repeatedly. Fifteen seconds passed before the sergeant grabbed his comrades and pulled them back.

"*That's enough!*" he bellowed. "Azeem, restrain him and bring him inside the compound. Stand guard while Badr and I call for transport."

"You've got it," Azeem said. He pulled out a pair of flexible cuffs from his cargo pocket, rolled Williams on his back, and bound his hands together. After he tightened the cuffs, he grabbed Williams by the arm, dragged him inside the gate, and sat him on the pavement with his back against the gate. Azeem angled himself to where he would have a good view of his surroundings and still have eyes on the prisoner.

Williams let out a short exhale and hung his head. He smiled.

CHAPTER TWO

Raleigh, North Carolina
10 July 2006
11:45 hours Eastern Standard Time (16:45 hours
Zulu)

THE SUN TOOK ITS pound of flesh as Williams worked the hammer. He placed the long nail along the ballistic rubber's seam, gave it a few taps to get it through the rubber, through the plywood sheet, and into the oak beam, and then moved his fingers clear and struck the nail hard repeatedly until the nail's head was flush with the rubber. He wiped his forehead with his arm and forced a short sigh past his lips. There was a slight breeze outside, but the walls kept it out, which left Williams drenched. His button-down plaid shirt had been removed and draped over the door, which left his attire as his jeans, boots, a wifebeater, a black Camelbak, and an worn royal blue ball cap with the old Broncos "D" logo worn backwards. He reached for his Camelbak's nipple, brought it to his mouth, and sipped water. It had been a smart move to fill the hydration bladder with ice water before he left his apartment. Williams cleared his throat as he finished his sips and returned the nipple to the hook on the Camelbak's shoulder strap.

Williams heard footsteps and automatically looked to the doorway. Lauren Kline wore a black tanktop, khaki cargo pants, and brown leather Ariat boots. Her long, dark hair was tied in a messy bun that rest beneath her dark Red Sox cap. The former CIA targeting officer held a hammer in her hand and had a determined expression on her face. Williams gave her a once-over, gave her a look, then turned back to the wall.

"What's with you?" Williams asked.

"Hoping to get off work in the next couple of hours," Kline said. "Sox are playing at one-thirty."

Williams shrugged as he began to work on the next nail. "Better get to work, then. Peyton and Verna are pretty adamant that we get this shoothouse operational."

"We seem to have been doing just fine without it," Kline said. She moved to the pile of ballistic rubber, grabbed a panel, and grabbed a naked piece of real estate.

"You shrug it off," Williams said. "Shooting skills aren't as emphasized on the spooky side of the house. Imagine Delta or SOG saying, 'Fuck it, static ranges are good to go.' You wanna play like the best, you've gotta train like the best. A proper shoothouse is critical."

"I still don't see the problem with the tire house," Kline said, referring to the poor man's shoothouse that Ronin Defense had been using for training for the past year.

"Lauren," Williams asked, "when's the last time you found a house made of tires out in sector?"

Kline bobbed her head from side to side, then pursed her lips in resignation. "Fair point."

"I'll tell you what it is," Williams said. He reached for another nail, lined it up, and gave it a few light taps with the hammer. "It's that you're having to do the leg work. That's why you want to settle for the house of tires."

"Hey, now," Kline said. "I don't have a problem with hard work. I have a problem with stupid work. If we've got the money to build the shoothouse, then why don't we have the money to hire contractors to build it for us?"

"Because we're not on rock solid ground yet," Williams said. "We've had a solid year of contracts, enough to keep us afloat, but if we start spending like sailors in a whorehouse, we'll go under real fast." Williams paused. "There's also the security issue. The less people who are aware of our facilities, the better."

"*Now* you're speaking my language," Kline said. "Wanting to control information makes sense. I could think of a few ways around that, but that's an acceptable answer."

"Good," Williams said.

"I still want to see the Sox game," Kline said. "It's the last of a four-game series with the Orioles. They won the first one, we won the second, and they won the third. We need a win going into the Yankees game on Thursday."

"I hate to be a pessimist," Williams said as he drove another nail into the rubber, "but don't y'all have a Curse of the Gambino or something that pretty much means you're not going to win shit?"

Kline snorted, then looked over her shoulder and said, "You don't watch baseball, do you?"

"Nah." Without looking, Williams reached with his left hand and pointed to his hat's logo with his thumb. "Football. Played it for two years in high school. Coaches said I had potential."

Kline's eyes narrowed. "Why only two years?"

Williams smiled as nostalgia fogged his mind. "Found that chasing skirts and making money was a better way to kill time than reading Shakespeare or solving for X."

"Typical." Kline rolled her eyes and said, "Anyway, for starters, Gambino is the name of a crime family. You're thinking the Curse of the *Bambino*. As in, Babe Ruth?"

"All right," Williams said.

"And for closers—"

"Coffee's for closers."

Kline cocked her head. "Huh?"

Williams chuckled, then shook his head and resumed work. "Nothing. For closers..."

"For closers, the Red Sox won the World Series in 2004. Swept the Cards. The curse is two years reversed."

"I stand corrected," Williams said.

"I'm gonna watch the game at B-Dubs," Kline said. "You should come with me."

"Like I said, not really a baseball guy," Williams said.

"I'll teach you what I know."

Williams put the hammer down, then turned to face Kline. "How about we grab B-Dubs to go, pick up some beer at Sheetz, and watch the game at your place."

Kline looked both ways before she shook an admonishing finger at Williams. "I'm onto your game, Williams." A smile spread on her face. "I'll take you up on it, but you're gonna sit there and watch the game. No funny business. You'll learn a thing or two."

The Nokia cell phone in Williams's pocket vibrated. As he dropped the hammer and stripped the gloves from his hands, he asked Kline, "I hope you've got some sort of incentive in mind for good students."

Kline raised her eyebrows. "Of course. You get to drink with me while enjoying America's pastime."

By that point, Williams held his phone in front of him and recognized the number. He hit the TALK button and held the phone to his ear. "Yes, sir."

"Blackstone's, thirty minutes. Come alone."

Williams stiffened. "Yes, sir."

Kline watched as Williams ended the call, placed the phone back in his pocket, and scratched his jaw. "Who was that?" she asked.

"Thrasher," Williams said.

Kline folded her arms. "What did he want?"

Williams raised his eyebrows and shrugged. "I don't know. I'm meeting him at Blackstone's. You want me to grab you something?"

"Just grab me a Gatorade on your way back," Kline said. "Gonna kick it into gear here so we can knock off early."

"Fair enough," Williams said. "A couple Praetorian snipers should be coming back from a known-distance range in a few. Shanghai them for construction duty if you need them."

"Can do easy," Kline said. "See you when you get back."

* * *

THE ESTABLISHMENT WAS BUILT just before the Second World War. It had been a condemned building during the eighties and nineties when a group of investors bought the joint and poured money into renovations. It was still down to earth and slummy in a dive bar fashion. The original wooden walls had been retained, for the most part, but behind the wood was solid concrete. Above the doorway was a white sign that read "Blackstone's Beers and Billiards," complete with a pair of crossed revolvers on either side of the text.

Blackstone's interior matched its exterior—the walls and floors were wooden, as were the tables, chairs, and stools. A couple of older televisions were mounted to the corners where two walls met the ceiling, and they streamed DirecTV. They were currently set to ESPN, where they usually stayed for the patrons to follow sports over beers and hot wings. Lights hung from the ceiling, providing just enough illumination to see clearly. There was also a couple of pool tables, a dartboard, and a miniaturized shuffleboard table. All of this furniture was hand-crafted, including the pool and shuffleboard tables.

From the front door, along the right wall was the bar, which sported an impressive collection of refrigerated beers and spirits. Shock Top, Landshark, Budweiser, Bud Lite, and Kiltlifter were the drafts on-tap. The bar itself was also handcrafted, made of a finely finished cherry wood. A lone television was mounted at the center of the wall and above the drinks. That afternoon, a couple of middle-aged working class types sat at the left end of the bar, nursing Bud Lites in a glass as they watched the baseball updates during an extended lunch.

John Thrasher's gray eyes analyzed the woman in front of him. Most people were put off by his willingness to stare beyond socially acceptable limits. It was not a leer or anything with perverse undertones, although the woman was indeed quite attractive. Thrasher's gaze was piercing, sizing her up. It also served as a catalyst: her reactions to his stare were telling as well. For the past twenty minutes, Thrasher had stared, and she had not blinked. He had to fight to smile. They did not make her type anymore, unflappable with a backbone. She looked young. If she was with the old breed, then she was the vanguard, the last of them before politics dictated her trade—*his* trade—was obsolete.

The door opened, and the woman's chestnut eyes moved to the door automatically. Thrasher watched her before he looked to the door himself. The woman knew how to case a room. The more he looked at her, the more familiar she was, but he could not place her. All she said was that she wanted both Thrasher and Ben Williams present. That put him on guard, but from the time he met with her, she had kept her hands in sight. The gesture did not put his mind at ease, but it was kind nonetheless.

Williams approached the table, dressed in a loose black T-shirt, jeans, and his work boots. Thrasher watched Williams's eyes acknowledge him, then drift to the left. He immediately made recognition and stepped forward, a smile dawning on his face.

"Lana?" Williams asked.

Lana Bouton stood and smiled. She wore a light-blue button-down blouse, tucked into jeans and completed with sneakers. Williams walked to her, and the two shared a friendly embrace. He stepped back, held her shoulders, and smiled.

"How the hell have you been?" Williams asked. "It's been like…what, five years?"

"Thereabouts," Bouton said. She brushed a strand of dark brown hair away from her right eye.

Williams's smile faltered. "What's the matter?"

"Sit," Bouton said.

"Now I know where I remember you," Thrasher said as he scratched his scraggly beard. "Bin Laden Issue Station. Bogotá before that."

"Very good," Bouton said. As Williams took a seat, she gestured to him. "I took the liberty of getting you water. That's basically all you're going to have time for."

"Is Langley contracting Ronin?" Williams asked. "I'm already not interested. I was dumb enough to take their contract after Tucson."

"Not Langley," Bouton said. "They don't know I'm here. Told them I was headed home for a few days, then switched flights on a cover ID."

Williams glanced ahead of him. A small mirror strip lined the wall, and in its reflection, Williams saw the two men at the bar. "You sure those guys aren't counterintel?"

"Positive," Bouton said. "Used a burner phone to touch base with Mr. Thrasher. Ran SDRs for an hour, ditched my rental down the street, and walked in from there. I've been here for an hour. Those guys have taken zero interest in me. They're too busy ogling the barkeep over liquid lunch."

"She's good," Thrasher said. "I believe her."

Williams looked at Thrasher. "That has nothing to do with the fact you probably cased the place yourself before you went in."

Thrasher took a sip of his water. "I haven't lived this long by being stupid."

Bouton gestured to the large purse that sat beside her. "I'm going to pull a portable DVD player out of her," she said for Thrasher's benefit. The DVD player was the side of a large hardcover book, with a four-inch folding screen and a headphone jack. Bouton slid it across toward Thrasher and Williams, then pulled out a set of earbuds and tossed them to Williams. He plugged the earbuds in, folded the screen up, offered an earbud to Thrasher, and placed the other bud in his right ear. Williams turned the portable player on, adjusted the volume, and hit play.

The picture filled the screen. Williams recognized an old friend's face as soon as it filled the screen. He had not aged much in the eighteen years that passed since they last saw each other. The major difference between then and now was that gray touched his beard, his hair was a little thinner, and worry was etched into his face.

"Peace be upon you, Benjamin, my friend," Ferran Anwar said. "I apologize for dispensing with the pleasantries, but I'm afraid I must get right down to business. My paternal cousin, Zaina, has been arrested. She has always drawn the ire of the ruling government with her opposition to their policies, but she took it a step further. She joined a group of like-minded individuals who initiated an underground radio station to speak out against government oppression. It lasted about a week before they honed in on the perpetrators. The Central Security Forces rounded them up in a series of raids and have imprisoned them in the Istiqbal-Tora Prison outside of Cairo."

Ferran looked over his shoulder worriedly, then leaned in closer to the camera. "I'm sure you're aware of how my government operates. When somebody is arrested for a political crime, it's the government's logic that their relatives are naturally implicated. In this case, that's completely untrue—I only found out the full extent of what Zaina was involved in after her arrest. However, the *Mukhabarat* could care less. They have already come looking for me. I've managed to stay off the grid, but I cannot file for asylum without my cousin. I cannot abandon her.

"I need your help, my friend. I need you to help us arrange political asylum, and I need you to break her out of prison. I will provide you with whatever operational funds and compensation you require, but I need to know as soon as possible whether you are willing to help. If I do not receive a response within a week of this message's recording, I will assume you are unwilling or unable to help, and will press forward on my own. God willing, this message will find you in a timely manner and you will find yourself in a position to assist me. Peace be upon you, and thank you, regardless of your decision."

Ferran looked over his shoulder once more before turning off the camera. Williams and Thrasher removed their earbuds, and Williams closed the DVD player before he slid it back across to Bouton. He interlaced his fingers, used his hands to prop up his chin, and let out a long sigh. After a long moment,

Thrasher took a sip of water and then broke the silence.

"From the way he spoke, he didn't sound sure whether or not you would come to his aid."

"That's because he is polite and unassuming to a fault," Williams said. "He knows I owe him big-time for the last time I was in Cairo." He looked to Thrasher. "You ran that op. You should remember."

"I remember," Thrasher said.

Williams returned his gaze to Bouton. "How did you come about this recording?"

"He paid a touring family two hundred dollars to deliver it to me," Bouton said.

"How does he know you?" Williams asked.

"He doesn't. He told them to deliver it to the Chief of Station."

Williams pursed his lips tighter together. He reached for his water glass, took a sip, and cleared his throat. "Give me the particulars on the woman."

Bouton removed a Palm Pilot from her purse, pulled the file up, and slid it across the table. Williams picked it up and read as Bouton spoke. "Dr. Zaina Ghonim Ishan Anwar, born 3 November 1961 in Philadelphia. Earned her bachelor's and her doctorate at Temple, and her master's at the American University in Cairo. She's lectured at both schools, as well as Stanford and the University of Bern. Until a week and a half ago, she was a tenured professor at the American University. No criminal record, no affiliations with any known terrorist groups. She's clean. Just another intelligent and idealistic educator imprisoned for sticking it to the man."

Williams leaned forward and studied the attached

photograph, presumably taken from the American University's website. She had shoulder-length black hair, tanned skin, and statuesque Semitic features. He only acknowledged her beauty in passing, instead electing to assess how long she would last in an Egyptian prison, which were not renowned for their human rights track record.

"What do we have on the prison?"

"Scroll left," Bouton said. Williams removed the stylus from its compartment and tapped the screen a couple of times. A grainy schematic filled the screen. Williams studied it as Bouton continued to speak. "The perimeter buildings are general population housing, with the exception of these three buildings on the north end. The two short ones, from west to east, are a prayer center and a library. The long building on the north side is their punishment block for troubled inmates."

Williams pointed to a set of buildings, and held the stylus in place as he turned the screen toward her. "What are those three buildings directly to the east of the soccer field?"

"One of them is a mess hall, and we're sure the two others are some sort of stock room or repair factory to put prisoners to work. The last building directly to the south of that, near the front gate, is the administrative building."

Williams faced the PDA toward him. Thrasher leaned over to study it. "You've got sniper towers with overlapping fields of fire, and a solid concrete wall surrounding the whole thing." Thrasher looked at Williams. "I know Istiqbal-Tora. It's Egypt's highest security compound. Not only are they fully staffed, there is a Central Security Force contingent on-site and a quick reaction force five minutes away. Sneaking in is damn near impossible, and any sort of assault is out of the question."

Bouton removed a small USB data stick and extended it toward Williams. "I'll be at the Sheraton Hotel until 21:00 hours tonight. If you're in, meet me before then. Don't take too long deciding. We've got a lot of mission prep and not a lot of time."

Williams looked at the data stick for a moment, then slowly reached out to accept it from Bouton. Once the stick was in his possession, Bouton retrieved her PDA and DVD player, packed both in her purse, then stood and nodded. "Gents."

Thrasher and Williams turned to watch Bouton walk out the door. Thrasher rolled his lips inward and shook his head. "Mmm. Solid tradecraft and a nice ass are the way to my heart." Williams gave him a look. "Oh, don't judge me. Acting like you weren't a horndog grunt once upon a time."

"Yeah, when I was a kid," Williams said. He shook his head. "Jesus, Boss."

"Though, really, she's not as hot as that Kline chick," Thrasher said. "Jesus tittyfucking Christ."

Williams said nothing. Peyton Neil, his section leader, had made clear for his shooters the penalty for sleeping with any of the female augmentee team members. Williams had kept his on-again, off-again arrangement with Lauren Kline subtle, and he had every intention of keeping it that way.

Williams changed the subject. "Let's get back to brass tacks. Most of my team is out of the country. I could take Lauren with me for operational support, but that's about it."

"Not on this one," Thrasher said with a shake of the head.

Williams's eyes narrowed. "What do you mean?"

"I mean that Ronin Defense Institute is barely over a year old," Thrasher said. "I mean that if we get caught up in an international shit storm like this, the Blackthorne-era bureaucrats embedded at Langley, State, and Justice will use this as an excuse to bring us all down. These are the same bureaucrats who won't lift a finger to help Zaina because one person is not worth jeopardizing a foreign partnership, particularly one that symbolizes one of our strongest allies in the terror fight."

"Why? Because they fight the Muslim Brotherhood? Partner of convenience, maybe. Ally?"

"You're also forgetting Israel. Our relations with Egypt get trashed, they get pushed toward a more radical bent, and you could be seeing the Six Day War, Part Two."

"That's such bullshit," Williams said. "It's not that hard to release her and just declare her *persona non grata*."

Thrasher held up his hands. "Don't shoot the messenger. The bottom line is they only care about politics. Aside from Lana Bouton and Ferran Anwar, the only ones who really give a shit about Dr. Anwar are you and me."

"And yet, I can't do anything," Williams said.

Thrasher paused, pressed his hands together, and held them in front of his lips. "I said Ronin couldn't get involved. I never said you couldn't go."

Double-talk was a language with which Williams

had grown familiar during his government service, first in the Army and later at the Agency. It was plausible deniability. Thrasher knew ordering Williams to stand down would be a deal breaker, but Thrasher needed Williams to know that if he went off the reservation, nobody would come for him. The thought would have terrified him as a young soldier, but it was business as usual for an intelligence officer. Thrasher knew Williams's reaction before Williams knew himself.

Williams picked up the water glass again and held it in front of his mouth. "*De oppresso liber*," he murmured as he took a drink.

Thrasher nodded, then slammed the rest of his water. "Good luck." He set the glass down, stood, and walked out of the establishment. Once Thrasher was out of sight, Williams dug into his pocket, pulled out the Nokia, and dialed a number from memory. The other party picked up on the second ring.

"You on your way back?" Lauren Kline said.

"I'm actually wondering how fast you can get to Blackstone's," Williams said.

"Probably in twenty, thirty minutes. Why?"

"I'm hoping by paying for lunch, I can make up for having to cancel on dinner."

Kline's tone changed on a dime. "What's going on?"

"Not over the phone." Williams killed the call, put the phone back in his pocket, buried his head in his hands, and sighed.

CHAPTER THREE

Istiqbal-Tora Prison
Cairo, Egypt
18 July 2006
08:00 hours Eastern European Time (06:00 hours
Zulu)

IT TOOK THREE DAYS for the police to process Williams. That time was spent in a cell, packed to the brim with other prisoners. There had been no room to lay down, so Williams had spent the entire time standing. The prisoners were not fed, and were sprayed down with a hose every day when the temperatures peaked. Most prisoners saw this as an opportunity to cool off and a chance to alleviate the collective stench. Williams would hold his mouth wide open and take in as much of the hose water as he could when it was aimed in his direction. The water was definitely not potable, but it was a basic survival rule that the body could not survive three days without water, so he drank every drop he could get. He had taken antibiotics in anticipation of ingesting the local water and food, but he couldn't determine yet if the rumble in his stomach was due to the water or the lack of food.

At six in the morning on the third day, Williams and fourteen others were finally released from the cell. Some fell over from the forced three-day stand, and others had trouble staying awake. Williams had forced himself to sleep for stretches at a time while standing, and had bent his knees as much as physically allowed to keep from locking up. His legs were wobbly coming out of the cell, but he quickly found his footing. They were escorted under arms to a blue armored van with no markings, and were told to board, one at a time. Once they were aboard, they were locked inside, and a few moments later, they were on the way.

Most of the inmates tried to catch some sleep during the ride. The rest stared around the compartment where they were housed, but none of them spoke. Williams was far too wired for sleep. He knew they were on their way to Istiqbal-Tora, and he was almost past the job's first hurdle. On top of that, he had no idea what kind of reception awaited them. Williams was no stranger to abuse in confinement—both in training and in real-world experience—and he knew that whatever the Egyptians had to dish out, he could take. That did not mean he would allow himself to be blindsided.

It was a silent thirty minutes before the van came to a stop absent the sound of other automobiles. The air smelled slightly cleaner than in the city, and Williams could hear the driver conversing with a gate guard. He adopted a blank stare and pretended not to understand the conversation. From the onset, Williams had decided to conceal his Arabic fluency, which would encourage the guards and the locals to speak freely in front of him. The two guards talked about transfer details and numbers, which were only peripherally important. Williams saved the information for later review.

The vehicle rolled forward again, and Williams steeled himself for what came next. As the van pulled to a stop, footsteps congregated by the door. After a moment of rustling, the doors swung open, and a guard climbed inside. That guard grabbed Williams by the shoulders and shoved him out of the back. Automatically, he tucked and rolled to absorb the shock. Other prisoners were not so lucky, and Williams thought he even heard one prisoner's wrist snap as he used his hands to break his fall.

Once the van was cleared of prisoners, the guards stood their new charges up and spaced them out. Working from both ends to the middle, they searched each body for weapons or contraband, such as cellular phones. Their search yielded no results, as the police officers at temporary lockup had confiscated all their contraband. Money, personal effects, and cash were allowed, though the guards helped themselves to some of the latter. The prisoners did not dare protest. Once they were cleared, the guards stepped back, and a short, pudgy, moustached man stepped out of the administration building. He wore the dark blue fatigues of the Central Security Forces, and sported an eagle and two stars on each epaulet. A black beret adorned his head, and he spoke with the tone of a man who mistook fear for respect.

"Listen carefully, you pieces of shit!" the officer said in Arabic. "I am Colonel Mustafa Mahdi Fath Abbas, and I am the warden of this prison! You *will* listen to me! You *will* do whatever I tell you! Leave whatever convictions you have right here, because until you leave the confines of *my* prison, *I am God!*" He had started to hyperventilate by this final portion, and took a moment to catch his breath. Abbas pulled out a handkerchief and patted down his brow. He cleared his throat, and then began to pace the line.

"You will not use cellular communications! You will not fight! You *will* take all direction from my guards! When they wake you up, you will be up! When they tell you it's time to eat, you will go eat! When it's time to sleep, you will sleep! If you are put on a work detail, then you *will* work! Any of you who refuse to follow direction will spend time in the punishment cells!" He stopped directly in front of Williams and locked eyes with him, his eyes lit with a sadistic glint. "You don't want to go there. Do you understand?"

All of the other prisoners screamed affirmatives, but Williams remained silent. This caused Colonel Abbas to lean in closer and repeat in Arabic, "*Do you understand?*"

"I don't speak Arabic," Williams said quietly.

Abbas reached for the pistol on his hip and trained it directly between Williams's eyes. Williams instinctively held his hands in front of his face and spoke rapidly. "*I don't speak Arabic, please don't shoot! I don't speak—I'm Canadian, for God's sake! I don't speak Arabic!*"

The warden studied Williams for a second, then lowered his pistol. "You have a passport?" he asked in accented English.

"Y-yes," Williams stammered. "I-it-it's in my p-p-pocket." He slowly reached into his back pocket for the dark blue booklet, stamped with the golden seal of Canada, then extended it toward the colonel.

"Darren Bowles," Abbas read aloud.

"Darren Bowles, yes," Williams repeated. "I'm a businessman. I-I sell technology."

"Why are you here?"

"I-I-I got into a little trouble with some palace guards. I-I took some photos, and they tried to take my camera, so I swung on one of them."

Abbas chuckled heartily. "You have courage! I like you!" His tone dropped a few octaves. "Don't try that here."

Williams held up his hands in surrender. "Absolutely, sir. You're the boss."

Abbas handed the passport back to Williams, looked to his subordinates, and gestured with his head towards the administration building. "Push these motherfuckers through!" he ordered in Arabic.

A rough hand grabbed Williams and shoved him forward. "Move!" the guard shouted.

Williams kept his head down, his hands up, and let out a deep, relieved sigh. He looked at the administration door, realizing that he was now inside, but the feeling of accomplishment was quickly replaced with worry-fueled brainstorming.

Now that I'm in...how do we get out?

* * *

THE FIRST ORDER OF business was to try and take advantage of the shower facilities, a luxury that nation's smaller prisons did not enjoy. The downside to them was that they did not work half of the time, and one had to bribe the guards to use them. Williams saw a guard posted by the shower building, casually smoking a cigarette, and immediately saw his in. He discreetly made his way over to the building and parked himself in front of the guard.

"Fuck off," the guard snapped in his native tongue. "I'm not letting you in."

"Do you speak English?" Williams asked.

"I guess you don't speak Arabic," the guard replied in English. "Fuck. Off."

"I need to use the showers."

The guard reached for his nightstick, and Williams held up his hands. "Hey, hey, calm down, man. Calm down. I've got some incentive for you." He motioned to the Royale cigarette, a popular brand in the Middle East. "You like smoking those?" The guard did not say a word, and Williams asked, "How would you like to smoke an American cigarette?"

That intrigued the guard. "Are you American?"

Williams laughed. "Oh, heavens, no. I live in Rutland."

"Rutland?" the guard asked.

"It's in Kelowna," Williams said. "British Columbia. I hop the border to Seattle and buy the American cigarettes. It's not that Canadian smokes are bad. The American ones just have a bit more *oomph* to the, you know?"

The guard was starting to catch on. "You let me try one, I let you shower."

"Certainly." Williams removed the pack from his pocket, opened it up, and handed a cigarette to the guard. The pack was then replaced with a lighter. Williams lit the smoke for the guard, who took a long pull off of it. The guard coughed a couple of times, looked to the cigarette, and nodded approvingly.

"That's good shit, eh?" Williams asked.

"Yes," the guard agreed. He gestured to the

shower. "Ten minutes. Any longer, and I come in after you."

Williams pressed his hands together graciously. "You are my hero."

The water in the showers was filthy and borderline scalding, but Williams wasted no time on complaints. He swiftly disrobed and took five minutes to wash away the grime and dirt from his most sensitive areas. He then air-dried his body for a couple of minutes and then clothed himself. There was a shattered mirror nearby, and Williams walked to it. He leaned in close and studied himself. There was a bruise on the left side of his face from the Republican Guard beating, and it was ginger to the touch. Three days of scruff had accumulated along his jawline, which added to his haggard appearance.

After he left the building, Williams fished the Marlboro pack from his pocket and tossed the guard another cigarette. "For your troubles."

"Thank you," the guard said. "A pleasure doing business."

Williams made his way to his assigned building on the prison's west side. When he stepped inside, he found the conditions to be exactly as he expected. It was a second class cell, reserved for the average and common criminal. There were ninety bunks, bolted to the cream-colored walls and grimy tile floors, and about a hundred and fifty some-odd prisoners within. All of them had been allowed to retain their clothing. The more dangerous prisoners and their cronies occupied the bunks, while the rest were forced to find a piece of real estate on the floor and doing their best to remain comfortable. He saw a handful of women mixed amongst the crowd, consistent with his research regarding the Egyptian penal system. Williams's eyes fell on each occupant as he sized them up.

"Hey, woman," a brute of a man barked. Williams could not see the woman and attempted to maneuver for a better view. "I've watched you sleep on the floor the last couple of nights. I think we could work something out where you could stay in my bunk."

"I'll pass," a woman's voice replied. Her tone was polite, but to the point.

The man yanked the woman into view, and Williams saw that it was not Zaina. He continued to watch. "You must really like the floor," the man taunted.

"That's not it—"

The brute cocked back and delivered a wicked backhand to the woman's face, which felled her instantly. "You like it so much, then stay down there, bitch!" Several of the brute's cronies guffawed heartily. Williams's blood chilled, but he turned his back as the thugs returned to shooting the breeze in the comfort of their bunks. *Not my problem.*

It was not the first time he had told himself that. It did not make it any easier.

* * *

DUSK HAD FALLEN, AND spotlights shone down inside the prison's walls. Every day at sundown, the guards allowed the prisoners to vacate the housing blocks for a football match. A peeling, barely inflated ball was produced, and several prisoners took to the pitch to engage in the world's favorite pastime. Williams stood off to the side and watched the game with feigned interest. While he could appreciate the game and the power it had over people, he was very American in that he preferred gridiron. That, and a greater preference to remain inconspicuous, motivated him to remain out of sight.

Williams's search for Zaina had been a dry hole. After a few hours, he had ventured to stroll the bunks and see if she were hidden, but had turned up nothing. That left Williams with one of three explanations— she was housed in another unit, she was in the punishment block, or she was not at the prison whatsoever. He pondered what his course of action would be if the third possibility were the case, then dismissed it as quickly as the notion came to him. He would cross that bridge once he reached it. All of his energy needed to be focused on investigating the other housing blocks and, if necessary, finding a way into the punishment block.

Across the pitch, Williams spotted the brute from earlier and his associates standing in a circle, each of them with a cigarette in hand. Williams stuffed his hands in his pockets and strolled in that direction. The group appeared to be the alpha dogs of the complex, and seemed like a good starting point for eavesdropping. Once he was about ten feet away from the group, Williams lit a cigarette and kept his eyes on the field while he listened in.

"I'm going to fuck that bitch soon," the leader insisted. "She knows it too. The only choice she has is whether she's willing or not."

"I'm surprised you did not take that shit from her earlier, Khalid," one of the subordinates said with a chuckle that came off as more of a nervous tick. "I mean, shit, you know nobody would have been stupid enough to break it up!"

"Use your head, Rafi," Khalid chastised. "We just got a new batch of prisoners and it was the middle of the day. You wanna spend time in punishment block? I know I don't, and I know I don't have enough influence to dodge that."

"Speaking of new guys, what do you make of him? The big guy. He's over there, smoking."

Williams could feel eyes on him. He did not say a word, nor did he turn to address them.

Khalid took a deep drag off of his cigarette. "That faggot? He's some kind of Westerner. I heard him speaking English earlier when he bribed his way into the showers. He doesn't speak Arabic. Probably some elitist bastard who got more than he bargained on vacation, right?" The group laughed in agreement before he continued. "He's no threat. As long as he doesn't fuck with how we do things and knows his place, we've got no business with him."

"What about that other bitch that speaks English, the one next door?"

"You mean that professor? Fucking cunt. Had the audacity to talk back to me, and then she ducked my slap! She thinks she's safe because she stays out of sight. I'll show that bitch. We'll see what good her fancy words do her when I have my cock in her ass and she's screaming for help."

The group howled with laughter at Khalid's

promise. Williams took another drag of the cigarette, dropped it in the sand in front of him, and extinguished it. With his description of an independent female professor and his intentions with her, Khalid had just made himself a person of interest.

* * *

SLEEPING AGAINST THE WALL with his knees bent was a huge improvement over sleeping standing up. At Williams's age, his back had started to affect him more than ever, particularly after over two decades of abuse for God and country, but he refused to let it bother him. When he became uncomfortable, he shifted his position and resumed his light sleep. Every so often, he would hear others shift, which would cause him to open his eyes and investigate. When he saw it was nothing, he returned to sleep as quickly as he woke.

What triggered his latest wakeup was something he had not heard all night: voices. They were hushed, but ineffectively so, and coupled with their footsteps, they were a herd of stampeding elephants. They were walking in his direction, toward the front door, so Williams narrowed his eyes and slumped his head. As they walked by, his suspicion was confirmed—it was Khalid and his four cronies. When they reached the door, Williams made out faint Arabic.

"Remember: you didn't hear a damn thing."

"You've got it, Khalid," the other voice—he assumed it was the guard—replied.

The footsteps faded away. Williams was on his feet and reaching for his pack of Marlboros. Once he reached the door, the guard blocked his path.

"Where do you think you're going?" the guard asked in English.

"For a smoke," Williams said. "Want one?"

"I don't smoke," the guard said sternly. "Back inside."

My luck. The only non-smoking guard in the entire fucking country. "C'mon, man, I just want a smoke."

The guard began drawing his nightstick. "Back. Inside."

"Okay, okay, okay," Williams said, reaching into his pocket. The guard tensed, and Williams held out a soothing hand as he cautiously produced a Canadian twenty-dollar note. He extended it toward the guard. "This buy me some smoke time?"

"No."

Williams sighed. He wanted to avoid hurting or killing the guards as much as possible, but if Khalid was going where he thought he was, he would kill this man and attempt to effect an *in extremis* extraction. The guard had one more chance before Williams was forced to escalate.

"Are you sure that this won't cover it? It's just as much as an American dollar, buddy."

The guard took a deep breath and said, "I'm sure that forty dollars would buy you some walk-about time."

Williams removed another twenty note, stuffed both in the guard's hands, and asked, "We cool?"

"Yeah, we're cool," the guard said. "Go ahead."

Williams stepped out the door and found the last

of Khalid's posse entering the adjacent building. He picked up a brisk pace and closed the distance to the next building, where another guard stood watch. As he approached, the guard said in Arabic, "What are you doing? Get back in your cell!"

"I'm sorry," Williams said quietly. "I don't speak Arabic." He produced another twenty note and extended it to the guard, then gestured toward the building's interior. "Money talks, yes?" The guard grunted in approval, then stepped aside to grant Williams access.

The layout was exactly the same as the building where he was housed. There was nothing he could use to improvise a weapon, which left him engaging the gang hand-to-hand if the situation escalated. Everybody was asleep, or at least pretending to be. Silence gripped the room. He immediately ducked right, and watched as Khalid's pack pulled a woman out of bed. The moonlight shone through the window and lit up the woman's face. She was startled, but her eyes held a glint that showed that she would not scare easily. Her features were foreign and familiar all at once, and her body matched the vitals that Lana Bouton provided.

There was no doubt in his mind. He had eyes on Zaina Anwar.

Talk your way out of this, Williams pleaded internally. *C'mon, please, talk your way out of this.*

"I told you that you'd pay for what you did, you fucking whore," Khalid rasped, his meaty paw locked around Zaina's jaw. "I've come to collect."

"Get your hands off of me or I start screaming," Zaina warned in flawless Arabic. Her voice wavered only due to the constriction on her mouth.

"I've paid off the guards," Khalid growled. "Nobody is coming to save you. Now, get on your knees."

"Last chance," Zaina stated, her tone resolute. "Let me go."

Stupid... Williams thought as he slowly stood and prepared to enter the fray. *Brave, but stupid.*

Khalid's grip on Zaina's jaw tightened. "Listen here, you fucking slut—"

His invective was cut off by a swift knee to the groin that doubled him over. Zaina then grabbed hold of Khalid's face and dug her nails into his eyes, and an agonized cry leapt from his throat. One of the flunkies stepped in and delivered a right straight to her ribs. The force of the blow was not enough to break bone, but it did stun her long enough for Khalid to grab a fistful of Zaina's hair and glare at her with red eyes.

"You'll pay for that, bitch!" he snarled as he suspended her in the air.

Williams materialized behind Khalid and grabbed him by the shoulders. His right leg made contact with Khalid's left knee and right shin and swept backward as he pushed forward. Khalid released Zaina to free his hands to make impact with the ground. Williams followed this move with a snap kick to Khalid's head, which elicited a sharp cry. Khalid huddled up to protect his head as he fought to regain his senses.

There was no time to celebrate. Williams immediately lunged for Zaina, grabbed her by the shoulders, and shoved her out of the battlespace. He glanced over his shoulder, found one of the four cronies close, and answered his arrival with a crisp back kick that caught the man square in the chin and knocked him out. Williams immediately transitioned to the next man, just in time to duck under a haymaker. He grabbed the assailant by the scruff of his neck and belt line, then spun and hurled him toward one of his companions, which sent the both of them on a collision course with a nearby bunk.

That left one thug in full commission. The flunkie threw a jab and followed it with a right straight. Williams slapped the jab away with his left hand, side-stepped, and grabbed the man's outstretched wrist with his left hand. He gripped his opponent's shoulder with his right hand to control him and doubled the thug over. With blinding speed, Williams put his right knee on the man's elbow, gripped the wrist with both hands, and torqued upwards. The joint dislocated with a sickening *crack*.

The man's shriek almost drowned out the sound of his two buddies scrambling back into the fight. Williams hurled the man under his control into the nearest attacker, then shifted his attention to the far threat. The thug threw a jab and a straight that were absorbed by Williams's forearms, then cocked back for a right haymaker. Williams blocked this with a left arm sweep, wrapped around and trapped his opponent's arm, delivered three brutal palm strikes to the man's chin, and then swung his right leg to his opponent's rear. Williams's leg swept while shoving the man's face forward. Once he hit the ground, Williams finished him off with a heel stomp to the chin.

That left Khalid and a lone associate in the fight.

Williams spun around in time to find the associate mid-bum rush. He retaliated with a swift jab to the nose, followed by a right straight, and punctuated with a solid front kick that crushed his opponent's ribs and lifted him in the air. The last criminal hit the ground, clutched at his chest, and gasped for air. Williams could tell from the breathing that the rib punctured the lung and that tension pneumothorax was imminent. The threat only had a few minutes left to live.

The distinct *click* of a switchblade locking in place caught Williams's attention, and he turned to see Khalid standing between the bunks. In his paws, the blade was a nail file. The murder in his eyes was real and familiar to Williams. It was the same look many opponents possessed countless times over. Khalid's mind was consumed with bloodlust and Williams was the focus.

By this time, all of the prisoners had awakened and were watching intently. Williams did not take his eyes off of Khalid, but he could only imagine that they had seen a similar spectacle more than once, and that Khalid had won without breaking a sweat. He backed away from the beds slowly and moved toward the center aisle. Khalid followed him into the aisle, as hoped. Williams wanted as much room to maneuver as he could get. Williams loathed knife fighting due to the sole cardinal rule.

Everybody gets cut in a knife fight.

Khalid parried with the knife, and Williams leaned back, narrowly avoiding the blade. Williams resumed his stance, and Khalid laughed menacingly. He waved the blade from side to side, his eyes never wavering from Williams's. Khalid took a step forward, and Williams remained in place. Neither man moved for what seemed an eternity. Finally, Khalid let out a battle cry and lunged forward. Williams side-stepped to Khalid's outside, but he did not move his left arm in time. The blade caught him on the forearm. The pain did not register as Williams side-stepped left, grabbed Khalid's head with his left hand, and neutralized Khalid's weapon hand with his right. He guided the brute into a support beam, and used Khalid's dazed status to twist the arm and guide the blade into the kidneys. As Khalid screamed, Williams pulled the knife from his body, placed his knee in the middle of Khalid's thigh, and applied pressure as he pushed his shoulders down. Khalid fell to his knees, and Williams grabbed a fistful of hair and yanked back hard to expose the throat.

In for a penny, in for a pound.

Williams plunged the knife into Khalid's throat and cut through muscle and esophagus as he severed the jugular. The gang leader's screams dampened as hot, sticky blood launched from his arteries, filled his windpipe, and stained the support beam and floor. Williams thrust the knife into the base of Khalid's skull and took a step back, watching his opponent's life fade rapidly from his carcass. He let out a deep breath and turned to face Zaina, whose horror-widened eyes were locked on him.

The lights came on, and several guards sprinted in, nightsticks at the ready. Williams immediately raised his hands and dropped to his knees. That did not stop the guards. As the first baton came crashing down on his side, Williams collapsed into a ball and waited for the beating to end. After thirty seconds, a shrill voice bellowed over the commotion.

"That's enough! Stand down!"

The guards stepped aside, and Williams moved his bloodied arm to look at who had called off the assault. It was Colonel Abbas, and he wore an irritated expression on his sleep-deprived face. That expression changed to a mixture of awe and disdain as he saw the carnage wreaked in the housing block. After a moment of inspection, Abbas folded his arms and looked Williams in the eye.

"Do you have an explanation?" Abbas asked.

Williams refused to meet Zaina's gaze, though he could see her out of the corner of his eye. He took a deep breath, decided on a narrative, and stuck with it. "They gestured that they wanted to smoke. When I stepped out to burn one, they dragged me over here, and they tried to beat me up, so I fended them off."

Abbas chuckled incredulously. *"Fend them off?* Mr. Bowles, I'd say you've done a bit more than just 'fend them off.' Where did you learn to fight? I thought Canadians were supposed to be polite?"

"We *are* polite, sir," Williams said. "Except when we play hockey."

"I see!" Abbas laughed again, and then his smile faded. He crossed his arms and rested them on his gut. "Well, you've killed one man, probably two from the looks of that gentleman across the way, and you grievously assaulted three others. How any of you managed to get past the guards on both buildings is cause for concern." He looked over his shoulder and motioned to the guards. "Take them all to the medical wing, get them patched up, and then escort them to the punishment block."

"Yes, sir," the guards said in unison. Two of them picked Williams up beneath his armpits and dragged him toward the door. His eyes met Zaina's as they pulled him past, and then quickly returned to the ground. He knew what came next. Extraction would be delayed by at least a couple of days, and he would have to hope that she could fend for herself until he got free.

CHAPTER FOUR

Istiqbal-Tora Prison
Cairo, Egypt
20 July 2006
04:15 hours Eastern European Time (02:15 hours Zulu)

THE SOUNDS OF SCREAMING women and crying babies were blared through the loudspeaker, a measure designed to psychologically break a subject down and inhibit sleep. Williams smirked when he heard it the first time, then took up a piece of real estate in the empty cell and slept. That was immediately after the medical ward on the first night, and it lasted all of two hours before the guards came crashing in, batons in hand. They worked him over for five minutes, then left him to contemplate his injuries. So far, he had managed to avoid any broken joints, a record he hoped to maintain.

Williams slept as much as he could during the night. During the day, when the temperature skyrocketed, he stripped out of the punishment block jumpsuit. At the heat's worst, when the guards were the most incensed, they entered his cell, beat him viciously, and screamed in Arabic about taking his clothes off or daring him to stand up and fight. He took the beatings and played the part of the scared tourist, but he was happy as a clam inside. He knew their playbook and knew they would not do anything that he could not withstand.

It was the early morning of the second day. They had taken his watch so he would not be able to gauge the time, but Williams had figured out a work-around. He remembered it was the very start of the nineteenth when he was taken to the medical wing, and thirty minutes had passed before his arm was patched up. Once inside the cell, he relied on the heat to tell the time. While his body was being pushed to its limits, his mental acuity was as clear as ever, which was the most important factor in resisting austere conditions and interrogations.

The doors swung open, and Williams automatically rolled into a ball. Between baton strikes on his back and legs, Williams considered how much time he had spent in this position in the past week. It was a sobering thought. Williams had a wealth of knowledge and experience that made him a particularly skilled operative. Yet, everybody from the police to prison guards took their pound of flesh from him. It reminded him of something one of the cadre members had told him when he attended the 22 Special Air Service Regiment's Selection Course as a foreign exchange NCO.

We are not supermen. We are not invulnerable. The purpose of this training is not *to make you think otherwise. We bleed, we take our licks, we lose limbs, and yes, we die. What you're here for is to learn how to do everything you can to prevent all of that from happening.*

The beating ceased. The guards stepped into the corridor and closed the door behind them. Instead of walking away as they usually did, the two conversed in front of the door.

"You know, I get the feeling we're being fooled," one voice said.

"How do you figure?" the other asked.

"Well...most of the guys we work over, they're begging not to be hit. They usually require a solid strike to get them to roll into a ball. This guy, he doesn't beg for leniency. He just rolls over and takes the beating. What'd you say he was again?"

"A computer salesman from Rutland."

There was a pause. "Where the fuck is Rutland?"

"I don't know," the other said. "Somewhere in Canada. Maybe near Toronto? That's not my point. My point is, how many computer salesmen do you know that are built like that?"

"You're grasping for straws. He's *Canadian.* You heard him the other night—he plays hockey. Those guys have to be buff."

"What if that's what he *wants* you to think?"

"You're paranoid. Don't worry about him. He's only got one more day before they return him to general population." The footsteps backed up. "C'mon, let's get some water..."

Williams smiled. *If only they knew.*

* * *

ZAINA GHONIM ISHAN ANWAR...Zaina Ghonim Ishan Anwar...

Each time he heard the name, he saw her face. At first, Williams saw her dossier photograph—calm, collected, poised, and stunning in the sense that her confidence and obvious intelligence supplemented her natural beauty. The name was spoken softly in

Bouton's voice and played on loop.

The image changed. It was a freeze frame, Khalid's meaty paws locked on her shoulders, and yet, she refused to capitulate. Her name echoed again, and it was the look in her eyes immediately after he had killed Khalid. She was revolted that somebody could kill so casually, and at the same time, she was grateful that he had done so on her behalf. Like the murderous glare Khalid locked him with, Williams had seen the look in Zaina's eyes numerous times.

His mind flashed from Zaina to the prison. He saw the schematics in his mind and matched them to where he had been, painting a mental 3D image. Everything was analyzed and reanalyzed. Williams thought about the guards patrolling the complex, and the few glimpses he caught of the riflemen in the towers. Colonel Abbas also came to mind, and Williams contemplated the ways that Abbas could impede the escape. He also hoped that Ferran had managed to evade the patrols thus far and would be present at the agreed rendezvous point.

The more he dreamed about it, the less he liked the plan. Too many "what ifs," too many things that could go wrong, too many things that *had* to go right. Williams wondered if he should not have accepted the assignment, but that thought was pushed aside. There was never any question about it, and Thrasher had to know it the moment he proposed the operation. Ferran was a friend, one to whom he owed his life. There was only one option—break Zaina out, link up with Ferran, and high-tail it to the embassy.

Williams heard the door open, and the two guards from the day before stood at the threshold. The one who had dismissed his friend's suspicions as paranoia leaned inside, motioned with his hand, and said in English, "Come, come. You go now. Done."

Slowly, he rose to his feet and approached the door apprehensively. The guard coaxed him further, and once Williams crossed the doorway, he took up a position behind him and just off to his right, while the other guard moved ahead and to the left. He suspected that they had heard how he had used Khalid's associates against each other during the fight, and did not want to suffer the same fate if "Mr. Bowles" elected to snap.

Colonel Abbas stood at the entrance of the punishment block, his hands behind his back. He had the look of a parent who had successfully taught their child a lesson. Williams suppressed the urge to break the man's neck.

"Not a pleasant place, is it?" Abbas asked.

Williams hung his head and shook it. "No, sir."

Abbas nodded sagely. "You know, it used to be much more brutal than it is now. But we've received proper instruction. We've learned from the best. Now, it is one of our more effective compliance methods, and is often the best tool we have in extracting information from people." He smiled and rubbed Williams shoulder. "But we don't have to worry about that from you. You mixed it up to defend a woman. Noble sentiment, and between you and me, it's one I agree with, but the rules are the rules. I'm sure you understand."

Williams nodded. "Yes, sir."

"All right." Abbas motioned toward the administration building. "Your clothing and personal items are in there. Just head in there and tell them you're coming from the punishment block. They'll help you out."

"Thank you, sir," Williams said quietly before he shuffled in that direction.

* * *

THE SUN SLIPPED BENEATH the horizon. The bays were empty, save from the odd loiterer who elected not to watch the football matches. Zaina Anwar was one of those loiterers—while she enjoyed the occasional football match, she preferred to stay inside and write in her journal, which the guards had allowed her to keep. She documented everything— her treatment at the hands of the guards, the people she met, the prisoners that accosted her, and now, the prisoner that intervened on her behalf. Most prisoners wanted nothing to do with the facility once they left, if they were allowed to leave, and feared government retribution if they spoke out. Zaina knew the moment that the CSF kicked in her door that she would blow the lid wide open on the affair, if she ever managed to get the word out. She had hoped her status as an American citizen would help make that possible, but with every passing day, it seemed as if Washington could care less about her well being.

Zaina scribbled furiously in her journal. Her heart pounded as she recalled when Khalid and his crew had grabbed her out of her bed, and what raced through her mind when the mysterious foreigner had swooped in to rescue her. She paused as she wrote down that last part and tapped her pen on the paper.

God, I'm such a damsel in distress, she groused internally. That was the last thing she wanted to be, but she knew her boundaries. She was an educator, not a fighter, and while that did not make her a pushover, she knew that there were much bigger fish in the sea. The stranger, on the other hand, was a force of pure violence. Everything he did screamed "fighter." His every move was brutally elegant, and when she watched him kill Khalid, she was equal parts appalled and amazed. Even when the guards dragged him away, Zaina had a feeling as to who was really in control. She knew that it would take more than a beating to break him.

"Care if I join you?"

Her heart skipped a beat as she looked up from her written musings. There he was, the stranger, standing in front of her, wearing the same raggedy clothing that he'd worn the night where he intervened on her behalf. He was sporting a hell of a shiner on the left side of his face, and his left arm was wrapped in a bandage, but aside from that, he looked and sounded completely normal.

"How did you know I speak English?" Zaina asked curiously.

"May I?" the stranger asked, gesturing to the space beside her.

"Please." He lowered himself carefully and gingerly rested his back against the wall. "Guess you're not Superman, after all."

"What?"

Zaina shook her head. "How did you know I speak

English?"

The man looked both ways before he responded in Arabic. "How do you know I don't speak Arabic?"

That caused Zaina to raise her eyebrows. "Playing dumb with the guards? Why?"

He removed his billfold—which was light forty dollars from when he was placed in the punishment block—and fiddled around with the inside. He opened a hidden compartment, removed a folded piece of paper, and handed it to her. Zaina inspected it cautiously.

"What's this?"

"The reason I'm here. Read it quickly, please, before somebody catches us."

Zaina unfolded the paper without another word. The paper turned out to be a photograph of her cousin, Ferran, with a half-hearted attempt at a smile, holding up a copy of the *Al-Ahram* newspaper, dated the 14th of July. She narrowed her eyes in confusion, then looked to the man. "What is this?"

"Proof that I am who I say I am," the man said. "I'll give you another minute with that if you need it."

"Who are you?"

"Darren Bowles," the man said. He took the photograph from her, removed his lighter from his pocket, and lit it ablaze. Bowles looked to her as he held the burning picture by his finger and thumb, then dropped it on the ground in front of him.

"I'd say that's about as authentic as your claim of being a computer salesman," Zaina said skeptically.

"That's all you need to know," Bowles insisted. "Ferran is waiting for us on the outside. We're running a little behind schedule, so we're going to have to speed things up."

"You mean escape?" Zaina said quietly. "In case you haven't looked around lately, we're boxed in and there are guards everywhere. There's a sniper on each corner, and we're well outside of the city. Escape doesn't seem to be quite within the realm of possibilities."

"Well, I suppose you'll just have to expand your realm of possibilities, won't you?" On cue, Arabic sounded off over the loudspeakers, instructing the inmates to finish their game and begin returning to the housing blocks. Bowles stood up and started making his way toward the door. "Make sure that burns, will you? I'll stop by soon. Stay vigilant."

Zaina took a moment to consider the meeting as she watched the photograph shrivel and burn. Ferran had never approved of her activism, which was a large reason why she kept her underground radio endeavor a secret from him, but in retrospect, she had inadvertently endangered him in the process. Yet, he was still doing all that he could to break her out. Zaina did not know much about Ferran's work, but she did know he was some sort of special forces soldier. Perhaps Bowles was an American he had trained with? Or maybe he really was Canadian? Either way, whoever he was, he was skilled and had promised her a way out.

As the picture finished burning, she looked up and sighed tiredly. *Maybe things are looking up.*

* * *

Egyptian General Intelligence Service Headquarters
Cairo, Egypt
21 July 2006
20:30 hours Eastern European Time (18:30 hours Zulu)

MOST EMPLOYEES HAD LEFT the building three hours earlier and made for home, where families would be waiting with home-cooked meals, or where single employees would hop in their showers, put on their best nightwear, and hit the decadent nightclubs in search of an inebriated one-night romance. The majority of the building's remaining occupants were the cleaning crew, supervised by a security guard at all times to ensure that none of them grew curious as to what lay beyond closed doors or on dormant computer terminals.

Colonel Abdullah Mahir Yusuf Agha was the other exception to the rule. There was no wife waiting at home, no dinner on the table, and no children wondering when Father would be home. His desire to cruise the nightclubs for the lithe, tan-skinned beauties had never been tremendously high to begin with, and as the years moved on, his desire to socialize diminished. It was not any sort of religious devotion—Agha had only been marginally interested in his Islamic upbringings as a boy, and grew into something of an agnostic over the years. Agha was married to his job, and his dedication paid off. At the ripe age of thirty-nine, he had been promoted to colonel and placed in charge of the Directorate of Counterintelligence, where he oversaw all such efforts, both domestically and abroad.

Agha was handsome, not in a movie star or rugged fashion, but in a quiet, contemplative manner. His body was lean, the result of an aggregate sixty miles of running per week and healthy eating. Short black hair covered his head, and he had grown and maintained a neat, thin beard, respectable enough to pass muster with traditional types but thin enough that said maintenance was minimal. With his rectangular reading glasses, white dress shirt with sleeves rolled beneath the elbows, gray slacks, and immaculately shined Oxfords, Agha looked more like an accountant or a business executive than the counterintelligence officer he was. This was intentional—he would much prefer to go unnoticed unless he made himself noticed, and his style of dress was no different from the average man on the street.

In his capacity as Director of Counterintelligence, Agha's job mostly focused on three areas: Israeli espionage attempts, both here and abroad, in violation of the 1979 peace accords; Muslim Brotherhood operatives attempting to wrangle control of the government from the Mubarak administration; and finally, dissidents within the country attempting to push for "democracy" in Egypt. He judged his targets dispassionately, and like a good soldier, he followed orders. There was no hate for the dissidents, the Muslim Brotherhood, or even the Israelis. He merely did what he was directed to do—root out all security leaks and take them out of commission through whatever means necessary.

His latest assignment had been to find the cause of the recent underground broadcasts speaking out against the government. That part had been child's play—the perpetrators were all educators, not hardened operatives. However, more than a few of them had been up to the task of playing soldier and had picked up weapons. The CSF paramilitary team he had brought with him lit the place up and killed both armed and unarmed dissenters alike. Only one dissenter survived the raid, and she had been swiftly arrested. By government standards, this was an acceptable outcome, but not to Agha's standards. It was not out of any sort of compassion that he regretted the outcome, but rather a matter of professional pride. Agha aimed for minimal bloodshed in his operations as a testament to his speed, surprise, and tenacity. Also, he knew the old adage "dead men tell no tales" to be painfully true. There was nothing in his arsenal that would allow him to download a corpse. Given that there was only the one survivor, Zaina Anwar, and there was no evidence that would suggest a second radio cell, Agha had turned his attention to hunting down her cousin.

First Sergeant Ferran Anwar was a member of Unit 777, and had not survived to attain his rank by being stupid. Agha attempted to bring Ferran in quietly, but the operator must have heard the rumors and went to ground. From there, it had been a waiting game. Either Ferran would slip up within the country and Agha would find him, or he would surface in another country and *Mukhabarat* operatives would deal with him from there.

Then, two things happened that caught Agha's eye. The first was the arrest of a Canadian, Darren Bowles, outside of Heliopolis Palace, five days earlier. He had been photographing the place, and while the pictures were at angles that could possibly be shared with any curious tourist, they were suggestive of a possible sniper recce. Coupled with the fact that President Mubarak had been scheduled to land only forty-five minutes after the arrest, and it seemed very suggestive. However, searches of his hotel room and history showed no links to any foreign intelligence service and no hardware necessary to carry out an assassination. None of the buildings he cased held anything that would incriminate Bowles, either. At that point, his only crime was being a belligerent Westerner—which was very odd for a man of his nationality—and picking the wrong day to photograph a government building.

The second had just made his way to his desk through one of his many sources within the penal system. A fight had broken out in Istiqbal-Tora that left two dead and three others severely maimed. Further investigation yielded that Bowles had been the man that wreaked havoc upon a hardened criminal and his friends, and furthermore, it was in the housing block where Zaina Anwar was housed. That, in and of itself, could have been coincidence, given that Istiqbal-Tora housed both extremely violent criminals and enemies of the state, but Agha had stopped believing in coincidence decades ago.

Several theories swam in Agha's head, but all of them required information he did not have readily available. That left one option. With his mind made up, he stood, donned his blazer, and made for the parking lot. Agha would need the sleep, as he had much work ahead of him in the coming day.

CHAPTER FIVE

Istiqbal-Tora Prison
Cairo, Egypt
22 July 2006
12:46 hours Eastern European Time (10:46 hours Zulu)

WILLIAMS KNEW THAT DESPITE the operation's misfortunes, there had been a lot of good luck in Zaina's detention at Istiqbal-Tora, and even more in that he had managed to be incarcerated in the same facility. Unlike the smaller prisons, there was a mess hall, and the prisoners received three meals per day. The food was eaten out of necessity rather than any sort of culinary appreciation, and Williams's digestive system punished him as it adjusted, but some nutrition was better than none, particularly after the three days spent in the punishment block. The antibiotic cocktail he had ingested a few days earlier did not fully alleviate the effects, but they did prevent uncontrollable bowel movements and regurgitation. He was still sore but felt a little better.

Inside the mess hall, the other inmates avoided Williams. He retained a table to himself. He did not go out of his way to intimidate people, but his reputation had spread. Those who did not witness his brutal dispatching of Khalid and his friends had heard the rumors. Nobody had told this to Williams directly, but he could tell from the looks on their faces. Williams accepted it for what it was worth. While it was not attention he wanted, it drastically reduced the number of people that would interact with him, which made his job easier.

Williams took his tray to the trash and emptied the contents within. He set the tray atop the receptacle and made his way outside. His eyes narrowed as the midday sun pounded the earth, and he glanced to his right, where he found Zaina Anwar leaned against the wall, a lit cigarette in her hand and a tired expression on her face. Williams approached her and found a cigarette of his own, grateful that the guards had taken only a couple of his smokes while he was in punishment block. He held the cigarette between his lips and took up a spot next to Zaina.

"I hope that you don't mind if I join you," Williams said. He ignited the flame, touched it to the tip, and inhaled.

"Maybe some of your reputation will rub off on me," Zaina said with a laconic smile. When Williams did not respond, she added, "They've given you a nickname: *Malak al-Moot*."

Williams snorted. He looked both ways before he confirmed the translation. "Angel of Death? A little melodramatic, wouldn't you say?"

"That's really the best way to describe your actions," Zaina said. "Most of these people have only seen that sort of thing in film or television, myself included. It was the most impressive display of violence I have ever seen, and I say that as a pacifist."

"It's not all that it's cracked up to be," Williams said. He took a hit off of the cigarette. "It's actually put a bit of a damper in my plans."

"How's that?" Zaina asked.

Williams saw a guard wander into view casually, his eyes on them. He took a deep breath and eyed the ground. "Wait five seconds, and walk around the corner. I'll follow."

Zaina said nothing. After the requisite time, she turned the corner. Williams followed her around and sidled alongside her. In a quiet voice, he said, "My original intent was to start a riot and use it as a diversion to facilitate our escape. Given my notoriety, that's next to impossible. Nobody's gonna stand their ground if I mix it up with them. I need another out."

"You don't have to be at the epicenter to generate a diversion," Zaina said. "Khalid's crew was not the only criminal clique in the prison. There are several others. They're just not stupid enough to fight you, given how you won in a five-to-one handicap match."

Williams looked to her with renewed interest. "I'm listening."

"Khalid's group was the largest of three main cliques. The other two squabbled with each other over minor things, and occasionally, it would escalate to violence, but at the end of the day, they fell in and toed Khalid's line. With Khalid and his second dead, and his three deputies in punishment block, there's a power vacuum. All it would take is one proper fight to ignite the powder keg."

Williams considered that information. He flicked away the excess ash and said, "Tell me about the other players."

"There's Aziz," Zaina said. "Thin guy, clean shaven, slicked hair. He was a racketeer on the outside, mostly stayed off the radar until somebody tried to cut off their protection rent. Beat the man to death and left him in the street, and that put the police onto him. His crew mostly consists of guys he had on the outside that got rounded up with him. He's brought his 'entrepreneurial' trade to the prison. He's got guards on the dole that smuggle him luxuries from the outside. With Khalid's passing, that leaves more guards ready to back him up."

"All right," Williams said. "Who's the other player?"

"Abu Bakr. Swimmer's build. Thick beard, thinning hair. Kind of tall. He's a trafficker. Bakr was connected to the opium networks in Afghanistan, and it was actually the anti-terror laws that got him arrested. As far as actual activity within the prison, he pretty clean. Most of his dirt is on the outside, and he's still running the business through cut-outs. He's got guards on his payroll, but not as many as Aziz. However, he's stronger in inmate numbers. Bakr's got enough pull on the outside to arrange for his foot soldiers to be transferred and assembled here."

"They almost seem complementary," Williams said.

"They could be, except there's tension from an incident a few months back, where an Abu Bakr soldier killed one of Aziz's associates," Zaina explained. Before Williams could ask, she explained, "There are prisoners who have been here longer than either group. I made some friends and figured a temperature check was in order."

"Sound policy."

"That's a large reason why Khalid had the autonomy he did before you killed him. He was a jack of all black market trades, and he knew how to do business. He saw their beef as an opportunity to align them under his rule. It actually played out like a peace conference. He assigned turf and gave them operating guidelines. All three groups actually flourished under this arrangement."

Williams nodded as he finished his smoke and extinguished the butt under his shoe. "It would be advantageous to both parties to continue the arrangement, but if old animosities could be inflamed, it could provide the opening we're looking for."

"Another thing—both factions have a long-standing rivalry on the pitch. Khalid kept it civil and friendly. If you caused an incident there, would be your best bet at bringing the house of cards down."

"You know, for an educator, you'd make one hell of a case officer," Williams said.

Zaina smiled. "Did you just hint at what you do for a living, Mr. Bowles?"

"Not at all," Williams said. "The turf. Break it down for me."

"Aziz is in a housing unit on the east side of the pitch," Zaina said. "Abu Bakr is in my block."

Williams nodded slowly. "You ready to step out of your comfort zone?"

"You want me to set the stage." It was not a question.

"If Abu Bakr has something of value that would send him over the edge if Aziz had it, that'd be optimal."

"I think that can be arranged."

He checked his watch. "It's 1:00 PM now. Think you can have it to me by three?"

"I'll give it my best shot, but no promises."

"I'll be outside my block for a cigarette," Williams said. "If you're not out by 3:05, then I'll come back out at four. If you don't have it by then, we'll have to push the plan back a day."

Zaina's brow narrowed. "Can Ferran afford to wait another day?"

"To be honest? Probably not. But what good will it be if they throw us both in punishment block or Abu Bakr catches and kills you? If you can do it, then do it, but don't go for it if it's not there."

"All right." Zaina uncrossed her arms and made her way back to the housing unit. Williams watched her walk away, then scratched his chin. He hated making things up as he went, but he knew from experience that when a plan fell apart, the successful operator compensated by developing the situation.

* * *

COLONEL ABBAS STOOD AT his window, his hands crossed at the small of his back as he overlooked the prison. It was a desolate place, one that would slowly eat at its occupants' souls, but that was what he liked about it. It would destroy the guilty, who would otherwise prey upon the nation's citizens. He knew that his job was unfortunately necessary, and that it served the greater good. It was that fact that made him swell with pride at the end of the day, knowing that what he did was good. That was what he clung to, what helped him sleep at night, and what allowed him to look himself in the mirror every morning.

The black phone on his desk sounded off. It was

his secretary, Captain Mansur. "Colonel, you have a visitor."

Abbas turned back to his desk and pressed the intercom button. "Who is it?"

"Colonel Agha from the *Mukhabarat* counterintelligence section and his deputy, Lieutenant Colonel Faris."

Abbas looked at his phone with surprise and curiosity. After a moment, he pressed the button and said, "Send them in."

A moment later, two men walked through the door. One was tall, thin, bearded, and intense in a quiet way, while the other was short, stocky, clean shaven, and sported the jowls of a bulldog. Both men wore khaki suits with open collars and no ties. As they made their way to Abbas's desk, he saw that the taller one was armed with a SIG-Sauer P226 in a cross-draw holster. The shorter man's handgun was not revealed openly, but Abbas could see it print against the fabric of his blazer. The taller man stepped forward with his hand extended.

"Colonel Abdullah Mahir Yusuf Agha," he said by way of introduction. "Head of counterintelligence at the General Intelligence Service Directorate." Abbas shook his hand, and then Agha gestured to the shorter man. "This is Lieutenant Colonel Uday Fa'iz Badi Faris."

"A pleasure to meet you," Abbas said reluctantly. "I received no notification that you were coming to the facility. Otherwise, I might have prepared a little better, perhaps had a lunch ready for you."

"The gesture is appreciated, but unnecessary," Agha assured him. "May we?"

Abbas gestured to the seats in front of his desk. "Please, please." Once they were seated, he asked, "What can I help you with today?"

"You recall a few weeks back, we brought you that agitator, Zaina Anwar?"

Abbas nodded knowingly. "Yes, yes, I do. Are you calling to check up on her? She's been nothing but well-behaved."

"Of course," Agha said. "I've been doing some following up. It seems that her cousin is a member of Unit 777, a First Sergeant Ferran Anwar. We've wanted him for questioning with regards to his cousin's dissident activities. He went off the grid soon after she was arrested."

Abbas looked at Agha carefully in an attempt to get a read on the man, but Agha's countenance was unmoving, made of stone. "All right?"

"On the fifteenth of this month, a Canadian was arrested for taking suspicious photographs of Heliopolis Palace a few hours before President Mubarak was due to land, as well as for assaulting Republican Guard soldiers. After his transfer to this facility, not even a day into his stay, he kills two men and maims three others, and according to my sources, he did this in the defense of one Zaina Anwar."

Abbas's face flushed darker. "You've been spying on my facility. How would you know any of this if that is not the case?"

"I prefer to look at it as an early-warning radar," Agha said casually. "Prevents red tape from interfering with national security, and it keeps people honest."

"Or breeds mistrust and an unwillingness to work

with your agency," Abbas said boldly, his eyes ablaze.

Agha offered the small smile of a chess player who knew exactly how many moves remained to checkmate. "Fortunately, I don't have that problem, Colonel Abbas." He crossed his legs and interlaced his fingers. "You see, people who don't work with me rapidly find themselves reassigned. It puts a major stunt on their career development. Many don't recover from it, and understandably so. Who wants to be known as the person who let his pride obstruct a national security investigation and thus became responsible for endangering the lives of millions of Egyptian citizens?"

Abbas looked from Agha, to Faris, and then back to Agha. He knew that they had him in a vise and that there was no room to maneuver. He had been in the Central Security Forces long enough to know when he had been out-politicked. Abbas took a deep breath, locked eyes with Agha, and gave him an artificial, polite smile. "What can I do to help you, Colonel Agha?"

"I'm going to need access to the prisoner, this..." Agha consulted his notes for appearance's sake. "Darren Bowles." Agha paused, then asked, "Did the Canadian Embassy return your request for a confirmation that he is indeed a Canadian citizen?"

"No, but I wouldn't expect an answer so quickly," Abbas said. "They confirmed that his passport was stamped at Customs, and the passport checked out, but it will be weeks until Ottawa gets back to us with a response. They're backlogged."

Agha shrugged. "It is of no matter. He will tell us

who he is and what he is doing here. Perhaps he is just a Good Samaritan, but I have to be prepared for the possibility that he isn't who he says he is."

Abbas nodded slowly. "I understand. I will put you in a room with the shift leader. He will provide you with the information you need."

"Thank you." Without further ado, Agha stood and left the room with Faris close in tow.

Abbas took a deep breath to suppress his rage. After a moment, Abbas hit the intercom button. "Captain Mansur?"

"Yes, sir?"

"Bring Sergeant Abdul to the administration building to talk with our *Mukhabarat* visitors. Tell him it regards one of our guests, and that Colonel Agha will bring him up to speed once he arrives."

"Yes, sir."

* * *

ZAINA FORCED HERSELF TO take deep breaths as she waited for Abu Bakr and his crew to depart. She had never felt more jittery in her adult life, and that included her first class as a teacher and her first post-doctorate lecture. She figured that her nerves were a result of being face-to-face with the legitimate possibility of death. Even when she had come up with the idea of the anti-Mubarak radio station, she knew that the government forces would not kill her, so long as she did not pick up a weapon and give them an excuse. That reminded her of her colleagues, and tinged her nervousness with a hint of sadness. She missed them, but they had been stupid to bring weapons to the station. Their purpose was civil disobedience, not armed insurrection.

Focus, she told herself. She knew exactly what she was going for, but she needed to be quick about it. If she spent too long in Abu Bakr's bunk area, then somebody would notice and, either hoping to impress Abu Bakr or under threat of harm, they would spill the beans and put Zaina firmly in his crosshairs. That possibility kept running through her head. She was not a coward, but she did have a healthy sense of self-preservation. There was still so much for her to do, things that she needed to accomplish, people that she could not afford to let down.

Ferran. He's waiting for me, Zaina thought. That thought slowed her heartbeat and gave her focus.

"Let's go have a smoke," Abu Bakr told his crew. On command, all of them rose from their various positions around the bunks and filed outside. Zaina waited a moment, then stood and moved to the edge of her bunk area. She peered around the corner and made sure that there were no stragglers. She checked her watch.

3:00 PM. Running out of time.

Zaina walked from her bunk and made her way to Abu Bakr's space. Her pace was neither fast nor slow, just enough that she did not draw attention. She did not look around or meet anybody's eyes. When she reached the bunk, she took a knee and slipped her hand beneath the mattress. Zaina had noticed Abu Bakr's nightly ritual and thought nothing of it at the time, but she knew as soon as Bowles had laid out his plan that this would be the catalyst.

Her hand brushed against glossy paper. *Got it.* She removed the paper from the mattress and found herself looking at a two-by-three sized portrait of an attractive woman, wearing a smile and not much else. A lipstick imprint of what she assumed to be the lady's lips were pressed over the picture, and a message was scrawled on the back. *Thinking of you every day, and longing for the day where we share your bed once more. -Nadia*

Never figured Abu Bakr for a romantic, Zaina thought, but she pocketed the picture and walked away. She stopped by her bunk to pick up her pack of smokes and then made her way to the door. Abu Bakr's crew stood around the door, but they parted the way for her to pass by.

Once she cleared the crowd, she placed the cancer stick in her mouth, lit up, and took a deep drag. The nicotine hit her bloodstream instantly, and what nerves remained quickly faded away. After the second drag, she glanced left and found Bowles outside of his housing block. He was nearing the end of his cigarette. Zaina tried to make eye contact with him, but he would not acknowledge her. She took another pull, and then began to move in his direction.

He quickly held up his left palm at his side, subtle enough that the casual observer would miss it, but a clear enough sign to Zaina. Bowles still refused to make eye contact, but he had seen her movement and had halted her advance. His posture seemed very relaxed, and yet, something in her gut told her that something was amiss. She leaned against the side of her building and continued to smoke as she waited to see what caused Bowles to halt her advance.

A moment later, four guards materialized from nowhere, each one taking a corner to block any avenue of escape. They knew enough about the Khalid incident not to get close unless they were all going to attack at once, but none of them felt like testing that operational theory. One of the men stepped closer and cleared his throat, his hand clutching his nightstick with a white-knuckled death grip.

"Mr. Bowles, I'm going to need you to come with me," the guard said in passable English.

"What's going on?" Bowles asked.

"Your presence has been requested in the punishment block," the guard explained. "I'm sorry. I don't have any further information. Please, come with us quietly."

Bowles extinguished his cigarette and held his hands where the guards could see him. "I won't fight. Lead the way."

"Thank you," the guard said, relieved.

As the four guards marched Bowles away, a thin, bearded man stepped into view, accompanied by Colonel Abbas. The man locked eyes with her, and a chill slithered down her spine. She thought she recognized the face, but she could not be sure. Regardless, Zaina knew that Bowles had caught this man observing him, and knew what came next. He had just spared her again, but at what cost? Without his assistance, she could easily start the riot, but there would not be a way to break out of the prison.

Zaina looked back to the door. She took a deep breath and made her way back inside. She needed to replace the photo and then sit back and wait. She could only hope that whatever this outsider had in store for Bowles was brief and relatively painless.

CHAPTER SIX

Istiqbal-Tora Prison
Cairo, Egypt
22 July 2006
15:39 hours Eastern European Time (13:39 hours Zulu)

WILLIAMS HAD BEEN LEFT to stew for the past thirty minutes. They had brought a chair and a table into the room, sat him down in the chair, and secured his hands behind his back with a pair of flex cuffs. He immediately recognized the tactic for what it was and remained calm. At the same time, he braced himself for the worst. In an American prison or a police station, leaving him alone to his thoughts would do half of the battle for the interrogator, and then the interrogator would win the other half through manipulation and the subject's own ignorance. The difference was, as he knew from both anecdotal and first-hand experience, the Egyptian government did not care much for human rights.

While he waited, he began to formulate a new way out of the prison. His plan to play the rival factions against each other was shot if he were held for any extended period of time. That left one option: an overt break. That option was full of flaws that could get Williams, Zaina, or both killed, but at the same time, he knew he was pushing the time envelope.

The door opened, and the thin man that he had caught scoping him out before entered the room, accompanied by a bulldog of a man, both dressed in similar suits. Once the door closed, the thin man took a seat directly across from Williams while the bulldog stood behind him and off to his left, a menacing glare in his eyes.

"I'm Colonel Agha with the General Intelligence Services Directorate, Counterintelligence Section," the thin man said. "This is my deputy, Lieutenant Colonel Faris. We have a few questions to ask you, Mr. Bowles."

"Counterintelligence?" Williams smirked. "Do you think I'm a spy, Colonel Agha?"

Agha smiled. "I don't know, Mr. Bowles. Why don't you tell me?"

Williams laughed, hung his head, then returned his gaze to Agha. "Colonel, I'm sure your expertise far exceeds mine. My knowledge of espionage is limited to James Bond and Robert Ludlum novels, but wouldn't a spy be trying to keep a low profile? I've made it no secret why I'm here. I'm just a tourist who's had some bad luck."

"Actually, you're correct, Mr. Bowles," Agha said approvingly. "A case officer or an asset would do everything they could not to draw attention to themselves. However, that cardinal rule can be disregarded if it serves a higher purpose."

Williams put on a perplexed expression. "And what would that higher purpose be, Colonel?"

Now it was Agha who laughed. "Mr. Bowles, you must think me inexperienced if you think I am going to lay all my cards on the table at once." He pulled out a notepad and a pen, clicked the pen into action, and cleared his throat. "When did you arrive in Egypt, Mr. Bowles?"

"The twelfth of this month," Williams answered.

"And what was the purpose of your visit?"

Williams squinted his eyes. "Can't you get all of this from customs?"

Faris rewarded his smart remark with an open-handed cuff upside the head. Agha pretended that he did not see anything. In a calm, neutral voice, he repeated, "What was the purpose of your visit?"

"Pleasure," Williams grunted, looking Faris up and down with an irritated look. "You mind calling off your attack dog? I thought we were having a civilized conversation."

"Well, that really depends on you, Mr. Bowles," Agha said pleasantly. "Answer all of my questions and our conversation will be civil and brief. Refuse to answer my questions, and I will be forced to resort to more...persuasive techniques."

Williams locked eyes with Agha. "You mean torture."

"Torture?" Agha looked to Faris, then back to Williams. "Torture's done without purpose, without aim. I believe the term used in your country is 'enhanced interrogation.'"

"That's an American thing," Williams said with a stiff upper lip. "Canada has a sterling record in regards to human rights. We would never sacrifice our moral high ground for security."

Agha shrugged as he scribbled something in his notepad. "Well, it must be nice to afford the luxury of human rights."

"They're human *rights*, not *luxuries*," Williams said. "They wouldn't carry the same weight that they do if they were abandoned at the first sign of inconvenience."

"Spoken like a true idealist," Agha said. "However, we are veering from the topic." He flipped back a few pages to consult his notes. "You were arrested three days after arriving in the country." Agha met Williams's gaze again. "Tell me what happened that day."

"What's there to tell?" Williams shrugged. "I was photographing Heliopolis Palace—a historic landmark—and I found the surrounding buildings to be a sight to see, so I snapped a few pictures. Out of nowhere, some asshole soldier is in my face and trying to grab my camera, so I sock him one good, and the next thing I know, he and his asshole buddies are kicking the crap out of me. They arrest me, keep me in lockup for three days, toss me in the back of a paddy wagon, and then, tada! I'm here."

"All right." He looked around the punishment cell. "This place really is draconian. If it were up to me, I would upgrade these punishment cells to something a little more modern." Williams said nothing, and Agha looked to him again. "You know a little something about these punishment cells, don't you?"

"Yeah," Williams conceded. "They suck."

"That's right," Agha said. "You've spent a bit of time in one, haven't you? Tell me about that."

"Some assholes managed to mime their way into convincing me that they had something to show me. Like an idiot naïve foreigner, I followed them. They then proceeded to kick the crap out of me, and I fought back."

Agha pointed to the bruise on Williams's face. "You definitely did not come out of the encounter unscathed."

Williams shrugged again. "You should see the other guys."

"I did see the other guys. Two dead, three seriously injured. You certainly know how to handle yourself in a violent situation, Mr. Bowles."

"What can I say? I'm a hockey player. I know a thing or two about brawling."

"Except that's the thing, Mr. Bowles." Agha set his pen down, interlaced his fingers, and twiddled his thumbs as he organized his thoughts. "When you were first arrested, you hit the soldier attempting to detain you, and were swiftly forced into compliance by the other soldiers. According to the sergeant on the ground, you threw a wide punch that allowed them an opening to take you down. Yet, against five criminals—one of them armed with a knife—you managed to make short work of them and kill two of them."

"If you'd notice my arm, you'd see it was anything but short work," Williams countered. "I got cut."

"Yes, you did, but you only got cut once, and it was a flesh wound," Agha said. "I read the medical report. You want to know what all of this tells me, Mr. Bowles?"

Williams rolled his eyes. "No, but I suppose you'll tell me, anyway."

Faris cuffed Williams harder upside the head, but he refused to give the counterintelligence officer the satisfaction of a show of pain. Instead, Williams clenched his jaw and took a deep breath. He looked at Faris for a moment, a fire in his eyes, then reluctantly redirected his gaze to Agha.

"There's a political prisoner here, Zaina Anwar.

She was arrested for sedition. Her cousin is in our special operations forces, and he has been on the run for the past three weeks. Something tells me that you know her cousin, and he asked you to break her out. You knew the only way to do so was to trick us into arresting you, and then making a break. Your final step would be to seek asylum from the US Embassy and arrange safe transport to the States. Does any of this sound familiar, Mr. Bowles?"

"Sure," Williams said. "Sounds like a straight-to-DVD action flick I saw last summer."

That statement earned Williams his first closed-fist strike of the afternoon, a solid right straight that left him hearing bells. He blinked rapidly as he tried to regain his bearings. Agha shook his head with a sad smile.

"As you can tell, Mr. Bowles, Colonel Faris doesn't appreciate your wisecracks. Personally, I find them to be humorous, the sign of somebody who tries to make the best of a bad situation. But, as I have no control over my associate, it would behoove you to abstain from the one-liners while in Colonel Faris's presence."

"Right," Williams said. "Where were you, now?"

"The Canadian Embassy hasn't returned our government's requests for identification verification, purportedly due to a backlog. Honestly, I think it's a waste of time. If you're a professional, your cover story will be back-stopped. If you're not, then your cover will fall apart and you'll be exposed as a foreign agent. Either way, your options aren't looking very good. So, let's start small. What is your name?"

"What?" Williams asked. He knew what came

next, but he would buy as much time as he could.

"Your name. What is your name?"

"You know my name, Colonel."

Agha's features were inscrutable, and his tone never betrayed a shred of impatience. "Your name, please. I will not ask again."

"Darren Rutherford Bowles."

"Very well, then." Agha stood and pocketed his notepad and pen. "Colonel Faris, would you do the honors? Meet with me in a half-hour to discuss his progress. I will be in the warden's office."

"You've got it, boss," Faris said.

Agha made his way to the door and knocked twice. The guard opened the door and allowed him to leave. As soon as the door was shut, Faris grabbed the table and hurled it across the room.

"Listen to me, you piece of shit," he snarled in heavily accented English. "I want to know your name. Tell me or suffer the consequences."

"Darren Rutherfor—"

The punch slammed into his solar plexus and knocked the air from him. A second blow followed close behind, followed by a right hook to the jaw. Faris grabbed Williams by the top of his head, digging his fingers into the bruise. Williams bared his teeth as the searing pain cut through his face, but he refused to let out a scream.

"What's the name?" Faris asked, his tone reduced to a deathly whisper.

"Already told you," Williams said. "Maybe you should listen a little better, pencil-dick."

Faris grinned wickedly. "I was hoping you'd say that," he said before he knocked over Williams's chair and continued his interrogative battery.

* * *

COLONEL AGHA SAT IN Colonel Abbas's office as he waited for another report from Faris. This was standard procedure, an extreme version of "good cop, bad cop." Agha rarely got his hands dirty with interrogations. He was not squeamish about the tactics, but he was far more effective with the psychological and analytical approach. Faris, on the other hand, was decidedly street-smarter than Agha. Pain was his art and an uncooperative subject was his canvass. Agha found it effective to use Faris to place the subject in a weakened state of mind via his liberal application of physical violence, and then use their state of heightened stress against them, a combination they had employed to great effect hundreds of times.

Yet, as Agha sipped from his *chai* glass, he had a feeling that they would have to go to greater lengths to break this subject. The subject was a tough man, probably trained to resist all forms of interrogation. That did not faze Agha in the least, as he knew the one fact that nobody, subject or interrogator, could escape.

Everybody has a breaking point.

Still, the subject fascinated him. If he had to place the man's profession, his best bet would be soldier. Agha knew beyond a shadow of a doubt that the man was not a civilian, and he seemed too refined to be a terrorist, at least of the caliber that he had dealt with during his career. "Bowles" also did not strike him as an intelligence agent. Most of those types were tougher than civilians, but not as tough as the subject. As he insinuated in the punishment cell, it was very likely that the subject was former special operations, which would make him a particularly tough nut to crack.

That's why you're enjoying this case, he told himself. *You love the challenge.*

Three knocks at the door tore Agha's attention from his musings. He looked to the door and said, "Come."

Faris entered the room, marched straight to his boss, and stood with his hands clasped behind his back. "Nothing. I've decided to give him a few hours to recuperate before I start back up again. I don't want to literally break him."

"Probably for the best." Agha checked his watch. "You've been working on him for seven hours straight. Not only does he need some time to heal, but you need rest. We can't have you burning out in the middle of questioning."

"You don't have to worry about me," Faris said dutifully. "I could continue pressing him for the time being if you want."

"Let him have his rest," Agha said. "But tomorrow, raise the stakes a notch."

Faris stood a little straighter. "What do you have in mind?"

Agha pondered the possibilities for a moment. "Try the cold water treatment. If that fails, try direct electroshock therapy. Burning comes next. If none of those break him, then we will adjust strategy. But for the time being, escalate slowly. Give each treatment at least a few hours' time before you move to the next. This is going to be a marathon. Bowles won't break easily."

"I'd like to bring First Sergeant Akram on to assist," Faris said. "Also, if anything comes up regarding Ferran Anwar, I'd like for Akram to take over in my stead while I follow the lead."

Agha nodded. "That's fine. If we capture Ferran, then that would render this whole Bowles affair irrelevant. We could put him down and rid ourselves of the problem. All we really need is the girl and her cousin."

"I agree completely, sir," Faris said. "Are you going to be staying here?"

"Yes," Agha said.

"You really should go home and get some rest, sir," Faris said. "I can handle things here. No need to stress yourself out at ground zero."

"A kind offer, but one I must decline," Agha said. "I need to stay close. Don't worry—I won't micromanage you."

"I'm not worried about micromanagement," Faris said. "I'm worried about *you* burning out."

Agha smiled. "Don't worry about me, my friend. I'll be fine."

Faris nodded. "In that case, I'll go and see if they have any spots in the faculty lounge for me to stretch my legs and get some sleep."

"Good idea," Agha said. "Go on, Uday. Get some rest. I'll come get you in the morning."

"Yes, sir." Faris turned on his heel and marched out of the warden's office. That left Agha to pick up

right now. And now, I feel nothing but despair. Mubarak's thugs are pervasive, all-knowing, and are experts in intercepting resistance before it grows. I am starting to acknowledge that there is a distinct possibility that I will die within the confines of this prison, and I can only hope that somebody will hear my story, that somebody will take strength in it and rise against the government to affect peaceful regime change. There is no government on Earth that can successfully silence the people when they speak as one. While it pains me that Mubarak may have won this fight, I have peace of mind knowing that he will not *win this war of ideals.*

Zaina put the pen down, closed the notebook, and placed both beneath her mattress. She pulled her feet close to her chest and took a deep breath. For all of her political activism, at the end of the day, Zaina was a realist. She knew that once the powers-that-be read the contents of her prison diary, they would burn it and buy themselves a term extension. However, she refused to cease her writing out of fear. So long as she was alive, so long as the diary was in her possession, she would continue to document everything she saw. She had to keep the voice of resistance alive, even if only in principle.

That goes for you, too, Bowles, she thought as she rested her head on her knees. *Keep fighting.*

* * *

Istiqbal-Tora Prison

Cairo, Egypt
24 July 2006
08:50 hours Eastern European Time (06:50 hours Zulu)

WILLIAMS KNEW THE PLAN as soon as the pair of guards brought the requisite materials into the room. He had seen this done before. Despite his knowledge, he tried his best to portray the frightened civilian. Agha, Faris, and Akram all stood together while one guard set up the interrogation and the other stood watch over Williams.

Agha looked at Williams. "We're moving onto the next phase," he said. "This will only continue to escalate until you tell me what I want to know."

"My name is Darren Rutherford Bowles," Williams said. "I'm a Canadian citizen." He fought against the restraints that kept him bound to the chair.

Agha smiled. Akram stepped forward with a knife in hand. He cut away Williams's shirt, exposing his bare chest. The knife was returned to its sheath, and then Akram reached back for a bucket. He removed a sponge from the bucket, squeezed most of the water from it, and began to touch it to Williams's chest.

"It's rather simple," Agha said. "Car battery and jumper cables. Minimal burning and scarring to your body, maximum pain inflicted." He then knelt to pick up the second piece of equipment and held it up. "We keep your body damp to ensure it conducts electricity. We increase the duration of the charge with every refusal or wrong answer."

Out of the corner of his eye, Williams watched Faris check his cell phone, then lean in close. He spoke in Arabic, but it was too inaudible to make out what was being said. Agha nodded to Faris, who immediately marched from the room and closed the door behind him. Agha cleared his throat and spoke.

"You are a tough specimen, Mr. Bowles, but you and I both know that every man has his limits. It is not a question of *if* you will break, but rather, a question of *when*."

"I don't know what the fuck you're talking about," Williams said angrily. "I am a computer salesman from Rutland!"

Agha looked at Williams with a mixture of admiration and pity. "You are quite the dedicated operative, Mr. Bowles. Sticking to your cover, despite knowing what lies in store. I almost wish that you were on my side. My country could always use another soldier like yourself."

"I am *not* a soldier," Williams hissed through gritted teeth. "I am a Canadian citizen and I demand to speak with my embassy, immediately."

"You will get that chance, once the Canadians claim you as theirs." He nodded to the guards, who brought the battery and jumper cables closer. Williams glared defiantly as one guard hooked one end of the cables to the battery. The second guard touched the other cables together, which elicited a sharp and audible spark.

"So, what will it be, Mr. Bowles?" Agha asked. "Your real name?"

"Darren Bowles."

Agha nodded, and turned to take his leave. "So be it."

Once the door shut, First Sergeant Akram said,

"Do it."

The guard took a step forward, cables in hand. His hands applied pressure to the clamps to open them up. In a swift motion, the guard touched the clamps to Williams's chest and released them. The clamps bit into his chest and the electricity rushed from the battery to his body.

For the first time since his imprisonment, Williams screamed.

CHAPTER SEVEN

Istiqbal-Tora Prison
Cairo, Egypt
24 July 2006
17:45 hours Eastern European Time (15:45 hours Zulu)

FIRST SERGEANT AKRAM STEPPED into the hallway and removed his cell phone from his pocket. He was overdue for a status report fifteen minutes ago, and figured he would just wait until the halfway point between the two check-in times to knock them both out. A medic had been brought in to treat the subject. While the main point was to induce excruciating pain, a secondary point was to keep the subject alive. The burn scars were small, but treating them helped to further break the subject down. No painkillers were administered, so Bowles felt every alcohol-soaked cotton swab. Even as he dialed Colonel Agha's extension, he could hear Bowles's grunts as the medical personnel did their work.

"Colonel Agha."

"Colonel, it's First Sergeant Akram."

"You were late with your report."

Akram looked back to the room. "My apologies, sir. I got distracted. There's nothing to report."

There was a contemplative pause. "He still hasn't talked?"

"No, sir," Akram said. "I pushed him particularly hard in the last few minutes of the questioning. Not a word. I called it early and had the medical personnel treat him."

"This only adds credibility to our working theory," Agha said. "Bowles is a well-trained operator."

"It's beginning to look like the only way to break him will be leverage," Akram suggested. "The first thing that comes to mind is to use the woman, manipulate the Western sense of chivalry against him to make him talk."

Agha was silent for a few moments. "Possible, but not something I want to commit to immediately. She does have declared U.S. citizenship and no military background. Nobody will bat an eyelash to our treatment of a rogue American operator interfering in affairs of state, but if we touch the woman, that may not be something we can rectify."

"Understood, sir." Akram cleared his throat. "Have you heard from Colonel Faris?"

"Last I heard, he was closing in on his objective. He'll contact me with any new developments. For now, come to my office and let's work out a plan of action."

"Yes, sir. I will be up there in twenty minutes."

"Very good."

Akram hung up the phone and took a deep breath. Contrary to the belief of bleeding heart organizations, a proper invasive interrogation was not carried out by a brainless thug. What was popularly known as "torture" was akin to a game of chess, an attempt to out-think the opponent and defeat them psychologically. The techniques employed were merely another tool in the interrogator's kit, a method to disrupt the subject's psychological processes and open a sieve through which critical information could be gleaned.

The door swung open, and one of the guards leaned out, his eyes wide and his breathing labored.

"First Sergeant!" the guard called out. "Come quick!"

Akram's face darkened. "What is it?"

"The prisoner has gone into convulsions!"

* * *

EVERY MUSCLE TENSED IN Williams's body. He leaned forward in the chair, his arms locked out and held in place by his restraints, his body shaking uncontrollably. Drool spilled from his lips as his eyes rolled into the back of his head. The medic knelt beside him, pulled out a penlight, and began holding back each of his eyelids as he shone the light on the eyes.

Akram barged past the threshold. "What the hell happened?"

The medic kept his eyes on Williams as he spoke. "I was dressing the prisoner's wounds. Next thing I know, he's hyperventilating and he's slumped forward."

"Uncuff him," Akram said. "I need him taken to the sick bay, *now!*"

One guard moved behind Williams, produced a handcuff key, and unlatched the handcuff. The other guard stood in front of Williams and propped him up by the chest. Once both wrists were freed, the guards moved to raise him from the chair.

Williams's eyes slipped into focus. He head-butted

the guard in front of him square on the nose, then swung backward with his left elbow and caught the rear guard in the temple. Williams shoved the front guard aside and rushed towards Akram. The first sergeant was ready for Williams, and caught him in the midsection with a left stab punch. Akram followed with a right hook that landed on the side of Williams's face, spun him around, and felled him.

Akram and the front guard both rushed Williams. He lashed out with a kick that caught Akram square in the groin, then spun on his lower back to face the other guard. Williams placed his hands on the ground beside his head, tucked his knees to his chest, and executed a textbook kip-up that caught the guard square in the chest. The guard stumbled backward and hit the wall as Williams's feet touched the ground. Williams spun around just in time to find the rear guard closing in, baton held high. He leapt forward and wrapped the assailant in a perfect spear, and once both men hit the ground, Williams scrambled forward and landed five solid elbows to the man's face. The guard's eyes rolled into the back of his head.

Both Akram and the remaining guard had found their footing and drawn their own batons. Williams scooped up the unresponsive guard's baton and held it slightly in front of him as he assumed a fighting stance. The guard attacked first, and Williams deftly side-stepped and applied a healthy helping of baton to his opponent's striking hand. His agonizing scream was cut short with a backhanded baton to the side of the head. Blood and gray matter flowed from the man's head as his corpse hit the floor.

Williams's eyes met Akram's. On instinct, Akram dropped his baton and went for his handgun. Williams rushed forward, cocked back, and batted the handgun away. He grabbed Akram by the shoulder and tossed him on the ground. He brought a hammer fist down on Akram's nose, then took a step back and swung the baton hard, connecting with Akram's knee. He repeated the blow to the other knee. Williams hefted the crippled Akram onto the chair, forced his hands behind his back, and secured him to the chair with handcuffs. He dropped the baton, grabbed the car battery, and brought it to the back of the chair. Akram craned his neck to look at Williams with a pleading stare.

"W-w-we can bargain," Akram pleaded, his voice stuffy. "Y-you don't have to do this!"

Williams stared at Akram, his eyes cold and empty. Akram knew what would happen, and shook his head briskly.

"No hard feelings," Williams said. He fastened the alligator clamps to the handcuff chair, and Akram's screams filled the chamber. It only took a minute and a half for Akram to expire, but Williams allowed him to fry while he retrieved the dead guard's keys and Akram's handgun. It was a flat-black SIG-Sauer, loaded with one in the pipe. It was not much, but fifteen bullets were better than none.

Williams disconnected the clamps and tossed them across the room. The Egyptians had done him a favor by cleaning and dressing his wounds, but he would need to re-dress them once he was on the outside. The important thing was that he had enough strength to effect the breakout. Time was running short and he had already missed his first rendezvous with Ferran.

Williams jogged to the door. Once he had crossed the threshold, he shut the door, locked it, and then tossed the keys in the nearby trash receptacle.

It was time to check out of Istiqbal-Tora.

* * *

NEARLY THREE DAYS HAD passed. Zaina could tell that the guards were keeping an eye on her, but none of them made a move. Her best guess was that whoever arrested Bowles had put out standing orders to keep eyes on at a distance. Perhaps they thought she had compatriots on the outside that were going to break her out. She rolled her eyes at the thought, but she knew that the regime treated any sort of dissent as a potential full-blown insurgency.

The desire to write in her journal had temporarily slipped away. She tried a couple times since her last entry, but Zaina felt that she had documented everything of importance. Instead, she went back and read through what she had already written. It was a mirror into her psyche, a display her indignation, defiance, resignation, and moments of hope during her incarceration. Zaina wished she could recapture the last feeling, the one she felt when Bowles informed her of his intent.

Rustling pulled her from her reverie, followed by the sound of a blunt object striking flesh. Zaina stood and moved to the edge of the bunk. The guard was thrown inside, and a large man swiftly followed him in and kicked him hard in the face. The man kicked the guard thrice more, studied the unconscious form for a moment, and then jogged towards Zaina. As he came closer, Zaina recognized who it was and her heart beat faster. Once he was only a few feet from her, that excitement turned to horror and shock.

"Oh, my God, Bowles!" she whispered. "What the hell happened to you?"

"I'll explain later," he said. "And my name ain't Bowles. It's Williams."

"Why—"

"Well, one of two things is about to happen: we'll be free or we'll be killed. At this point, keeping you in the dark is irrelevant. I'll explain once we're free."

Zaina's eyes fell on the bruises that adorned his body, as well as the two small burns on his torso. She could see the pain carved into his countenance, how the only thing keeping him going was sheer willpower. After a hesitant inhale, she said, "Are you sure you're good to move?"

Williams started to chuckle, then grabbed his midsection and winced. "No, probably not. But that's irrelevant. We *have* to move, *now*, while the evening match is in full swing. It's our best chance of getting out of here." He turned and made for the door. "Let's move."

"Wait!" Zaina took a knee beside her bed, grabbed her diary, and held it in her left hand.

Williams eyed the book. "What's that?"

"Prison diary. This is how I'm going to blow the whole thing open."

"Uh-huh." He drew the SIG-Sauer from his waistband, cocked the hammer, and then motioned with his head toward the door. "Time to go."

"What's the plan?" Zaina asked as they moved to the door.

"Huh?" Williams focused on his area scan, the SIG-Sauer held close at chest-level with his finger alongside the trigger guard.

"How are we getting out?" she repeated. "There is no back gate, the front gate is heavily guarded, and there's no access to the sewers. The grates are bolted down tight."

Williams stopped and gave Zaina a look.

"What? I got desperate my first week."

"Ah." He reached the door and peeked out. Once he saw the coast was clear, he pulled back and looked at Zaina. "We are not going out the front and we are *definitely* not trying to swim in a fucking sewer."

"Then how are we getting out?"

He flashed her a brief smile. "We make our own way out."

* * *

AGHA CHECKED HIS WATCH as he sipped his *chai*. Akram was late, but he knew the man. Much like his immediate superior, Colonel Faris, Akram was a workhorse who immersed himself in the task at hand. If he felt a breakthrough was imminent, then he would forego the check-in to press harder. It was the attitude that Agha instilled in his men that made them so efficient. While they were good soldiers that followed orders, they also were self-starters, men that took initiative, men that knew when it was acceptable to bend the rules to accomplish the mission. So, while Agha valued punctuality, he valued results even more, which was why he did not grow vexed by the missed check-in.

His *chai* glass ran empty, and he refilled it. After he mixed a spoonful of cane sugar in with the steaming hot drink, Agha took a sip from the glass, set it down, and fixated on a point on the wall as his mind wandered. He pulled in all of the factors to that point: Bowles's incompetence at the Heliopolis Palace, and then his combat prowess against a gang of hard criminals. That contradiction was supplemented by his ability to withstand physical coercion.

Ability to withstand coercion? Agha thought back to Bowles being interrogated, reflected on the reports that Faris and Akram had given him. It was more than having a high pain threshold. The look in his eyes, his demeanor...it brought to mind something Faris had told him after the dunk treatment.

"Our average subject reaches a point where he begs for us not to touch him, where he is afraid of us and what we will do to him. With Bowles, we do not hold back, we do not cut him any slack, and he just seems like he is ready and waiting for more."

*He's playing with us...*Agha slammed the rest of his *chai* and stood. He placed his hands behind his back as he paced. Somebody who was caught would be much more worried about *if* they would ever break free. Bowles, on the other hand, seemed to know that his incarceration was only temporary, that the pain would come to an end...

He knows that he'll break free. He's just looking

for the right moment.

Agha pulled out his cell phone and dialed Akram's extension. It rang for four tones, then went to the preprogrammed voicemail greeting. He closed his phone, marched to desk, and punched the intercom button on the desktop phone. "Hello?"

"Colonel Agha, this is Colonel Abbas. What can I do for you?"

"I need a runner sent to the punishment blocks. I want a status update on Mr. Bowles."

"I'll do it," Abbas said. "I need to check on the status of my other prisoners."

"Check Bowles first," Agha stressed. "This is non-negotiable. Do I make myself clear?"

Abbas barely kept his tone in check as he replied, "Yes, sir. I'll get back to you."

"Contact me direct over the net," Agha ordered. He released the button and ran a hand over his hair. His heart rate had picked up as two questions gnawed at him.

Am I leaping to conclusions, or have I caught on too late?

* * *

WILLIAMS BRACED HIMSELF WITH his right arm and gripped the SIG-Sauer in his left hand. He peered around the corner. As predicted, all eyes were on the pitch. His eyes shifted to the next housing block. The guard was not at his post, which was the norm for the matches. Most of the guards opted to keep eyes on the pitch rather than guard the doors, and it was a strategy that was allowed to help take some of the pressure off of the tower riflemen. It would also allow Williams to move closer to the exfiltration point, just beneath the northwest tower.

He looked over his left shoulder and made eye contact with Zaina. "You ready?"

Zaina swallowed nervously. "Suppose I don't have much of a choice, do I?"

Williams shook his head. "Nope. C'mon."

He lunged around the corner and jogged the distance between the housing units, switching the SIG-Sauer from his left hand to his right. The pistol's barrel moved in sync with his eyes as he scanned up and down, left to right. Once they reached the building, Williams transitioned his weapon to his left hand and braced his right hand against the wall for support. He winced and gritted his teeth as he caught his breath.

"Are you all right?" Zaina whispered.

"Yeah," Williams breathed. He shook his head briskly. "Let's move."

The pair moved forward and ducked beneath windows as they approached the door. Williams signaled for Zaina to hang back. He took a couple of preparatory deep breaths, then launched himself to the top of the stairwell and quickly stepped inside, his gun tucked close. The housing unit was empty, and Williams rejoined Zaina outside.

"All right," Williams said. "Next stop is the wall. We'll be relatively obscured from the sentries around the pitch, but if the tower guards get a glimpse of what we're doing, then it's gonna be a long shot, if we're not picked off immediately."

"Okay," Zaina said. "You still haven't explained how you're going to break us out."

"I'll show you here in a second," Williams said. "Wait here."

He peered around the corner, and then immediately ducked back around, the back of his head pressed against the wall. Zaina looked at him curiously. "What?" she asked quietly.

"Colonel Abbas," Williams breathed. "Heading for punishment block."

Her eyes widened. "What's he going to find?"

"Nothing, initially. I locked the guards' bodies inside the room."

"So he won't find them?"

He shook his head. "He's the warden. He'll get inside sooner or later."

"Then we need to move before that happens," Zaina said flatly.

Williams gave her a look that said *no shit* before peeking around the corner. "Okay, we're clear. Stay here."

* * *

COLONEL ABBAS MARCHED INTO the punishment block. He was immediately on guard when he saw that there were no sentries posted outside the door, nor were there any noises coming from the cell. He picked up his pace a little bit, reached the door, and tried to open it. The knob did not give. He reached for his radio and held it to his lips.

"Punishment block, this is Colonel Abbas."

He heard a voice respond, but something caught his attention. A moment passed before the other party keyed up again, and he knew exactly what he was hearing. On the other side of the door, he heard radios, but no response. Abbas's heart pounded in his chest as his worst suspicions raced to mind.

"Punishment block, this is Colonel Abbas. Bring me a set of keys, now."

"Roger," the sentry said. "On the way."

Abbas tried the door a few more times to no avail. He pressed his ear against the door and heard dead silence. His impatience ate at him, and he slammed his fist into the metal door five times in rapid succession.

"This is Colonel Abbas!" he called out. He pounded on the door again. "This is Colonel Abbas! Open up!"

"Colonel!"

Abbas turned to find a young soldier rushing forward, a ring of spare keys in hand. Once he was within arm's reach, Abbas snatched the keys from the soldier, found the right key, and slid it into the lock. Abbas twisted the key to the right and pushed the door open. His mouth dropped as he took in the scene before him. One guard was out cold. Another's brains were leaking from his cranium. If that were not enough, First Sergeant Akram's body was slumped in a chair, his hands cuffed behind his back, his eyes rolled into the back of his head. The putrid stench of charred flesh reached his nose, and it took every

113

ounce of willpower to refrain from emptying the contents of his stomach all over the floor.

"What the hell?" the young soldier asked beside him.

Abbas took command and pointed to the soldier in the corner. "Wake him up!"

"Yes, sir!"

As the soldier rushed inside to resuscitate his compatriot, Abbas marched toward the punishment block entrance. "All points, this is Colonel Abbas. We are on high alert. I say again, high alert. Mr. Bowles has escaped from confinement. This facility needs to be locked down at once. Return all inmates to their housing blocks and begin a block-by-block search for Darren Bowles. I say again, lock this prison down and find Bowles, *now!*"

* * *

AGHA CONTINUED TO PACE the room when the call came in over the radio. "Punishment block, this is Colonel Abbas. Bring me a set of keys, now." He stormed over to the radio, snatched it from the desk, and held it to his ear as he listened anxiously. A full two minutes passed without any further updates. When Abbas came back on the net, his voice was strained, almost haunted.

"All points, this is Colonel Abbas. We are on high alert. I say again, high alert. Mr. Bowles has escaped from confinement—"

That was all Agha needed to hear. He clipped the

radio to his belt and drew his SIG-Sauer. His hands moved mechanically as he removed the magazine to ensure it was full, replaced it, and then pressed the slide back slightly to confirm that a round was chambered. Satisfied, Agha bolted from the office and made his way to the courtyard.

It was time to go hunting.

CHAPTER EIGHT

Istiqbal-Tora Prison
Cairo, Egypt
24 July 2006
18:00 hours Eastern European Time (16:00 hours Zulu)

WILLIAMS REACHED THE WALL and tucked his SIG-Sauer into his waistline. He removed his belt from his pants, unscrewed the hilt of the buckle and removed it, which allowed him to pull the buckle free of the belt. There was enough of a gap between the two pieces of leather for Williams to fit his finger inside, which allowed him to tear the belt apart at the seams.

From the belt's carcass, he removed two thin, long strips of faded tan putty with gray backing. Williams looked over his shoulder to check that nobody was meandering into the area, then removed the backing from a strip to reveal an adhesive surface. He looked for the crack in the wall and found it exactly where he had imagined it during his pre-mission ground reconnaissance. Williams pressed the strip to the wall, then ran his hand along the strip to ensure there were no gaps between the strip and the wall. He repeated the process with the other strip and placed it perpendicular to the first to create an "X." Finally, Williams removed a cap from the bottom of the hilt, embedded it in the center of the "X," and twisted the cap's top. He was rewarded with a stark green light.

Williams pocketed the rest of the buckle and jogged back towards Zaina. That was when the alarms sounded, and Colonel Abbas exited the prison block, right in Williams's field of vision. On instinct, Abbas turned and met Williams's eyes. As the warden opened his mouth, Williams's hand blurred as he drew the SIG-Sauer from his waistband. He extended the Swiss handgun directly in front of him, placed the front sight on Abbas's chest, and squeezed off two rounds in less than a second. Before gravity had a chance to pull Abbas's body to the ground, Williams shifted aim directly between Abbas's eyes and stroked the trigger once more. The 9mm slug punched through skull and gray matter, and created a pink mist around his crown. Abbas' eyes rolled into the back of his head, and he fell where he stood, his bodily fluids staining the desert soil.

The moment his final shot had registered, Williams turned towards the distant tower and fired off two rounds in rapid succession. He knew at that range, the 9mm round was unlikely to hit the target, but it kept the rifleman behind cover, which is what Williams needed. Turning on a heel, Williams sprinted back to Zaina, yanked her off the stairwell, and shielded her body with his own. He reached into his pocket, removed the belt buckle and pressed a button on its corner.

The miniature radio detonator sent a signal to the blasting cap embedded in the center of the cross-strips of C4 plastic explosive. The blasting cap sparked the explosion, ripping through the structural weakness in the wall and created a gaping hole. The tower position mounted to the corner creaked as it lost its support, and the sentry within screamed as the tower gave and crashed to the ground.

"C'mon!" Williams shouted. He grabbed Zaina by the hand as he lunged from cover and raced for the exit. Gunfire saturated the air around them as they skirted the outside of the felled tower and sprinted past the wall. The terrain outside the prison was rugged, barren, and expansive, with no natural cover to speak of. His recce had highlighted this dilemma, and he knew that however he managed to breach the wall, their movement to the hard point would be the most dangerous portion of the escape.

Behind him, he could hear Zaina gasp for air as they crossed the desert expanse. He tightened his grip on her hand and pushed forward. Fire burned within his legs, a culmination of the beatings, lack of nutrition, and the sudden stress he forced upon them. His back screamed protests, the welts and burns opening and sweat pouring into the sores. Williams felt his body telling him to pass out, to quit, that he had come farther than any normal man could and it would be acceptable to die right there.

Hell no. Williams bared his teeth and snarled as he picked up the pace. He could feel his arm locking out as Zaina started to fall behind, and he pulled her closer, just hard enough for her to keep up but gently enough that she did not trip over her own feet. Finally, they reached what they had aimed for: an odd-shaped tan object, virtually invisible from a distance.

"Wha...what...what is this?" Zaina asked breathlessly.

"Our ride out," Williams said. He grabbed two fistfuls of cloth and yanked back hard to reveal a tan Land Rover Defender. Williams immediately opened the back, and before he reached inside, he looked to Zaina. "Get to the driver's side. Keys are in the visor. You're driving."

"What? I don't even know where the hell we are!"

Williams extended a blade hand across the roof of the Land Rover. "That's due west," he said. "Drive that way, but watch where you're going. There's a giant ravine that'll fuck our day up."

Zaina jogged around the front of the Rover as she asked, "Why aren't you driving?"

"This," Williams said as he opened a black case to reveal an M4A1 SOPMOD carbine, equipped with a Knight's Armament flip-up rear sight, a Trijicon Advanced Combat Optical Gunsight 4x rifle optic, a forward grip, and a PEQ-2 infrared optic mounted just behind the front sight post. He extended the buttstock to its full length, seated a thirty-round magazine in the well, and ripped the charging handle to the rear to chamber a round. Williams grabbed a bandoleer full of loaded M4 magazines, slammed the door, and took the shotgun seat. As the engine roared to life, Williams opened the sunroof and stood on the seat to emerge through the roof. His back grazed the edge of the sunroof, which caused him to scream and clench his eyes shut as he worked past the pain.

Gunshots brought him back into focus. Williams shouldered the carbine and peered through the ACOG. The tritium-illuminated chevron made it easy to line up the sights with the enemy, but he'd had to tape over the fiber optic wire to block the light and keep the chevron from being blindingly bright. One guard raised his rifle and began to open fire. Williams placed the tip of the chevron just beneath his sternum and stroked the trigger. A 5.56mm missile raced from the barrel and caught the rifleman in the chest. A follow-up shot hit a quarter of an inch above the first entrance wound and dropped him.

Williams shifted aim to the far tower and placed the base of the chevron at center mass to adjust for the three hundred meter distance. On his exhale, he squeezed the trigger twice in rapid succession, and both rounds ripped through the sentinel's chest. The sentry stumbled over the edge of the tower and plummeted to the ground, head first. Williams turned back to the exit he had created, flicked the selector switch to AUTO, and began tapping out three-round bursts towards the crowd that had congregated there.

Zaina shifted gears and pressed the pedal to the floor. "Hang on!" she cried out. She peeled out in reverse hard tail-end right and the force of the movement thrust Williams's back into the edge of the sunroof again. An agonized howl filled the air, and he looked down at Zaina, his expression a mixture of pain and vexation.

"Take it easy with those spin-outs!" he growled.

"You wanted me to drive!" she spat in response.

"It was either drive or shoot, and you don't look like a shooter!"

"I think I'd surprise you!"

Williams rolled his eyes and readjusted himself in his makeshift turret. "Just shut up and drive! Give us some distance!"

* * *

AGHA MADE IT TO the courtyard as fast as he could. A thin film of sweat covered his skin by the time he reached the blast site. Most of the guards were posted by the housing blocks to deter the inmates from making a break for it. A couple guarded the hole, their MISR rifles at the ready as they tried to draw a bead on the escapees, and a couple more stood over one of the fallen bodies. Agha slowed his pace as he came closer to the fallen man. Enough of the face was left to know who it was, and the man's shoulder rank confirmed it.

"Colonel Abbas." Agha looked to the nearest soldier and asked, "What happened?"

"I heard gunshots, I left the punishment block, and I found the colonel dead and a prisoner with a weapon," the guard said. Agha was amazed at the young soldier's ability to remain calm. "When I went to respond to the threat, I heard a loud explosion, and once the smoke settled, two of the prisoners had escaped. They ran out about two hundred meters and uncovered a vehicle. The prisoner who had been wielding the pistol produced some sort of rifle and killed two more men before laying down suppressive fire to cover their escape."

Agha could not help but feel a bit of pride, not only at the young soldier's composure, but his ability to recall details clearly and factually. He got a quick look at the soldier's nametape. "Good job, Private Ghazi. Carry on."

"Yes, sir."

Ghazi only made it two steps before Agha said, "Private Ghazi! What channel is your QRF frequency on?"

"Channel Two, sir."

"Thank you." Agha removed the radio from his belt, switched it to Channel Two, and held it to his mouth. "Any station on this net, this is Colonel Abdullah Agha. Please respond."

"This is Sergeant Khalifah, QRF commander," a voice came back immediately. "Who are you?"

"I'm the new commander of Istiqbal-Tora," Agha announced calmly. "A high value target has escaped the prison and has killed several guards in the process, including Colonel Abbas. Subjects are headed due west. I repeat, due west. You need to scramble your QRF to intercept immediately."

"It will take some time to mobilize the ground force, but we have a helicopter unit here on station," Khalifah said. "They'll get a bead on them and continue to follow while the QRF main force moves to intercept."

"I want a status update every two minutes," Agha said. "This is a matter of national security, Sergeant. We cannot allow these targets to escape. Am I clear?"

"Yes, sir."

Agha clipped the radio to his belt and moved to the hole. As he came closer, a strong odor akin to asphalt reached his nose, and he immediately recognized its source. "C4?" he asked himself aloud. His mind knew the conclusion, but he lacked the evidence to make the case, and plastique residue only served to further tease him. He looked out the hole at the vast desert that surrounded the prison.

Standing at that hole, Agha felt something that he had not felt in a long time. It was an uncomfortable feeling, and one that threatened to engulf him.

That feeling was anger.

* * *

ZAINA GRIPPED THE WHEEL with white knuckles, her teeth bared and her eyes wide as she navigated the open desert. The terrain was bumpy, and while the suspension system and off-road tires did a lot to lessen the impact, the Defender still jostled her and Williams about as they raced westbound. Every few seconds, she heard Williams grunt or shout as his wounds were aggravated, but after the initial criticism, he had remained otherwise silent while he scanned the dusk sky for threats.

"Where are we going?" she asked.

"We're gonna hit El Nasr Road," Williams replied. "Once we get there, make a hard right onto the hardball and take it north. That will take us to Al Abajiyyah. From there, we'll lay low at a safe house."

"Will Ferran be there?"

"No. He was there a few days ago. Since then, he's moved onto another one, as was the plan. We'll establish radio contact once we reach the Al Abajiyyah safe house, lay low for a few hours, and then rendezvous with him."

"And then?"

"We're off to the embassy and we're home free."

"I don't have my passport," Zaina said.

"I've got a contact inside the embassy. She'll get us inside, no questions asked. From there, a day, maybe two at the embassy, and then a diplomatic flight to D.C. Your refugee status begins, and you two are home free."

Zaina fell silent for a moment. "Seems like a waste, really."

"What's that?"

"Fleeing to the States, evading the government. I've conceded the fight."

"Not my problem."

That comment elicited an irritated scoff from Zaina. "Of course it isn't your problem. There aren't any natural resources for the United States to come and exploit for financial gain. I shouldn't have expected anything less of a government yes-man."

"Shh, shut up," Williams said. "I think I hear something."

All Zaina could hear was the steady hum of the motor. Then she heard it, faintly at first, but then it grew in crescendo. It was not a sound she was accustomed to, but she knew it. Rotorthrob was hard to mistake for anything else. Up top, Williams could make out the movement in the dark sky, and he immediately ducked back into the vehicle.

"Should I try to outrun it?" Zaina asked, her breathing shallowed.

"No," Williams said. He set the M4 behind the passenger seat and began digging in the back. "I knew this would happen. I just wondered how long it would take them to scramble the bird."

"Wait—you *knew* they were going to send a helicopter after us?"

Williams continued to rummage through the back seat as he spoke. "That's the vanguard of their quick reaction force. They send the chopper ahead because it covers more ground and allows them to put eyes on a target before the ground force is on-site. Theoretically, they should even be able to disable a threat before the ground force arrives."

"Again, you *knew* they would send helicopters, and using a *car* was your idea of a logical prison break?"

Williams looked over his shoulder and glared at Zaina. "Next time, I'll let *you* plan the prison break. Until then, shut your mouth and keep driving."

"Right," Zaina snorted. "Keep calm until their machine guns cut us to ribbons."

Williams said nothing as he found the items he was looking for. He brought them to the front seat and prepared them for employment.

Zaina glanced over as Williams affixed an AN/PAS-13 optic to the Picatinny rail mounted to the side of the tube on his lap. "What's that?"

"My idea of a logical prison break," he deadpanned. He turned on the optic and switched it from white-hot to black-hot, and then removed an 85mm grenade and slid it into the business end of the RPG-7 rocket-propelled grenade launcher. Unlike the common RPG, this one was specially modified for use with Unit 777, which had access to American technology, such as the PAS-13. It was made completely of parkerized steel and sported rail attachment points for the optics of choice. Atop, it also had iron sights for daytime use or in case the optics malfunctioned. The grips were encased in rubber to ensure a slip-free handle on the weapon in any condition and to make it more comfortable to brace against one's shoulder.

With the weapon prepared, Williams leaned the spare rocket-grenades against the back of his seat and rose through the open sunroof. Once the weapon had cleared the opening, Williams checked his backblast, then shouldered the launcher and peered through the PAS-13. He could make out the helicopter, clear as day. It was an Mi-8 Hip, a Soviet design and the most widespread helicopter in the world. Williams could see a man attached to a harness and leaning out of the left side of the helicopter, his shoulder pressed to a mounted machine gun. As he centered the sight on the Hip's cockpit, the chopper gunner sighted in his range and held down the trigger. A stream of 7.62mm rounds sought flesh and metal as they peppered the area just ahead of the Defender.

"Holy fucking shit!" Zaina cried out. She swerved the car hard left to avoid the incoming fire. At that same moment, Williams began to pull the trigger on the RPG. The sudden movement threw the rocket off course to the far right, and simultaneously dug the sunroof further into his raw back. Williams reached down for another rocket grenade as he attempted to balance himself amidst Zaina's interpretation of evasive driving.

"Hey!" he shouted. "You need to keep this motherfucker steady."

Zaina took a deep breath and readjusted her grip on the wheel. "All right."

"You can do this," Williams assured her. "Keep it steady."

Without another word, Williams reemerged from the sunroof, RPG cocked and ready to go. The gunner had realized that he led the vehicle too much on the first burst and dialed back his sights. The rounds were coming in much closer. One tore through Defender's roof, whizzed past Williams's leg, and exited through the car's floor. That caused him to flinch, but he kept his aim on the chopper. The Hip was centered in his sights, and he dug his back into the edge of the sunroof for extra stability, ignoring the accompanying pain. He confirmed his sight picture, took one final breath, and squeezed the trigger.

The rocket grenade left a deafening *boom* around the vehicle as it left the tube and raced towards the helicopter, a trail of smoke in its wake. As it closed in on its target, the pilot saw it coming and managed to bank hard left to narrowly avoid it. Just as the pilot and co-pilot breathed sighs of relief, he spotted a third rocket that Williams had loaded and fired almost immediately after the second. With the remaining distance left to target, the pilots could do nothing but stare in horror.

Once it made impact, the rocket grenade ripped through the cockpit and exploded, instantly killing both pilot and co-pilot. The chopper gunner was thrown violently from the bird by the shockwave, and the remnants of the Hip spiraled to the desert floor, engulfed in flames. Williams allowed himself a grim smile of macabre satisfaction as he watched the fire light up the sky.

The moment was short lived. The adrenaline in his bloodstream started to thin, and the pain that had been held back rushed through his body. Williams let out a crazed growl as he lowered himself into the seat. He tossed the empty RPG in the back, grabbed the M4, and held onto it as tightly as he could. Williams told himself he was getting ready just in case the ground force caught them before they reached the safe house, but he knew better.

"What's wrong?" Zaina asked. She looked over at Williams. Perspiration drenched his body and soaked through the bandages. His eyes were clenched shut and his breathing was labored. Slowly, he forced his respiration in through his nose and out through his mouth to slow his heartbeat to a more reasonable range.

"Safe house," Williams breathed. "I'll guide you in."

A few moments later, Zaina reached the hardball. She turned the Defender right, hit the improved road, and stepped on the gas.

* * *

"COLONEL AGHA, THIS IS Sergeant Khalifah."

Agha grabbed the radio from his belt. "Give me a status report."

"He shot down the helicopter, sir."

For a full minute, Agha said nothing. He was not sure whether he was stunned that Bowles had managed to break out *and* shoot down a gunship, or absolutely livid that he had not pushed Bowles to his breaking point from the get-go. It proved what he already knew—Bowles was a professional. He knew he should have never let up on the interrogations, and that he could have led a few himself if he wanted constant, twenty-four/seven interrogation. Instead, he had opted to play it by ear, and now, several of his dead countrymen littered the desert.

"Are you there, sir? Colonel Agha?"

"Return to base," he said quietly. "They're gone."

"Yes, sir."

Agha clipped the radio to his waist, then reached into his pocket for his mobile. After two rings, the other party picked up.

"Colonel Faris."

"Situational update. Bowles is on the loose. He took the girl with him and killed ten people doing it. First Sergeant Akram is amongst the casualties."

There was silence on the phone. Faris had recruited and trained Akram decades earlier and the two had been tight. "What's our next move?"

"Give me your current status."

"I think we've located the target. We'll be moving in once we've confirmed. After that, we'll immediately commence on-site interrogation. I will provide you situation reports every quarter-hour."

"Very well," Agha said. "I'm returning to headquarters. I need to generate and disseminate a nationwide all-points bulletin for Bowles and Anwar. I want every cop and soldier in the city to be looking for them. Keep your eyes peeled, as well, just in case they come to you."

"Yes, sir," Faris said.

Agha closed the phone, pocketed it, and stared at the blaze in the distance. His jaw clenched as he associated the flames with the deaths of ten men, his countrymen, sworn to the same duty, the defense of the Egyptian homeland. Their lives had been taken by this dissident, a traitor who felt subversion was the answer for change. As Agha exhaled, he made a promise.

Your crimes against my country will not go unanswered, Bowles. When the bill is due, I will be the one to collect it.

CHAPTER NINE

Al Abajiyyah, Cairo, Egypt
24 July 2006
19:03 hours Eastern European Time (17:03 hours Zulu)

"TURN HERE," WILLIAMS SAID, using considerable effort to point out the house. It was in a shanty area, with houses of poor adobe construction. The one Williams pointed out had a wooden shack acting as a makeshift garage adjacent the building. Zaina pulled the Defender into the parking space, half of which was occupied by a beat-up silver 1985 Fiat Argenta. She looked to the Fiat, then to Williams.

"That's our next ride," he said to answer the unasked question.

Once Zaina put the vehicle in park, Williams opened his door and attempted to step out of the vehicle, the M4 in his left hand. A blade of pain plunged into his back's nerves and his muscles locked, which caused him to fall to the asphalt and suppress a shout. Zaina quickly killed the vehicle, hopped out of the driver's seat, and sprinted around the front to meet Williams.

"Are you okay?" she asked, the concern stark in her voice.

"Help me up," Williams growled. "There's a first aid kit inside."

Her eyes wandered to the bandages, which were now stained with his blood. She took a deep breath, and then draped Williams's left arm across her shoulders. Williams picked up the M4 with his right hand and used the buttstock to help Zaina lift him to his feet, and then the two of them hobbled to the door. It was unlocked, and both of them stepped inside.

"This building doesn't have electricity," Zaina pointed out.

"Switch to the generator is on the wall to your left."

Zaina reached out with her left hand and patted the wall until she felt something that broke the texture pattern. Her fingers found a knob atop a metal block that was held to the wall with what felt like duct tape, and she turned it to the left. The generator began to hum, and slowly, mounted florescent lighting reached full luminosity. Zaina began to make out the features of house. To her left, she could see the fuel generator, and beyond that was a closet. In front of them was a kitchen, which from initial impressions looked remarkably clean, given the living standards of the low-income area. She and Williams limped their way past the kitchen, through the spartan living room, and directly to the bedroom. There was an army-issue cot in the corner of the room, and Zaina gingerly lowered Williams to a seated position on it.

Williams pointed across the room to a metal case with a red crescent moon on it. "There's the kit. Bring it over."

Zaina fetched the kit off the wall and was surprised by its weight. When she set it on the cot and opened it, she was immediately able to reconcile its weight— given the sheer amount of supplies within the box, it was more of a field surgical kit than a simple first responder set-up. Williams immediately grabbed a wooden tongue depressor and placed it in his mouth, near the back of his jaw.

"What do you need me to do?" Zaina asked.

"We need to clean the burns, wrap my ribs, and clean and redress the cut on my arm."

"All right." Zaina cleared her throat.

Williams looked to her. "Have you done this before?"

"I can dress a wound," she assured him. "The rest seems self-explanatory."

"Then let's get to it."

Williams took deep breaths as he braced himself for the discomfort to follow. Zaina sat beside him and found where the medics had fastened the bandage. "Give me your arm," she instructed, and Williams did so, his molars digging into the tongue depressor. Zaina unfastened the bandage and unwrapped it, layer by layer. She undressed the wound as quickly as possible with complete disregard for the blood that stained her hands.

"If you have HIV, I'll kill you," she deadpanned.

"Well…" Williams said with faux hesitation.

Zaina gave him a look and pulled extra-hard on one of the bandages, which caused him to suck air through clenched teeth. "Bitch," he grunted.

She smiled sadistically. "Amongst other things."

Another moment passed by in silence. Zaina cringed as she exposed the wound. With its exposure to open air, she heard Williams suck air through his teeth. Her eyes fell on the stitches and she nodded once.

"I'm not a medical doctor, but that's not too bad for a prison stitch job," Zaina said. "It should heal fully."

Williams nodded. "I agree. That was at Abbas's

direction. He gave an honest effort. I think he actually liked me."

Zaina glanced to Williams. "Yet, you were still able to kill him."

"Me or him. I don't regret it."

Zaina removed cotton balls and a bottle of rubbing alcohol from the kit. As she dipped the tip into the alcohol, she said, "You don't regret much, do you?"

Williams gave her a tired look. "Don't pretend you know me, Ms. Anwar. Just clean over and around it and wrap it back up."

She soaked the cotton ball in the alcohol and ran it over the wound. He winced but refused to complain. Once she was sure she had gotten all the grime from on top and around the wound, Zaina applied redressed it. She then turned her attention to the burn marks on his chest. Blood and pus accumulated where they had attached the alligator clamps to his chest. Zaina cleaned those wounds, applied antibiotic ointment, and then grabbed the bandage and wrapped it tight around his chest and back.

"I figure those will be permanent," Williams said in an attempt to predict what Zaina was thinking. "I'm still operational. It's just going to hurt like a bitch."

"I've seen similar scars," Zaina said quietly. "Not on myself, but on people I know, fellow Egyptians, family members."

Williams gestured to the door. "Across the hall, there's a mini-fridge. There should be some water in there."

"Good idea," Zaina said. "We both need to hydrate." She rose and disappeared into the other room. When she returned, Zaina held a bottle of water in each hand. She extended one to Williams, who accepted and cracked the bottle open.

"Thank you," Williams said. Zaina nodded, and Williams drank half of the bottle before he cleared his throat and wiped his mouth off with his good arm. "Where have you seen these kind of scars before?"

"I'm not the first member of my family to be imprisoned by the government," Zaina explained. "Mubarak is one of many Egyptian leaders who resorted to heavy-handed tactics to retain his power." She paused. "How much do you know about Egyptian history, Williams?"

"Not a lot," Williams admitted between drinks. "Just the CliffsNotes—Nasser takes over in '56 and causes the Suez Crisis, then the Six-Day War in '67. Nasser dies, Sadat takes over, and he shifts allegiances from East to West. The Yom Kippur War in '73, then Sadat gets whacked, paving the way for Mubarak."

"Textbook answer," Zaina said. "What history class doesn't teach you is that ever since Nasser's takeover, Egypt's been a boiling pot. The gap between the wealthy and the impoverished has steadily grown over the past five decades. Our government is corrupt and ineffective. Get in trouble with the police? Pay a bribe. Need paperwork pushed through? Pay a bribe. The poor can't afford bribes, and find themselves imprisoned with no way out."

"The poor, and political prisoners," Williams said.

Zaina nodded. "Piss off the government, threaten the balance of power, and there is no bribe that can save you from incarceration."

"That seems to be the trend amongst authoritarian

powers."

"The worst part is the despondency of the Egyptian people. People demand change, and their voices are unheard. The more charismatic voices are imprisoned. Protestors are met with brutal police riot suppression. Most people endure the government's oppression because they would rather live the illusion of freedom rather than face brutality or incarceration for speaking out against the reality."

"Which is why you created your radio station."

Zaina nodded again. "Yes. The government controls the media and ensures that only approved messages reach the airwaves." She sighed heavily and pursed her lips. "That was a project several months in the making. It started when I overheard some of my colleagues airing their grievances with the government. Grievances turned to collusion, and collusion turned into action. It all came about on the concept that the people are infinitely more powerful than any government. If the people band together and revoke their consent to be governed, the powers-that-be will have no choice but to bend to their will."

"Dangerous words in today's world. One man's freedom fighter is another man's terrorist."

Zaina shrugged. "I believe in the power of civil disobedience. It's the only way the Egyptian people can effect the change they want and need. If we take to arms, the government will hunt us mercilessly and the world will turn a blind eye. But if the people challenge the status quo through intellectual warfare, when the government cracks down, they will be exposed for the tyrants they are, and the international pressure will be too great for them to retain their power. This is one struggle that can only be fought with words, with ideals." Zaina's expression darkened. "Until the rest of the people join the struggle, it will always be one side equipped with ideals, and the other side with guns."

Williams looked Zaina in the eye. "Well, you've done your part. Once you leave this country, you can never come back. If things are truly as desperate as you say, then the people will find their voice, but there's nothing more you can do here."

Zaina held her tongue. Her eyes fell to the tribal tattoo on his left pectoral and shoulder.

"You're Samoan," she said.

"Partially."

"I knew a Samoan guy in college," she explained. "I got curious about his tattoos." Her eyes wandered to the skull on Williams' right shoulder. Atop its head was a cowboy hat, and in its hands were two smoking revolvers. "What's this one for?"

"Family crest."

Zaina raised her eyebrows. "I'm sure they have an interesting motto."

"Outlaws: shoot 'em in the face."

"That's cute."

Williams raised his eyebrows. "Yeah, well. You have any tattoos?"

Zaina nodded. "One, on my right side, on my ribs. It's in Arabic."

"What does it say?"

"Well-behaved women seldom make history."

"Laurel Thatcher Ulrich."

"Very good, Mr. Williams," Zaina said.

"I read from time to time."

Zaina took a moment to gather the used bandages, gloves, and tongue depressors, and toss them all in the trash. Next, she went to the bathroom and washed the blood and grit off of her hands, and ran some water over her face. Zaina grabbed a towel and dried herself off. Feeling a little better, she returned to the room and sat down next to Williams.

"Who *do* you work for?" she asked. "The CIA?"

Williams shook his head. "Nope."

"FBI?"

He started to laugh, but it turned into a grimace. "If the FBI were involved, do you really think I'd have infiltrated the prison? I'd have shown up with an order for your release."

"NSA?"

"Crypto-geeks. Don't believe what you see in Hollywood."

"Military?"

"Nope."

"You've got to give me a hint," Zaina said.

Williams took a sip from the water bottle. "All right. Out of your four guesses, I used to be two."

Zaina raised her head and took in a deep breath. "Mercenary."

Williams pursed his lips. "Sounds more honest than 'independent contractor,' doesn't it?"

"Haven't enough people made a business out of death?" Zaina asked coldly.

"I wouldn't be so quick to condemn," Williams said. "Nobody on the government payroll was gonna go off the reservation for you, and the government sure as hell wasn't going to intervene, at least not until they could have worked out some kind of tit-for-tat with Mubarak."

"And that's why the rest of the world hates Americans," Zaina said, her activist passion creeping into her tone. "You stick your noses where it doesn't belong. You make backroom deals with tyrants and despots. You care about nothing and no-one but yourselves, and expect everybody to welcome you when you invade their countries to 'liberate' them."

Williams nodded, to Zaina's surprise. "You know what? You're absolutely right. We do stick our noses where they don't belong. And that's why we need to hang up the world police badge."

"Well, I wasn't expecting that answer."

"But that's not all. Just because we hang up the badge doesn't mean we're obligated to play global social worker, either." He shook his head. "I say fuck 'em all. Let every nation forge their own destiny. We shouldn't go running to the aid of another country at the first sign of an earthquake or a tsunami. Let them fend for themselves. Not our responsibility to put together food packets for the starving or lead rescue efforts."

Zaina stared daggers at Williams. When she spoke, her tone was a dangerous whisper. "What's the point of being a superpower if you don't use that power to leave the world a better place than you found it?"

"We have natural disasters and starving and homeless in the good old US of A. Our focus has always been on trying to help the world while we neglect our own. Fuck that. Let others get their shit in order while we square our own shit away."

"That's a false dichotomy," Zaina insisted. "The United States can resolve its issues at home while helping others abroad at the same time."

"Doesn't work like that," Williams said flatly. "You can't expect us to stay at home militarily but beg us to fork over our cash. That's a double standard. Either we play the world's nanny or we keep to ourselves and leave others alone."

""Then one day, when the United States needs help-"

"-we'll be fucked," Williams cut her off. "We didn't need help for Afghanistan or Iraq. We just put together a coalition to make it look like it wasn't a solo US effort. If a situation arises that we can't handle on our own, there's no amount of foreign help that will save us."

Zaina nodded, her face the personification of the phrase, *If that's how you want it...* "I'm going to clean up."

"Fine."

Zaina cleaned up the area, threw the trash into the waste bin, and then returned to Wililams. "All right, I'd say you're all ready to go."

"Good, because I have work to do." He reached in the medical kit for a bottle of Percocet and poured himself two pills.

"Wait...you're going back out there?"

"Ferran's waiting for us," Williams said. He started to stand, but Zaina moved in front of him and gently placed her hand on his chest.

"Reality check, Williams," she said firmly. "You look like shit. You just went through hell and a half. I had to help you walk inside. If you go back out without some rest, then you'll get us both killed."

"If we don't go now, we'll get Ferran killed,"

Williams argued.

"No," Zaina said. "Your best bet is to get a few hours of sleep, get some food in you, and then we'll go looking for Ferran. I know him well enough to know he would tell you the same thing."

Williams looked Zaina in the eye and knew that the topic was not open for discussion. Slowly, he replaced the pills in the bottle, capped it, reached to his belt line for the SIG-Sauer he had taken from First Sergeant Akram, and extended it towards Zaina, butt-first. "You know how to handle one of these?"

"Dad taught me and my siblings how to shoot," Zaina said. She accepted the pistol, kept her finger off the trigger, dropped the magazine to check how many rounds she had to work with, and then pressed the slide back slightly to ensure there was a round in the chamber. Zaina loaded the magazine once more and held the SIG-Sauer at her side. "I'm a little rusty, but I remember the basics."

"Well, I'm not expecting you to hold off a squad," Williams said. "If somebody comes in and it isn't Ferran, kill him. If you think you hear something, then tell me."

"Do you think Ferran will come back to this safe house?"

"He shouldn't, but just in case. Be mindful of your surroundings."

"You've got it."

Williams pointed to the desk on the right hand side of the room. "That's a SINCGARS radio," he explained. "It's on standby, and the freqs and COMSEC are already loaded."

"I don't speak military," Zaina said.

He took a deep breath. "Right. There's a knob on the lower-left hand corner. Right now, it's on S-T-B-Y, for standby. Twist it to T-S-T for test, wait until the screen says, 'Good,' then switch it to ON. Don't touch any of the other knobs. There's a piece that looks like a telephone headset. That's your hand mic. On the right side, there is a button—that is your press-to-talk transmitter. On the hour, every hour, you need to hold that down and said, 'Pharaoh, this is Outlaw, radio check, over.' If he responds, you wake me up and hand the mic to me. If he doesn't, you try three more times, each time a minute apart. If that doesn't work, then leave it and wait for the next comm window. Better?"

"Yeah, I've got all of that," Zaina said.

Williams checked his watch. "It's 7:35 PM right now. Wake me up no later than 1:00 AM. We need to be on the road by 2:00 AM if we're going to check the other safe houses for Ferran. We don't want to be caught out and about at daybreak if we can avoid it."

"You've got it."

"And one more thing. *Don't fall asleep.* If you're getting sleepy, wake me up. But if I wake up and catch you sleeping, we're going to have a problem. Are we on the same page here?"

"Got it. Stay awake."

"There's Red Bull in the fridge if you need it to stay awake. Try to save some for me if you can."

Without another word, Williams laid down on his belly. His left arm hung over the side of the cot while his right hand gripped the M4 by its heat shield. He passed out before Zaina had even settled in at the radio desk.

CHAPTER TEN

Al Abajiyyah, Cairo, Egypt
25 July 2006
01:00 hours Eastern European Time (24 July 23:00
hours Zulu)

THE MOMENT ZAINA'S HAND touched his shoulder, Williams's eyes shot open, and he moved to bring his M4 to bear. Two things stopped him: the startled look in Zaina's eyes, and the sharp pain that seized his torso as he turned. He bared his teeth as he slowed his movement, and a moment later, he kicked his legs over the edge of the cot. Williams rubbed his temples with his left hand and sighed.

"How are you feeling?" Zaina asked.

"Like shit," Williams answered honestly. "I should have taken those Percs before I racked out." He popped the top on the pill bottle, poured himself two, then grabbed a bottle of water and downed them.

"You going to be okay taking Percocet?" Zaina asked.

"What do you mean?"

"Won't that impair your thinking?"

Williams shook his head. "I'll be fine, so long as I'm ingesting it. If I chewed or crushed the pills, then I'd be going for the high. I just need to be able to move."

"Are you expecting trouble?"

"I'm always expecting trouble, but something's been bothering me."

Zaina folded her arms. "What's that?"

"During the interrogation, the number two man,

Colonel Faris, took a phone call. He never came back."

The news caused Zaina's eyes to widen. "You don't think they're closing in on Ferran?"

"It's a distinct possibility," Williams said. "That's if they haven't captured him already."

"I thought he was special forces. Should that make him harder to catch?"

"Harder, but not impossible. He's hardly a ghost. I'll tell you one more thing: escape and evasion in a non-permissive environment usually involves leaving said environment. Leaving the city is all right. Leaving the country is optimal, and leaving the continent is ideal. He's been on the run in one city for half a month now, more than enough time to disseminate his photograph and vitals to local law enforcement. With the kind of dragnet they'll be throwing over him, it's not a matter of *if* they catch him, but a matter of *when*."

"Then what do we do?"

Williams went into the closet adjacent the cot. He pulled out a black tough box and dragged it next to the cot. A moment later, he had opened the box and produced a small yellow package. He tossed one to her, and then kept another for himself. Zaina inspected the package.

"Shower wipes?"

"Think of them as five-star baby wipes," Williams said. "You'll actually feel like you've taken a shower after you've used a few of those babies. Designed for athletes, soldiers, and fugitives who just don't have time for a shower." He glanced to the bathroom. "Or, in our case, if you're lacking running water."

"What about clothing?" Zaina asked.

"Ferran managed to grab an outfit from your confiscated items once they brought them down to the police station," Williams said. "Luckily, Anwar is a pretty common name. This was before they started actively hunting him."

"Not sure how I feel about my cousin rummaging through my clothing," Zaina said. "Still, suppose beggars can't be choosers."

Williams smirked. "Now you're catching on."

"Where are my clothes?"

He reached into the tough box and removed a plastic bag. Within the bag were blue jeans, a white short-sleeved button-up blouse, a black bra, black bikini panties, socks, and running shoes. "There are some basic hygiene products in there, too. Ferran tried his best to exercise sound fashion judgment, but you'll have to forgive us because...well, we're men."

Zaina smiled as she reviewed the contents of the bag. "It'll suffice. I'll go clean up."

Once she left the room, Williams closed the door and stripped down. He pulled out wipes, two at a time, and focused on his groin, armpits, and feet. Once those areas were clean, Williams wiped down his face, legs, and as much of his torso he could while working around the limitations of his injuries and the bandages that covered them. He finished his clean-up and tossed his wipes in the trash.

Next came clothing. A pair of white boot socks and black boxer-briefs started him off, followed by khaki cargo pants, which he held up with a black rigger's belt. Williams fetched a white T-shirt and gingerly pulled it over his head and the bandages. A pair of tan Belleville hot weather boots were next. Once his boots were tied, Williams hid the tops in his pant legs. Finally, Williams retrieved a Timex Ironman watch and a handmade paracord bracelet, and fastened them to his left and right wrists, respectively. He held the watch to his face. *01:14*. They were good on time, but that did not mean he was going to take his time getting ready. Less time preparing gear made more time available to look for Ferran.

Williams and Ferran had packed the tough box before he infiltrated the prison, so he knew what it should contain. He also knew that while there were no signs of intrusion, his gear was not something he wanted to leave to chance. Williams personally put hands on every piece of equipment—even if he had to pull it out of a pouch—and made sure nothing had been tampered with.

As he finished his inspection, Zaina walked in the room. While she would not be strutting her stuff on a New York catwalk, her clothes were meant for her body. He was sure that in her current attire, she could walk in a club alone and walk out with a man in hand. Zaina placed her hands on her hips and sighed tiredly.

"How do I look?" she asked.

"Sufficient," Williams said flatly. "You ready to go?"

"Whenever you are."

Williams placed the M4 in the tough box and closed it. He went to the table, picked up the SIG-Sauer, and tucked it in his waistband at the small of his back, beneath his shirt. His last order of business at the table was to set the SINGCARS to zero mode, which cleared the radio of all encryption keys and frequencies. He took one last look around the room to ensure they had not left anything of strategic importance behind, and then he took his position at the rear of the tough box.

"Help me load this into the Fiat," Williams said. Zaina picked up her end, the muscles in her arm taut as she led the way to the vehicle.

* * *

Warraq Al Arab, Cairo, Egypt
25 July 2006
04:05 hours Eastern European Time (02:05 hours Zulu)

"ZAINA. WAKE UP."

ZAINA stirred and automatically used her forearm to wipe some drool from the corner of her mouth. She used the edge of her palms to wipe the rheum from her eyes and blinked a few times. Her eyes wandered to the window and found they were in an urban residential neighborhood, with apartments around for miles. Zaina leaned back in her seat, forced an exhale through her mouth, and looked to Williams.

"Where are we?" she asked.

"Warraq Al Arab," he replied. "This is it."

"When did I fall asleep?"

"Almost immediately after we started driving. Figured you could use the rest."

"How do you know this is it?"

Williams pointed down the street to two black SUVs. "Government plates and unmarked cars." He shifted his aim to two men at ground level, clad in black uniforms and wielding MISR rifles. "Central Security Forces providing the muscle."

Zaina swallowed nervously. "Does this mean he's been captured?"

"It doesn't look good," Williams admitted. In his hands was a flat black SIG-Sauer P226, which he had retrieved from his kit box. This one differed from the one he had given Zaina a few hours earlier in that it had an extended threaded barrel. While his right hand held the pistol steady, his left screwed a Knight's Armament sound suppressor into place. Once it was affixed, he gave it a solid tug to ensure it was snug, then conducted a press-check. "It's not the only outcome. It's possible that they found the safe house and that he's still on the lam." He shrugged. "There's only one way to find out."

"You're going in."

Williams sighed. He rest the SIG-Sauer in his lap, fetched a bottle of water, and downed a quarter of it. He licked his lips as he calculated his actions on the objective. "Stay here. If I don't come back in ten minutes, then drive to the embassy. It's west of here in the Garden City. Drop the car a few blocks back and walk the rest of the way. They'll detain you otherwise. You'll find a passport in the tough box, as well as a number you need to call. You call them and relay the message that I didn't make it." He looked over to her. "You still have that pistol?"

Zaina reached into the glove box and removed her SIG-Sauer. "Yes, but, Williams, you honestly think—

"

"Ten minutes," he repeated.

Williams dismounted the vehicle and quietly closed the door behind him. His right hand was concealed behind his hip, the pistol's hammer cocked back to convert the stiff trigger slack of the double-action mechanism into a smooth single-action squeeze. He approached casually, unconcerned as to whether anybody would recognize him. It was still the late twilight hours, and the first hints of the morning sun had not yet started to creep over the horizon, which limited the enemy's field of vision. While he rehearsed his actions in his mind, his eyes were constantly scanning for any threats he missed in the car, and looking over his shoulder to make sure nobody walked up on him. The advantage of the early hour was that most civilians were still asleep, and the mosques had not started the call to prayer. That reduced the likelihood of civilian casualties. Williams had no issue with killing Egyptian soldiers. It was the cost of doing business, and he knew they would do the same to him if the roles were reversed. Civilians, on the other hand, did not ask to be involved.

He was close now. Williams picked up the pace just enough to close with the two ground-level sentries but not enough to draw their attention. When he was within twenty feet of them, he moved his gun hand from behind his hip to adjacent his thigh. Once he reached fifteen feet, one of the guards noticed his approach, leaned towards him, and squinted to make out his visage. That was when Williams extended the SIG-Sauer in front of him, lined up the tritium sights with the first guard's head, and stroked the trigger.

The 9mm Parabellum hollowpoint round tore through the guard's skull and exploded out the back, shredding the medulla oblongata and cerebellum. As the body fell to the floor, Williams shifted aim and fired on the second guard. The can on the Swiss pistol trapped most of the gasses and reduced what would have been a sharp *crack* to a muted *thwock*. The second brass casing hit the asphalt in cadence with the *thump* of the corpse hitting the ground.

Williams stepped over the bodies and held the SIG-Sauer with both hands tucked over his sternum. He hugged the wall and peered around the corner. Nobody greeted him, so he rounded the corner and jogged up the stairs, moving on the balls of his feet to minimize his footfall. As he approached the top of the flight, Williams walked sideways and peered over the edge of the banister. There was no threat, so he made his way up the next flight. The safe house was on the third floor, and Williams knew that if the *Mukhabarat* operatives were worth their salt, they would have placed their CSF augmentees in a tight security formation by the entrance.

As he came up the third flight and peered over the banister, his assessment was confirmed. The first thing he found was a roaming guard that had his back turned to Williams. He held off on the roamer, instead following him to the corner. The roamer turned the corner, and Williams peeked. The guard walked right past two more CSF troopers posted on either side of the safe house front door, their MISR rifles held at the low ready.

That was when he heard it. It was quiet enough that the average sleeper would be able to tune it out, but a light sleeper or anybody awake would not be able to mistake it for anything else. It was the sound of muted screams. Williams's eyes narrowed as he listened in. It was a male voice, and in the right pitch range. Ice hit his veins as the worst case scenario was confirmed.

They have Ferran.

Williams spun around the corner and pushed the SIG-Sauer in front of him as he advanced on the door. The roamer was first in his sights, dispatched with a lone 9mm slug to the back of the head. Williams shifted targets, took up the trigger slack, and tagged the closest door guard with a shot just above the ear. Williams side-stepped left to acquire a clear sight picture on the third CSF trooper, who had just started to react to the deaths of his two colleagues. He cut the Egyptian paramilitary's response short with a hollowpoint between the eyes. Gray matter smeared the wall behind the sentinel as his back hit the wall and he fell to a seated position, his head drooped against his left shoulder.

As he moved to the left side of the door, Williams removed and pocketed the magazine in the SIG-Sauer and replaced it with a fresh one to give himself fifteen-plus-one rounds going into the house. With the pistol held in his right hand alongside his chest, Williams reached out with his left hand and gingerly tested the doorknob. It offered no resistance, and he let out a short preparatory breath.

Williams pushed the door open and lunged inside right behind it. He immediately found two CSF soldiers in the the living room, one standing off to the side while the other had slung his rifle and was using a pickaxe to create an avenue to search for contraband. Williams engaged the soldier off to the side first, putting a single round through his forehead, and then transitioned to the pickaxe-wielding soldier and put him down with two rounds to the chest and one to the head. He traversed right to clear the corner, then spun one-eighty to clear dead space to his left. Williams caught it at the last moment: a third guard had been in the blind spot, and brought his rifle to the ready. He spun back and dropped to the floor as the CSF trooper opened up with his MISR rifle, 7.62x39mm rounds chopping through the walls and air above him.

Williams spun onto his back, bent his knees, and trained the SIG-Sauer directly in front of him as footfalls closed in on him. The CSF trooper rounded the corner, ready to fire, when two 9mm slugs caught him in the chest. As the rifleman stumbled back, Williams used his weak hand to press off the ground and scramble to his feet, then aligned his sights and finished the rifleman with a round between the eyes.

Shuffling from the hallway drew Williams's attention. Two more CSF soldiers materialized, their rifles at the ready and killing in their eyes. Williams took a step forward and strafed left, saturating the hallway with lead as he moved to concealment. He took a knee behind a couch and, spotting his pistol's slide had locked to the rear, he dropped the spent magazine, retrieved a fresh one from his belt, slammed it home, and stroked the slide to chamber a round. Williams vaulted over the couch as the CSF troopers left the hallway. His move placed him at their flank, and he utilized the advantageous position.

He shot the closest man once, traversed to the second and serviced him with two to the chest, then returned to the first soldier and shot him once more. Both men fell to the ground, the hollowpoint rounds making short work of their lungs.

Williams stood over their bodies and shot each man once in the head, then continued into the hallway. At the far end was a space with three doors: one to his left, one directly in front of him, and one to his right. The door to his right was ajar, and a glimpse inside revealed a sink and a toilet built into the ground. That left the door to the front and the one to the left. Williams slowed his breathing and listened carefully. After a moment, he heard it: a muffled grunt, faint but audible. He took a step closer to the left door and paused. A few seconds later, he heard it again.

Door number one, Williams thought as he cocked back and thrust his boot just offset of the knob. As he passed through the fatal funnel, he kept his pistol tucked in close to prevent from being disarmed. That turned out to be a wise move: as soon as Williams stepped through the door, a man in a business casual suit attempted to grapple with him. Williams drove the heel of his palm into the assailant's sternum, side-stepped right to avoid the door, and placed four shots center-mass into the man. In his peripheral vision, he saw a man tied to a chair at the center of the room, his head drooped over. Williams's eyes widened as he feared the worse, and he started moving to the man.

An unseen force clubbed Williams over the head, sending him falling to the floor, the SIG-Sauer slipping from his grasp. He hit the floor, chest-first.

The burn scars seared through the Percocet dullness and encouraged Williams to quickly spin onto his back. He found Lieutenant Colonel Faris standing over him, SIG-Sauer drawn as he moved in on Williams.

"So good of you to join us, Mr. Bowles," Faris said. "I believe we have unfinished business."

Williams waited until Faris was just beyond his leg's reach, and he stared the colonel in the eye. "Williams."

Faris was caught off guard. "What?"

"My name's not Bowles. It's Williams."

Faris gave Williams an intrigued look. "Well, that's a productive start—"

Williams thrust himself forward and drove his heel into Faris's kneecap hard, then flipped on his left side and swept Faris's legs from beneath him. He crawled on top of Faris and started with elbow strikes, but Faris managed to block each one. Faris then edged his torso to the left as Williams came down with another strike, catching him off balance. Trapping Williams's foot and using his own momentum against him, Faris spun Williams around and ended up in his guard. The counterintelligence officer started his assault with a flurry of punches that Williams managed to fend off. Each time, Williams tried to grab ahold of Faris's wrists to set him up for a triangle choke, but Faris was savvy to the technique and kept his punches swift.

Switching tack, Faris grabbed a fistful of Williams's shirt, planted both feet on the ground, and assumed a squatted position. With this base, Faris hefted Williams off the ground and then thrust him downward, his hands maintaining their points of contact with the shirt. Faris refused to relent, and repeated the slam twice more, growling and snarling with each repetition. The final slam stunned Williams, leaving him rolling on the floor and growling. Faris took the opportunity to extricate himself and dive for his SIG-Sauer. He grinned as he palmed the Swiss handgun and turned it on Williams.

A shot rang out, and Williams flinched, but he could not feel the gunshot. Faris fell to the ground and screamed as a bullet punched through his hip. Three more barks filled the room, and Faris lay still, bullet wounds in his abdomen and one in his chest, through his heart. Williams looked up to find Zaina in the doorway, a smoking handgun in her trembling hands. Sweat coated her skin and her mouth was agape, both amazed and horrified at what she had just done.

Williams grabbed the nearest object—the leg of a desk—and used it to pull himself to his feet. He braced his lower back with his hands and forced himself to stand up straight. He grunted as the pain intensified. After a moment, he looked to Zaina, who had managed to lower the gun to her side, stand up a little straighter, and breathe normally. Williams knew the the look he saw in her eyes, and also knew now was not the time to address it.

"You were supposed to stay in the car," he said quietly.

That drew a sharp look from Zaina. "I just killed a man to save your life. Unless your next words directed to me are, 'Thank you,' then shut the fuck up, Williams. I don't want to hear it."

Williams opted to pick up his SIG-Sauer from the

floor rather than continue to chastise her decision. He looked to her and said, "Stay right there. Don't move."

"Okay, tough guy," Zaina snapped.

He ignored her as he stepped back into the hallway and kicked in the door he had passed earlier. It was the other bedroom, and it had been completely ransacked. The bed had been cut apart, and holes had been picked in the wall. Aside from the wrecked furniture, the room was empty, so Williams returned to the other room.

Zaina's eyes were locked on the body in the chair. She was afraid to approach it. Williams could see the question in her eyes, and rather than discuss it with her, he went directly to it. As he approached, he could see that Faris had put the man through the wringer. Chunks of the man's flesh were missing from his torso, littered on the ground around him. The instrument of choice—a pair of pliers—rested at his feet. He could see the man was not moving. Williams reached out with his left hand, cupped the man's chin, and lifted his head.

The facial features were badly bruised, and one of the eyes was completely swollen shut. However, Williams remembered the face well enough to recognize the man past the marks of physical abuse. Gently, he lowered Ferran's head, and then pressed two fingers into his neck to check for a pulse. There was no feedback.

"I'm sorry," Williams murmured. He turned and looked at Zaina. Tears rolled down her cheeks, and the tremors in her hands intensified. Williams stuck the pistol in the back of his waistband and grabbed

Zaina by both shoulders. She looked him in the eyes with a gaze that cut through his gut.

"We have to go." He tried to soften the blow of the statement as much as possible, but he could see the damage his words had done.

"We can't just leave his body like this." Zaina was adamant.

"We can't take him with us," Williams said. The statement showed in his slouched shoulders, pained expression, and perspiration-drenched face. "We get pulled over by the police with a dead body in our car, and they've got us dead to rights."

"They will—"

"What? Desecrate his body? They've already done that. They have nothing to gain from further mutilation. If anything, one of the government's own, they'll probably cover it up, say he's a hero or something. But I can promise you that if we try to bring him out, we'll be caught when reinforcements arrive, and that's if a concerned citizen doesn't try and call it in first. The best thing for Ferran is to get you to the embassy."

Zaina said nothing. A few moments later, she gently shrugged out of Williams's grasp and walked over to Ferran's body. She lifted his chin and studied his face for a second, and began murmuring in Arabic. Williams turned away to give her privacy. Fifteen seconds later, she planted a kiss on Ferran's forehead, took a deep breath, and wiped her eyes dry. When she marched back to Williams, there was purpose in her gait.

"Let's get out of here," she said coldly as she breezed past Williams.

CHAPTER ELEVEN

Warraq Al Arab, Cairo, Egypt
25 July 2006
05:30 hours Eastern European Time (03:30 hours Zulu)

COLONEL AGHA'S BLOOD BOILED as he entered Bowles's safe house. He had already passed the bodies of five troopers on the way in, and his anger stewed as he found five more cadavers in the common area. The look was etched into the faces of the CSF team he had brought with him to secure the location. They knew the men that laid slain at their feet. They had trained and worked with them, had blown off steam with them in their shared off-time. They wanted to hunt Bowles down almost as badly as Agha did.

That anger increased as he entered the bedroom and found the bodies of Colonel Faris and one of his subordinates on the floor. Decades of memories flashed before his eyes as he knelt beside his old friend's corpse. He remembered their first case together, hunting down an Israeli spy network. Their friendship had not always been balmy, but over time, he came to respect Faris's gruff style, and Faris came to respect Agha's calculating methodology. They had stuck by each other, case by case, and not just on a professional level. The man in front of him was his brother, not by blood, but through fire. A lone tear trickled down his cheek as he squeezed Faris's shoulder one last time.

"Goodbye, brother." Agha wiped his cheek and

cleared his throat. He looked to the nearest soldier and waved him over. He removed a business card, handed it to the soldier, and said, "Inform them that Lieutenant Colonel Uday Faris has been killed in the line of duty. Make sure to inform his immediate survivors."

"Yes, sir," the CSF trooper said solemnly.

"And keep the card," Agha said. "If you or any of your men have any troubles with burial arrangements, then let me know. I will clear the path."

"Yes, sir." The trooper looked to Ferran's body in the chair and asked, "What should we do with him?"

"Process him and ensure he is given a proper burial."

"But, Colonel—"

Agha held up his hand. "He's dead. Desecrating his body won't bring back our comrades. Our entire focus must remain on Bowles. Is that understood?"

The soldier swallowed. "Yes, sir."

Agha left the room. His mobile phone rang, and he answered it on the second ring. "Yes?"

"Colonel Agha, Captain Darzi." It was the voice of his personal assistant, a young man he had taken under his wing. "As requested, I took the prisoner's mugshot and cross-referenced it with all known Canadian law enforcement, military, and intelligence operatives. The search yielded no results."

"I figured as much," Agha said as he trotted down the stairs. "Widen the search and continue looking."

"Already ahead of you, sir," Darzi said. "I thought perhaps he was American military, so I ran his photograph against our files on American operators that trained with First Sergeant Anwar during the

Bright Star exercises. Got a match."

"Good job," Agha said. "Who is he?"

"Benjamin Williams. He was with 5th Special Forces Group during Bright Star 1989. He was held prisoner for six months by Saddam during the Gulf War, and left the service shortly thereafter as a sergeant first class. He worked with First Sergeant Anwar twice: once during Bright Star, and once in 1999."

Agha quickly put two and two together. "He's a spy."

"Was," Darzi said. "The details are scant. From what we can put together, he was recruited by Langley sometime after leaving the Army. Apparently, during the American presidential election in 2004, there was some kind of scandal that forced President Blackthorne to abdicate the candidacy. Williams is reported as leaving the CIA. Analysis believes that he had something to do with that. After he left the CIA, he worked in civilian freight for a few months." Firas paused. "Do you remember the terrorist incident in Tucson, Arizona last year?"

"The one that involved internal anti-government extremists?" Agha asked.

"The very same," Darzi said. "Apparently, Williams was caught up in the event and helped bring it an end. From there, rumors indicate that he became a private military contractor. A mercenary."

"An American general once said, 'Old soldiers never die. They just fade away.' He's just killed twelve people single-handedly. Keep digging and find me everything you can. I want to know if he's acting alone or if he's back on the dole."

"Yes, sir."

"Good job," Agha repeated. "I'll be back at headquarters in forty-five minutes. Have whatever you can gather ready for me by the time I arrive."

"Yes, sir."

Benjamin Williams... Agha mulled the name over. He knew that he should have heard of him, but the name paired with a face did not immediately leap out at him. That was the sign that Williams was a true professional. Competent operators of his caliber were not well known outside of their community. Agha did not dwell on not knowing him for too long. They had a name and a face, and more importantly, they had a nationality.

Benjamin Williams... I'm coming for you.

* * *

United States Embassy
Garden City, Cairo, Egypt
25 July 2006
09:30 hours Eastern European Time (07:30 hours Zulu)

LANA BOUTON HAD NOT been home in over twenty-four hours. On her way out of the office the day before, word had gotten out that two suspected terrorists had escaped from the Istiqbal-Tora Prison. Everybody that worked on the embassy's third floor knew that the Egyptian government's definition of a terrorist could either mean a legitimate threat or a political dissident, and as the Cairo Chief of Station, it would fall on Bouton to discern to the best of her ability which category the two escapees fell under.

There was only one problem. She already knew who the escapees were, and she was waiting for their call.

After the initial buzz, things quieted down, and most of Bouton's colleagues went home to grab some sleep. On the other hand, she stayed in her office and remained awake as long as her body allowed. When she woke up an hour later, her forehead was imprinted from where she had rested her head. That was when Bouton decided that any rest she got would be better had on her lounge couch. She slept fitfully throughout the night. Moments after she finally abandoned the notion of sleep, she received a phone call that set the tone of the day.

Three Mountain Dews, two cups of tea, and dozens of phone calls later, Bouton sat at her desk and contemplated the paperwork in front of her. She rubbed her temples and glanced at her reflection in the computer monitor. Bouton would never be an ugly woman by any sensible man's standards, but she was undoubtedly at her worst. Bags had formed beneath her brown eyes, and her long brunette locks screamed to be washed and brushed. She wore the same white button-up short-sleeved blouse and khaki slacks from the day before. When she tried to sleep, she had kicked off her brown flats, and had not bothered to put them back on upon waking. Bouton wished she could entirely blame her disheveled appearance on fatigue, but she knew she would be lying.

The phone rang again, and Bouton snatched it from the receiver halfway into the first ring. "Hello?"

"It's me."

Bouton sighed heavily, and then said, "Going secure." She pressed a green button on the receiver and a red light flashed for five pulses. On the sixth, it went dead, and a green light took its place. "What's going on? You never told me the breakout was going to be this loud. What the hell were you thinking?"

"Not my choice," Williams said. "I've had this counterintel colonel crawling up my ass. Anyway, I've got me plus one pax. I need you to reel us in."

Bouton took a deep breath as she grabbed her words from the pit of her stomach and forced them to the surface. "That's not going to happen, Ben."

Williams scoffed sarcastically on the other end. "Look, just because things got a little messy—"

"Things are more than just 'a little messy,'" Bouton snapped. She inhaled hesitantly and repeated the words that all case officers and operators feared. "You've been compromised."

There was a long silence on the phone. Finally, Williams asked, "How?"

"They ran your face against a list of personnel in our bi-annual joint exercises. Your name came up. Bright Star 1989."

"Hmm." He let out a drawn out sigh. "In that case, I'm surprised they didn't find it sooner."

"I'm issuing denials, and Ambassador Lantos has declared you *persona non grata*, with the full understanding that, should you arrive at the embassy, we are to turn you over to the *Mukhabarat*." She paused. "It's strange."

"What is?"

"When she read me in on her intent to turn you in, Ambassador Lantos seemed more...involved than usual. If I didn't know any better, I'd say she's got a hard-on for you."

Williams chuckled. "You don't know the half of it."

"I guess I'll have to ask sometime." Bouton pursed her lips. "I'm sorry, Ben. My hands are tied here."

"You did all you could," Williams said. "I suppose this will be the last time we speak for a while."

"Unless you've got a bottle of political white-out in your kit, more than likely," she sighed.

"I'll leave that battle to my betters," Williams said. "Take care, Lana."

"Ben?"

"Yeah?"

Bouton looked to a photo on the wall. "Stay frosty. Give 'em hell."

"Yes, ma'am." He terminated the connection.

Bouton hung the phone up and walked over to her wall, which she had jokingly named her "I Love Me" wall. On it were an assortment of photographs, ranging from her days on her high school track and field team, to her tenure as president of the College Republicans at her alma mater, the University of Arizona. There was a photo of her graduation from the Clandestine Service Trainee course, and then several snapshots from her time as a case officer in Colombia and while on assignment with the Counterterrorism Center.

The photo that had caught her eye was taken five years earlier in the Hindu Kush, by Afghanistan's

Khyber Pass. Bouton could see that her olive skin was tinged red in the cheeks from the austere environment. She was covered in a black fleece jacket, with tan cargo pants protruding from beneath and a watch cap covering her head and ears. An AK-47 was slung across her chest, and despite there being a war on, she had managed a smile, as had her large, bearded companion in similar kit and clothing: Ben Williams, then a paramilitary operations officer with Ground Branch and one of the Jawbreaker team leaders.

That photo was taken the last time she had seen him prior to approaching him for the job. An hour after that photograph, they had gone out on patrol to look for Taliban, and they had found them in force. It was not the first time she had seen Williams in combat, but it was an affirmation that even as the years rolled by, he had not lost it. She knew that the Egyptians had another thing coming if they thought they could bring him down.

"Good luck," she said quietly.

* * *

Izbat an Nakhl, Cairo, Egypt
25 July 2006
09:50 hours Eastern European Time (07:50 hours Zulu)

WILLIAMS HUNG UP THE phone, a rueful smile on his face. Putting aside his personal grudge for

Agha, he had to admire the man's competency. The counterintelligence colonel's play would certainly complicate things at home, but that was a worry for when he got there. He realized that the game had become a chess match, and it was his move. An idea was already stewing, but Williams put it on the back burner. There was something else he wanted to address.

For the past few hours, Williams had allowed Zaina to grab some rest while he checked gear and waited to check in with Lana Bouton. The entire time, he had heard rustling and labored breathing. He had an idea of what was going on, but he let her try to fight through it. When he got off the line with Bouton, he heard a loud gasp, punctuated with heavy panting. Williams slipped the cell phone in his pocket and stood in the doorway. As predicted, Zaina sat upright on the cot, her knees to her bosom, sweat accumulating on her brow. After a moment, he pulled up a fold-up chair and took a seat.

"You all right?" he asked quietly.

Zaina fixed him with a look that would have scared an ordinary man. "What do you think? My cousin is dead and I killed a man." She took a deep breath. "I shouldn't feel bad about this. He's the son of a bitch that killed Ferran, and yet..." Her voice trailed off for a moment, and she pursed her lips. "Yeah, he's an extension of Mubarak's reign. Yeah, he killed Ferran, and he's probably done the same to dozens, maybe hundreds of others, but that didn't make it my place to take his life." Zaina hung her head and exhaled audibly. "What makes me any better than him?"

Williams pressed his hands together and stared off at the wall. "I killed my first man nearly twenty-four years ago. My unit was on patrol with the Salvadoran National Guard, looking for members of the FMLN. We're walking through the woodline, and the enemy opens up with tracer fire. Here I am, this twenty-two year old kid, scared out of his mind but doing his best not to show it.

The patrol leader gets us out of the killzone and rallies the survivors. All the Americans are still alive but we've lost a few of the Salvadorans. He tells us that we're gonna have to hold the line while the weapons squad gets consolidated. I take my three guys and we find cover, and we're burning through mags. Can't really see if we're hitting anything at this point, and to tell the truth, I don't think any of us were trying, because none of us knew if we were ready to cross that line." He chuckled wryly. "It's always the guys that brag about wanting to mix it up with the bad guys that shit their pants when it hits the fan. We talked a big game back at the FOB, but now we had hot lead snapping and cracking over our heads."

Williams met Zaina's eyes. Her attention was fixated on his every word. "That's when I see him. He's lighter skinned than the Salvadorans and wearing a different uniform. He's a Russian, and he's sticking himself out from behind cover. He's got his AK pressed to his shoulder and he's picked up a target. I've got this guy, dead to rights. Suddenly, I reach this point and I…" He struggled to find the words. "I don't care any more. I don't give a shit if one of those bullets hits me. None of it matters. My entire world at that moment is the man in my sights.

"I pulled the trigger," Williams continued. "I see my round hit, just above the left eye. I fire again, and I see the second round punch through his nose. I fire one more time, and I hit him through his right cheek. He falls behind cover, and all I can see is his hand, still gripping his rifle, but he's still, unmoving. All I can feel is this cold, but I don't dwell on it. I can't dwell on it. I find another man wearing the wrong uniform and I kill him, too. My firing is mechanical. My reloads are mechanical. My orders to my men are mechanical. *I'm* mechanical."

He took a deep breath and eyed the ground. "After we've secured the battlespace and I've taken care of my men, I start to think. That first kill, that Russian adviser. He probably wasn't too different from me. He probably had a woman waiting back home. Maybe he had kids. He was somebody's son. I feel a little sick thinking about it, but then I realize something. He *wasn't* different from me at all. He signed on to carry a weapon for his country, just like I did for mine. He knew the risks. I wasn't responsible for his life. I was responsible for my men and my men only. At the end of the day, I did what I had to do."

Williams sighed, interlaced his fingers, and looked back at Zaina. "I got lucky. I know men who've crossed that line and couldn't live with it. I've known men who froze up at the line and got killed because of it. The people I know who've killed and lived with it come to grips with the cold logic that it was either them or the other guy."

"Can I go back?" Zaina asked.

"What?"

"Can I go back to the way I was before?"

Williams shook his head. "No, no, you can't. But you can find a new normal. You can find a way to live with yourself. You can accept that you did what you had to do and you can move forward."

Zaina looked away. "That doesn't sound much different from the rationale that Mubarak's thugs use to justify their actions."

Williams stood, hands at his side. "That becomes the trick, doesn't it? You've crossed the line and there's no going back, so the struggle becomes finding the right balance to keep from becoming no different than those you initially justified killing." He paused and then added, "I think you'll be fine."

A drawn out breath fell from Zaina's nose. "We'll see."

"I think it runs in your family," Williams said.

"What do you mean?"

Williams folded his arms. "The last time I was in Cairo was back in 1999. It was a joint op between my team and Unit 777. We'd tracked an al-Qaeda operative to a compound. Both our units hit the place. I entered a room and I see this guy. I service him, but he's still moving, so I move to finish him off. I was drawn. Ferran spotted a pair of tangos that crept up on me and he shoved me out of the line of fire. He took a bullet to the leg for that and still managed to kill both of them." He nodded, then added, "You're not the first member of the Anwar family to save my life. I accepted this job because Ferran cashed in a debt. Now, I owe you one."

Without another word, Williams made for the door. Zaina sat up a little straighter. "You're leaving?"

"Just getting a little privacy," Williams said without breaking stride. "I've got a phone call to make."

* * *

Raleigh, North Carolina
25 July 2006
03:07 hours Eastern Standard Time (08:07 hours Zulu)

TO SAY THAT JACOB Stickles's day had been long would have been an understatement. Between providing support and analysis for a hostage rescue contract, gathering intelligence reports and sifting through them, and his daily shake-and-bake of his old contacts in the intelligence community for any new tech, there was not much time for Stickles to catch his breath. Upon returning to his single bedroom apartment in town, Stickles had promptly changed into shorts and a blue T-shirt that bore his alma mater, the New York Institute of Technology; made his way to his bedroom; and crashed on the bed, face first.

That was four hours earlier. The shrill, obnoxious sound of his work cell phone dragged him out of his sleep. Stickles slowly lifted his head and reached for the phone. He saw that the number was blocked, which gave him cause for hesitation. After a moment, he figured that only another co-worker would know his number. Stickles yawned and flipped the phone open.

"Hello?"

"You know who this is. Don't say another word until you've encrypted the call."

The voice cut through Stickles's grogginess. He reached for an attachment that plugged into the bottom of the phone, connected it, and turned it on. A moment later, the light flashed green, and Stickles held the phone to his ear again.

"Williams, where the hell are you?" Stickles asked. "The guys have been asking about you."

"I'm off the reservation," Ben Williams told him. "Unsanctioned job. Thrasher's tracking. The buck stops with you. You tracking?"

"Mum's the word," Stickles assured. "But where the hell are you? Are you safe?"

"I'm in Egypt," Williams said. "I've escaped from prison and have retrieved a VIP. The Egyptians have positively identified me and have issued a BOLO. The embassy is tracking the situation. They've considered us *persona non grata*."

"Wait, wait a second," Stickles said. He swung his legs over the bed and assumed a seated position. "The Agency hung you out to dry?"

"Not necessarily," Williams said. "I blame the State Department more than anything. Chief of Station is a friend of mine, but her hands are tied with the Ambassador."

"Which is where I come in," Stickles said. "What do you need me to do?"

"Access the list of active Agency operations in Cairo and find me one to piggyback."

"Stand by," Stickles said. He got out of bed, walked over to his ruggedized custom laptop computer, and woke it up. Next, he brought up his government intranet emulator and a custom IP cloak program. Then, he opened a list of log-in names and passwords. "Hmm...who should I be today?"

"I'm sure the lead BIR analyst would love to be of assistance today."

"Cairo chief of station, Bureau of Intelligence and Research..." Stickles scrolled down his list until he found the name. "Greg Miller." He adjusted his IP cloak to emulate log-in from a Cairo-based terminal and entered the corresponding username and password. "I'm in."

"Lay your cards on the table," Williams said.

"Any specific parameters?"

"I'd prefer something that isn't a joint op with the Egyptian government, but if you have to piggyback one, just make sure the *Mukhabarat* are not directly involved."

"Let's see..." Stickles scrolled the list of active operations and clicked on one that looked promising. "Not an Agency op, but you've got DEA working with Border Guard forces to interdict a major drug shipment."

"Nah, no cops," Williams said. "Need somebody who's willing to bend the rules a little."

"Okay..." Stickles continued to scroll. "Got Agency working in tandem with the *Mukhabarat* attempting to bring down a Muslim Brotherhood financier. From the particulars, it looks like the Agency's working their own leads while the *Mukhabarat*'s running down their own, and they're sharing notes."

"Too close for comfort. Next."

"All right…" A minute passed by in silence. Something on the screen caught Stickles's attention, and he leaned in closer. "Hmm…that's interesting."

"Talk to me."

"Langley's running a stand-alone op, arranging an arms deal between them and a Brotherhood big wig, guy by the name of Jafar Abdul-Rahim. Notes that Abdul-Rahim has ties to al-Qaeda."

"I thought that the Brotherhood and AQ weren't on friendly terms."

"Turns out that Abdul-Rahim is a hardliner." Stickles skimmed the notes. "He toes the party line, but he's working to push the Brotherhood's agenda further towards armed insurrection. AQ's more than willing to give him a bit of a helping hand to gain another foothold in the region."

"We can work with that. Give me the point man's particulars."

"Hmm…" Stickles scrolled some more. "Seems that he isn't so much of a point man but rather a lone wolf operative. Doesn't provide a photograph or a name either."

"This must be some sensitive shit, then."

"It does provide a call-sign for the man on the ground. Tin Man." The line was quiet for a solid fifteen seconds before Stickles asked, "Hey, Williams, you still with me?"

"Yeah, Stickles, I'm still here," Williams said, his voice reluctant.

"I can dig up the particulars on this Tin Man if you want."

"That won't be necessary." Williams took a deep breath and said, "Keep this conversation to yourself.

Either I'm coming out with my principal or I'm not coming out at all. There's too much at stake here."

"Keep my mouth shut and avoid an international incident," Stickles summarized. "Got it. Watch your back over there, dude."

"Always," Williams said before he killed the line.

CHAPTER TWELVE

Shubra Al Khaymah, Cairo, Egypt
25 July 2006
14:00 hours Eastern European Time (12:00 hours Zulu)

WHEN TRANSLATED FROM CYRILLIC, the name on her passport was Ekaterina Lazarovna Korovina. In her passport photo, her hair was short and black, and her eyes were an empty bistre color with a facial expression to match. Her declared occupation was imports and exports, and she claimed to be based out of Moscow. When she had entered the country a week earlier, the customs official had given her a skeptical look, which was melted away by her brilliant, even-toothed smile and batted eyelashes. The official had stamped her passport and sent her on her way.

The thing was, Ekaterina Korovina was not her real name. It was close enough, though, much closer than some of the legends she had adopted over the past nine years. She was not from Moscow, though she spoke fluent Russian with a Muscovite accent. The only true statement she had made at the customs desk was that she was in imports/exports, which was only in the loosest definition of the industry. The lie of Ekaterina Korovina, businesswoman, was only the frosting of the fabrication cake. Beneath that layer was Ekaterina Korovina, arms dealer, and the woman whom a faction of the Muslim Brotherhood believed could deliver them enough arms to launch an insurrection against the Mubarak regime.

At her core, she was Karen Cockayne, a CIA non-official cover operations officer, a fact she had to force herself to remember from time to time. Like any other competent undercover asset, she knew that only the legend was true. Because of all of the deceptions she had crafted over the years, it became a chore to sift through them all to reassemble the pieces of herself that she had embedded in those deceptions. She figured that would explain why she had taken no more than a week off between missions over the past two years.

The task at hand was simple: meet with Jafar Abdul-Rahim Muslim Brotherhood, get a feel for the man, gain his trust, and get him to open up about his like-minded compatriots within the. Langley hoped this operation would expose the collusion between the Muslim Brotherhood and al-Qaeda. Thus far, the public assumed that they were in collusion, but there was more than enough chatter to suggest that a public denouncement of al-Qaeda could happen within the next year, a sign of love lost between the two organizations.

Cockayne suspected that the play would be capitalized upon to try and wipe out the entire Muslim Brotherhood, which would solidify Mubarak's hold on the region. Personally, she could not care either way. Mubarak was the typical Middle Eastern autocratic leader who conducted the charade of democracy, while the Muslim Brotherhood held hardline, oppressive perspectives and were no friend to the United States. It was the factions within the Brotherhood that colluded to return the political party to its armed insurrectionist roots which made Abdul-

Rahim her concern.

The meeting place was a building in the Shubra Al Khaymah district, a public café that intelligence suggested was friendly to the Brotherhood's cause. It was low-key enough that it had not drawn government attention, but the rumors were there, and Abdul-Rahim asking to meet there only lent credibility to those rumors. He would want to set the pace of the talks, which was fine by her. Cockayne knew that Abdul-Rahim would not attempt to double-cross somebody who could help him realize his ambitions of an Islamist state through a violent overthrow.

Cockayne traveled alone. Her section chief had offered a Special Activities detachment to pose as her muscle, but she had declined it. The only person she relied on was herself, and that attitude applied to everything she did in her life, personally and professionally. She was also unarmed. The mission was strictly reconnaissance: meet the man, develop the situation, adjust strategy from there. An unarmed arms marketeer would make Abdul-Rahim feel much more at home than if she elected to show up with an entourage. If he became belligerent, then she had something to fall back on: her reputation in the arms realm. She was a strong proponent of the theory that often times, the threat of violence was stronger than actual violence.

She spotted the café off to her right, maneuvered her Fiat into a parking spot adjacent to the cafe, and dismounted the vehicle. Cockayne was dressed conservatively in her blue jeans and white button-up long-sleeved blouse. A sleek black *hijab* wrapped around her hair and neck and all but concealed her features. What she could not conceal was her physique, which was obvious even with her modest clothing. She knew every red-blooded male had eyes on her as she walked down the street. What those males did not know about was her intellect. It bolstered her sex appeal and gave her a significant advantage with manipulation.

As she slid her aviator shades over her eyes, she spotted Abdul-Rahim. He was a tall man, handsome and impressively built, who sported a black short-sleeved shirt and olive-drab cargo pants. A *keffiyeh* was draped around his neck, and a cigarette—Royales, by the pack on the table—hung from his lips. She looked in his eyes and could feel the anger they held. Cockayne smiled politely as she took her seat at the table.

"Peace be upon you, Ms. Korovina," Abdul-Rahim greeted in Arabic.

"And peace upon you, Mr. Abdul-Rahim," Cockayne replied in the same language. She knew better than to offer a handshake. "How does today find you?"

Abdul-Rahim smiled. "Optimistic. Your reputation precedes you, Ms. Korovina. Our brothers in Chechnya speak very highly of your services and your professionalism."

"I aim to please, sir, and I'm more than happy to equip the freedom fighters of the world," she said.

"Discretion, timely delivery, and reasonable prices are the three bottom lines of your business model, as I understand it."

"As well as insurance," Cockayne pointed out. "I

have contacts in international law enforcement and intelligence circles that allow for one hundred percent guaranteed, hassle-free delivery."

"Very good," Abdul-Rahim said. He leaned forward and interlaced his fingers. "I also hear your catalogue runs the gamut."

"For your region, anything from small arms to shoulder-fired missiles. If it fits in a small enough box, I can deliver it. What will you be needing?"

"As far as small arms goes, we're covered. We will be needing ammunition for the weapons. However, our largest concerns at the moment are RPGs, explosives, and grenades, all of which we are in short supply."

"Do you mind Soviet stockpiles?"

"We prefer Soviet stockpiles. That is what our men are most proficient in."

Cockayne cleared her throat. "I can get you Semtex by the kilo, as well as blasting caps and detonators. RPGs are also not a problem. As far as hand grenades, I can secure an excellent deal on a stockpile of RGD-5s."

Abdul-Rahim smiled as he contemplated the weaponry. "This all sounds very good."

Cockayne sensed that something was up, as the meeting was going far too smoothly, but she elected to play along. "Well, perhaps we should talk about prices and delivery."

"Well...here is the thing." Abdul-Rahim placed his index fingers perpendicular to his lips. "I may have heard good things about you, but I have never worked with you directly. I believe that as a sign of good faith, you should arrange a demonstration of the merchandise. Once we see that what we're getting is a quality product, then we can move onto the actual purchase."

She raised her eyebrows. "Mr. Abdul-Rahim, I understand your reluctance, but I would advise you not to horse-trade with me. I can give you a demonstration, absolutely, but you may want to hear the prices first, as they are not up for negotiation."

Abdul-Rahim nodded. "Then perhaps we are wasting each other's time."

Cockayne smiled and rose from the table. "Perhaps we are. Have a good day, sir. Peace be upon you." She took five steps, and then turned and stopped on cue. "You have my contact information. I would appreciate it if you informed me of when you've placed your order with a competing buyer so that I may inform how much you would have saved were it not for your attempts to force me to undercut my product prices." She continued forward and made it four more paces.

"Wait."

Damn, Cockayne thought to herself. *Called it one pace short.* She turned back to face Abdul-Rahim. "Yes?"

Abdul-Rahim gestured for her to return to her seat. "Come, let's discuss prices. We can do that much."

"I would like that," Cockayne said cordially. She returned to her seat and crossed her legs. "Let's talk about the RPGs first. They're the priciest item. How many are you looking to buy?"

Before Abdul-Rahim could answer, one of his men furrowed his brow, as if he had heard something. The bodyguards were smart—they'd purchased ear buds for their radios to prevent outsiders from eavesdropping. One of those guards approached Abdul-Rahim and whispered in his ear. Cockayne studied his facial expressions while he received the news, and halfway through, his face darkened. That look was never a good sign in all her years working undercover.

Abdul-Rahim pulled away from his subordinate and smiled at Cockayne. "Come, I have something to show you."

"How far away is it?" she asked.

"Not far," he said. "Just inside the building."

Cockayne forced a smile. "Lead the way."

She noticed how the bodyguards formed a box around her as she followed Abdul-Rahim. By itself, it was not cause for concern, but when combined with the message from the subordinate, it did not bode well. Abdul-Rahim led them through the dining area, past the kitchen, through the storage room and into the alley. The first thing Cockayne saw was one of the Brotherhood leveling a Glock 17 at an unseen target. When she passed the doorway and saw who was being held at gunpoint, it took every ounce of discipline she had to adopt a neutral expression.

"I found him up there," the guard said, pointing to a rooftop that had a clear vantage point overlooking the café patio. "And I found him with this." The guard unslung a modified M4A1 and handed it to Abdul-Rahim.

Cockayne looked to Abdul-Rahim, who had produced his own Glock in his hands. He pointed the weapon at her, and then to the large man. "Do you know him?"

"Never met him in my life," Cockayne deadpanned.

"And yet, he's caught covering you with a scoped rifle during our discussion? Do you think I'm stupid?" Abdul-Rahim leveled his pistol in her face.

Cockayne shrugged. "I don't know what to tell you, and I don't know what kind of organizational model you run when the person who has the hardware you need, at the prices you need, is on the business end of your gun."

"You said it yourself," Abdul-Rahim said. "There are other merchants. I'll find another."

"There are other merchants," the man held at gunpoint by the guard said loudly, in Arabic.

Abdul-Rahim tore his eyes from Cockayne to face the man. "What did you say?"

"There are other merchants," the man repeated. "I work for one of them."

Abdul-Rahim lowered his gun and approached the man. When he was close, he stuck his gun up under the man's chin, finger on the trigger. "Tell me which merchant you work for and I'll make it quick."

Ben Williams's left hand shot up, grabbed the Glock's barrel, and twisted hard as he side-stepped. Abdul-Rahim's trigger finger snapped. Williams stripped him of the pistol, and immediately turned and fired a round into the shooter who had apprehended him. One of Abdul-Rahim's bodyguards stepped in to fire, and Cockayne sprung into action with a firm foot to the side of the knee. She tore the Glock from the man's hands and gunned him down. Cockayne spotted a gunman trained on Williams and instinctively drew down on him, placing two in his chest and one between the eyes. Three more shots whizzed past her, and she automatically focused on the source, only to find Williams in his shooting posture. Cockayne looked left and saw the body of the last guard, blood flowing from newly formed perforations.

Footsteps sounded from within the building. Cockayne sprinted to Williams's side, and gunshots sounded off as the first of the Brotherhood's remaining force hit the ground. She spun on a heel, thrust the pistol in front of her, and picked up a second gunman in her sights. Her finger stroked the trigger twice, and the man joined his comrades on the alley floor. Williams grabbed Abdul-Rahim by the scruff of his neck, stuck the pistol in his back, and backpedaled toward the alley entrance with Cockayne in tow. Once they reached the street, they side-stepped in opposite directions to seek cover, and Williams threw Abdul-Rahim to the ground, safely out of the line of fire.

Three more Brotherhood shooters joined the fray, two with pistols and one with a Kalashnikov, but none of them had a chance to fire. The Glocks in Cockayne's and Williams's hands barked as they saturated the alley with 9mm rounds. A trio of corpses hit the ground, and a moment of silence passed. Cockayne exhaled and glared at Williams.

"What the fuck are you doing here?" she hissed in English.

Williams stuck the Glock in his waistband, moved back into the alley, and retrieved the M4 from the ground where Abdul-Rahim had dropped it during the struggle. He then returned to Abdul-Rahim, grabbed him by the shoulder, and jabbed the M4's barrel into his back. "Helping you capture your HVT."

"You fucking idiot! He was supposed to help me network his buddies!"

"Then take him to a black site and download him," Williams said indifferently. "Or hand him over to the *Mukhabarat*—they'll pull it out of him. Either way, I'd rather not discuss this in a bloody alley with automatic weapons and nine dead bodies. Would you?"

Cockayne scowled at Williams. She walked over to him, grabbed Abdul-Rahim by the arm and dug her Glock into his ribcage. She leaned in and said in Arabic, "You make one wrong move, and the doctors will spend the next few days reconstructing your guts and declaring you a paraplegic. You savvy?"

"Yes. I am savvy."

"Good." Cockayne looked to Williams and reverted to English. "You drive here?"

"Nah, took a taxi. Left my car at the safe house."

Cockayne reached with her free hand and tossed him the keys to her Fiat. "You're driving. This had better be fucking good."

* * *

Egyptian General Intelligence Service Headquarters
Cairo, Egypt
25 July 2006
14:45 hours Eastern European Time (12:45 hours Zulu)

AGHA WAS GOING ON thirty-two hours without sleep, and yet he was wide awake. His eyes were bloodshot, and his usual expression had metamorphosed to a concrete glower. He had not eaten and only drank water as he pored over information. All that he could get his hands on was the scant dossier compiled by the *Mukhabarat* during Bright Star 89, as well as a joint CIA/Unit 777 operation in 1999. It was not much, but it provided enough of an insight into his quarry.

The after-action report from Bright Star 89, written by the Unit 777 squadron commander, stated:

The training exercise was a resounding success. Our own operators performed admirably, and the American contingent maintained their usual level of competence and professionalism. The unit cohesion between both contingents is incredibly promising, and is noteworthy for potential joint operations in the future.

One American soldier that should be noted by name is one Sergeant First Class Ben Williams, whose knowledge was imparted to great effect, both with our unit's operators and his own. In particular, his commensurate skill in maneuvering within a non-permissive environment is not only considerable, but based in experience: he has worked in insurgent environments in Latin America, and also worked in Northern Ireland during an exchange tour with the 22nd Special Air Service. His unique perspective has proven to be a valuable training tool, and I would suggest formalizing it into an internal text for current and future operators to draw education from.

Agha set the after-action report down and thumbed through the photos taken during the exercise. There were several photographs of Williams and Ferran Anwar working together. Williams was younger and had more hair, but he looked much more haunted than the man he interrogated in Istiqbal-Tora. His face in the photo was that of a man who had seen hell, but whose mind had not caught up with the reality. Agha paired that with his experience staring down the man and knew that Williams had grown stronger in the wake of tribulations past.

Next, Agha picked up the after-action report from the 1999 joint operation. The mission had been a failure, as the team had been forced to kill the target they had been tasked with capturing, but Ferran had nothing but praises for Williams:

As far as the American special operations contingent assigned to my team for the operation, they cannot be blamed for the result of the operation. They have upheld their reputation for exhibiting the utmost professionalism. Under fire, all of the Americans kept their cool, but none more so than their team leader, Ben Williams. I have worked with him in the past during the Bright Star exercises, and he has only grown more skilled with time. He adapted to the situation when the mission fell apart and exhausted every possible alternative before making the choice to terminate the target. While the mission to capture the target was unsuccessful, Williams and his team conducted a thorough site exploitation that produced leads that showed promise of actionable intelligence for future missions.

Agha set the file down and stood. He paced back

and forth as he reflected on the reading. *A survivor, capable of working on his own or within a team, a sharp mind, expert in non-permissive environments.* Yet, he could not predict what Williams's next move would be. The objective was the same: exit the country. To that effect, he had issued a nationwide BOLO for both Williams and Zaina Anwar, and had appealed to the director to increase security at all ports and on the borders. However, Williams had to know that would happen, and would find a way around it. He wondered if Williams had the resources necessary for multiple contingencies or if he was improvising.

Three solid knocks sounded through the door. "Come."

Captain Darzi walked through the door and snapped to attention. Since neither one of them was in uniform, neither man saluted, but Agha did gesture for Darzi to relax.

"What is it, Captain?" Agha asked.

"Local police have responded to a shootout in Shubra Al Khaymah," Darzi said. "Nine dead, and initial reports state that all of them are suspected Muslim Brotherhood operatives."

Agha let out a sigh. "Pass it off to somebody else. We need to focus on Williams."

"Hear me out, sir," Darzi said. "The shooting went largely unwitnessed, as it happened in an alley behind a café. However, moments after the shooting, a large man and a woman were seen escorting a third person to a black Fiat and driving east."

That caught Agha's attention, and he stepped towards Darzi. "Did they get a better description of the man?"

"They seem to think he's Arab," Darzi said. "They said he was speaking both English and Arabic fluently. Bit of a scraggly beard going. They noted that when the man got into the car, he lowered himself slowly, almost like he was in some sort of pain."

"That's him," Agha said. "Spin up a chopper. I want to be on that crime scene in the next thirty minutes."

Fiaras snapped to attention. "Yes, sir."

* * *

Izbat an Nakhl, Cairo, Egypt
25 July 2006
15:09 hours Eastern European Time (13:09 hours Zulu)

WILLIAMS PARKED THE BLACK Fiat in front of the apartment complex, behind his blue one. He got out of the car first, his M4 now safely in a duffel bag in his left hand and his right hovering where he had stashed the Glock. His eyes scanned the area for anybody taking a particular interest in their activities. Once he found nothing, he motioned for Cockayne to bring Abdul-Rahim out of the car. Abdul-Rahim was out first, and Cockayne was hot on his heels, her weapon still trained on him. Once he heard the door shut, Williams led the way to the safe house, four stories up.

At the door, Williams signaled with his left hand for Cockayne to stop. He knocked four times, waited two seconds, knocked three more times, waited five seconds, and then knocked another four times. As soon as his knuckle hit the door the last time, Zaina opened the door, SIG-Sauer at her hip but trained in the direction of the door. She stepped aside and motioned with her head for the guests to enter.

"Good job," Williams said as soon as Zaina opened the door. "You did great."

"Wasn't that hard," Zaina said. "Point a gun at the door, and if they mess up the code, take cover and wait."

"You'd be surprised how many people get that wrong. You're cool under fire, you know that?"

"You saying I should make a living of this?" She shook her head emphatically. "Fuck that. Give me back my classroom."

"I hear you, Professor," Williams said, setting down the duffel bag.

Zaina stuck the SIG-Sauer back in her waistband and pointed to the newcomers. "Who are they?"

Williams took a deep breath. "One of those people is an angry, secretive soul with a capacity for deceit and a hatred of everything that I am. The other one's a member of the Muslim Brotherhood."

Zaina raised her eyebrows as she turned to look at Williams. "Ex-girlfriend?" When Williams gave her a look in return, she said, "Honey, I'm a woman. I can sense that kind of drama a mile away."

"No," Williams said. "Not an ex-girlfriend. We…" He looked back to Cockayne, who had just finished duct-taping Abdul-Rahim's ankles together and his hands behind his back. She looked over and glared at Williams, which caused him to turn back to Zaina. "We had a misunderstanding once."

"Uh-huh." Zaina crossed her arms. "Well, I see you've got that all under control. I'll leave you two to talk shop."

"Much appreciated," Williams said. As Zaina started to walk away he said, "Hey. How are you holding up?"

Zaina looked back. The hurt was in her eyes, but she kept a stiff upper lip. "I'll manage."

"Good." He nodded. "Off you go."

Cockayne finished locking down Abdul-Rahim and placed a strip of duct tape over his mouth. She removed her *hijab* and ran a hand through her hair as she walked into the kitchen. Her first stop was the fridge, where she removed a can of Mountain Dew. It looked exactly the same as its American counterpart, except that half of the script was Arabic and it had a peel-off top. She cracked it open, tossed the top away, and took a swig of the soda. Williams helped himself to a bottle of water from the fridge and slowly lowered himself into a chair at the table.

"You hurting?" she asked, her tone borderline on taunting.

"You could say that. Been keeping myself going with Percocet."

Cockayne gave him a faux pout. "Aww. You poor thing."

Williams cracked the cap off of the water bottle and had a drink. "You can sit down, you know."

"I can. I'd rather not." Cockayne leaned against the countertop. "How did you know where to find me?

Last time I checked, you were a green badger, and not one in good standing, not since that incident with the Shedlock Group. Langley wouldn't read you in on my op unless I specifically requested otherwise."

"A magician never reveals his secrets."

Cockayne snorted derisively. "Right. You want my help, and you start off playing coy." She took another sip. "Why don't we try this again?"

"Put yourself in my shoes, Karen. If you were on the outside and you reached out to somebody for help, would you want to lay your cards on the table, be at someone else's mercy?"

Cockayne shook her head. "No. But I'm not the one asking for help. Now, tell me how you managed to piggyback my op."

Williams scratched his beard while he fixed Cockayne with a disapproving stare. "How do you think? Just like anybody else with the technical know-how would. I hacked my way in. And for the record, don't even think of trying to report that to higher. You won't find the proof."

Cockayne raised her eyebrows at that and eyed her Mountain Dew. "Wow. You must be in some pretty deep shit if you're willing to come clean that quickly. What's this all about?" The last word betrayed her Minnesotan upbringing.

Williams had intended to provide only the minimum level of details, but Cockayne knew that she had him in a vise. He let out a long exhale, took another swig of water, and cleared his throat. "Friend of mine's cousin was arrested as a political dissident. Asked me to break her out and get them to asylum in the States."

"Okay." Cockayne nodded and paused. "Where's the friend?"

"Dead. Didn't survive the *Mukhabarat*'s interrogation."

"Why didn't you make few calls to the embassy to secure safe passage?"

"I did," Williams said with frustration. "They've got some counterintel colonel chasing me. Agha. Somehow, he pieced two and two together and figured out who I am. I'm *persona non grata* at the embassy and I'm to be turned over if I show up."

"And you decided to get me involved?" Cockayne laughed incredulously. "Do you know how much drama you're dumping on my doorstep? I'm a NOC. The *last* thing I need is the Egyptians discovering *my* identity. You know what kind of international shit storm this could cause?"

"Couldn't really give two shits at this point," Williams said. "I'm here to do a job. That's it. I promised my friend that I'd get her out. The diplomats can eat a fat dick, for all I care."

"Spoken like a true grunt," Cockayne said. "And now, you can bet they're looking for me. They saw what car we were driving in. How do you propose I work my way out of this situation?"

"Well, first of all, you should have taken that case officer position that Thrasher offered you," Williams said. "Your cover was blown with the Shedlock affair. And yet, you keep looking for assignments. You knew the risks when you signed back up for UC duty, so don't expect me to shed a tear if you get burned."

"Fuck you, Ben."

"And secondly, it's because you're still in the field that you'll be able to work your way out of this. I've already given you your target. What I need from you are your contacts. You have an asset that runs a cargo service, a layover from your stint with Rezanov. You saved him from *mafiya* types, flipped him, made him official."

"What of him?"

"I know you trust him enough to let him know who you really were. If he has that level of trust with you, then he's exactly what I need."

Cockayne shrugged. "Maybe I don't know where he is."

Williams slowly rose from his chair and sauntered towards Cockayne. "He's based in Cyprus and handles your operations in the Mediterranean, the Middle East, and northern Africa. He runs legitimate furniture shipments on the regular to avoid raising suspicion with the prying eyes of the authorities. He'll drop everything at the first sign you need him for something because you've got that poor man wrapped around your finger." He stopped inches from Cockayne's face and spoke in hushed tones. "He knows *who* you are, but he doesn't know *what* you are."

Cockayne set her Mountain Dew on the counter, placed her palms on the edge of the counter, and leaned back. "Enlighten me. What am I, Ben?"

Williams locked eyes with her. He knew this would be counterproductive to acquiring her cooperation, but he did not care. "You're an emotional parasite. You use somebody and feed off their emotions because it's the only way you can feel anything. Your intellect and your sex are weapons at your disposal. The knowledge you can completely corrupt somebody's mind and bend them to service your every whim emboldens you. It empowers you."

Cockayne spread her lips to reveal her brilliant smile, cocked her head to her left, and bit the corner of her bottom lip. "You feel better now?"

Williams shook his head. "This was a mistake." He turned heel and marched towards the common area.

"He's actually due in port in a couple of hours," Cockayne said.

He stopped, closed his eyes, took a deep breath, and turned around to face her. "Where?"

"Alexandria. He was bringing in a weapons shipment. I don't need him now that I've got Abdul-Rahim. I can make a call and tell him to expect you."

Williams folded his arms. "What's the catch?"

"We swap cars."

Williams smiled. "They know your car. They don't know mine. You want me to draw fire."

"How else am I supposed to get him out of the country under their noses?"

"With the kind of dragnet they're throwing over the city, it's gonna be hard to get to Alexandria."

"That sounds like a personal problem," Cockayne said. "There's my offer. You take my car, you get the boat. You take your car, then I hope it can grow fins and swim."

"Sounds like you want me to get caught."

Cockayne laughed. "This isn't the first time I've heard the name Abdullah Agha. The man's like James Jesus Angleton, except he's not paranoid. He's just that damn good. America's prodigal son versus Egypt's top spy hunter. It should make for a hell of a showdown."

"Better hope I win," Williams said quietly. "They catch me again, there's no reason why I shouldn't give you up as the bigger catch."

Cockayne finished her soda, tossed the can in the nearby receptacle, and walked towards Williams, her hands in her back pockets. "You wouldn't do that."

"Why's that?"

"You may play the part of the cynical mercenary, but I see past the steely glint, clenched jaw, and tough talk. You never took to the hard calculus of the intelligence world. End of the day, you're still the same golden boy altruist who'd jump on the grenade. You're a soldier. You wouldn't sell me out."

"Think what you will," Williams said, with less swagger than he'd had moments earlier.

"So, am I gonna make that call?" She stood in front of him, looking up at him with what those unfamiliar with Karen Cockayne would mistake for adoration. He saw it for what it was—the look of a satisfied woman who knew she had what she wanted, and it was only a matter of time before her prey caught up to the fact.

Williams stepped out of the kitchen, grabbed the keys to the blue Fiat, and handed them to Cockayne. "Make the call."

CHAPTER THIRTEEN

Shubra Al Khaymah, Cairo, Egypt
25 July 2006
15:20 hours Eastern European Time (13:20 hours Zulu)

THE MI-8 HIP CHOPPER shuddered as it made its descent. Agha looked out of the window and watched the rotorthrob blow dust up in the air. He reached into his pocket, removed a pair of aviator shades, and slipped them over his eyes as he felt the gentle rock of the helicopter's wheels touching the pavement. Agha unbuckled himself from the seat, slid the door open, and hopped out. He kept low until he was fifteen paces from the helicopter and slowly rose to an erect posture. The senior Cairo Police officer on the scene stood at parade rest to wait for the counterintelligence colonel, and turned and walked in step when he moved on line with him.

"You have nine bodies killed by small arms, no murder weapon, no sign of return fire." Agha shouted to be heard over the rotorthrob.

"That's correct, Colonel," the cop—Sergeant Mufeed, by his rank and nameplate—said. "It looks like 9mm rounds, judging from what the deceased were packing, but all of the shell casings suggest that whomever they were congregating around did all of the shooting. Also signs of a physical struggle, which could indicate that the deceased could have been disarmed by the shooters, judging by the types of injuries."

"That fits my target," Agha said. "Any additional

dispositions taken since my office was informed of the shooting?"

"No, sir. We have held the people that did see something if you wanted to conduct any follow-on interviews."

"I'm sure that won't be necessary," Agha said. "I just want to see the bodies."

"Very good, Colonel." Mufeed waved to his comrades guarding the alley, and he led Agha into the alley. Agha knelt to the closest body and inspected it. The shot groups were tight, like they were with the fallen at Istiqbal-Tora. All but one of the bodies showed only gunshot wounds. The last body showed a dislocation of the knee. There were four groups of casings: two at opposite ends within the alley, and two by each corner of the alley. Agha took in all of this and put the pieces together.

"The woman with him was a shooter," Agha said. "Not the woman I was looking for, though. She knew enough to take down a man who was probably much larger. They were held at gunpoint, disarmed the shooters, and killed them before they could get in the fight. Then, they sought cover and killed the rest as they funneled through the door." He stood and waved to all nine bodies. "I know these men. Not by name, but I know their leader. Jafar Abdul-Rahim, suspected cell leader with the Muslim Brotherhood. Was his body found at all?"

"No."

"Williams must have taken him."

"Do you think your man is linking up with the Brotherhood?"

Agha shook his head. "Not in his nature. He's

helped kill them before. If even one recognized him, they'd gun him down in a heartbeat." He walked the scene, both of his hands behind his back as he studied and formulated theories. It took him a moment, but he found a theory that fit the frame. "He wasn't here for Abdul-Rahim. He was here for the woman. She's somebody he knows. American, maybe Israeli."

"Then why did he take Abdul-Rahim?" Mufeed asked.

"Because the woman was after him," Agha said with certainty. He looked to Mufeed and told him, "You didn't hear any of this."

"Hear what, sir?" Mufeed asked innocently.

"Precisely." He looked to the edge of the alley. "You said that the shooters were headed east."

"Yes, sir. All units in the region are on the lookout for the black Fiat."

"All right. Good job." He walked to the edge of the alley, removed his mobile from his jacket pocket, and selected a speed-dial entry from his contacts.

"Captain Darzi."

"It's Colonel Agha. Williams has linked up with somebody here, a woman."

"It's not Anwar?"

Agha shook his head. "No. This woman knows how to kill. That's beyond Anwar's skill set. I'm thinking either American or Israeli, somebody who knows the country and has the resources necessary to get him out of the country."

"I can check our contacts and see if any known networks have been activated," Darzi volunteered.

"Go ahead, but I doubt it will produce anything," Agha said. "Williams knows we keep close tabs on the Israelis and we conduct joint intelligence operations with the Americans. He also knows if he tries to piggyback one of those ops, I'll catch him. His options are narrow with the Israelis, but a little broader with another American. It's got to be a NOC operation, and if he lucked out, he'll have found one without any connection to the embassy. I'm sure of it."

"What are you going to do, sir?" Darzi asked.

"I'll be with the chopper, coordinating with local police forces. Contact Central Security Forces and get in touch with Special Operations. I want a response team fueled up and on standby in case the locals can't contain the situation."

"Yes, sir."

Agha killed the connection. He took one last look around the area, his eyes narrowed as he hoped to catch even a glimpse of Williams. His mind visualized drawing the SIG-Sauer on his hip, extending it in front of him, and his finger twitching twice. He imagined two fresh holes in Williams's chest as he fell to the ground. Agha's jaw clenched at the thought, and a shudder ran down his spine. After a deep breath, he shook the thought from his head and jogged towards the helicopter. He knew the moment would come; he needed to set the stage first.

* * *

Izbat an Nakhl, Cairo, Egypt
25 July 2006

15:38 hours Eastern European Time (13:38 hours Zulu)

ZAINA STOOD IN THE living room, arms crossed, while Williams ferried equipment to the black Fiat. She had offered to help, but Williams had popped a couple of Percocet and insisted on doing the work. She could see Williams through a window. He loaded up the black Fiat with the gear from the house, then shifted focus to the blue one and transferred items from one car to the other. Zaina had no idea what kind of deal Williams had struck with the woman, but from the expression on Williams's face, she could tell that it probably benefited the woman more than it benefited them. A drawn out sigh fell from her lips as she waited for the go-ahead to load up.

"He doesn't want you helping?"

Zaina looked to her right and saw the woman standing next to her. Her arms were also folded, and a smirk adorned her face.

"What's your name again?" Zaina asked.

"Karen Cockayne." She saw the look on Zaina's face and chuckled. "No, that's not pseudonym, and yes, I've heard all the jokes."

"I'm actually surprised you'd give me your real name," Zaina said. "I figure you intelligence types would keep that kind of information close to your chest."

Cockayne smiled and looked back to Williams. "I figure that if the *Mukhabarat* catch you, they'll kill you before you surrender. If you flee the country, Ben will make sure you don't divulge my identity."

Zaina raised her eyebrows. "His first name is

Ben."

"He didn't tell you? Hmm. Probably just for brevity's sake. He may be a spook, but not the kind that keeps secrets for keeping secrets' sake. He's a soldier to the core. Everything he does or says has an objective behind it. He may play in my world, but at the end of the day, he's just an expanded skill set soldier. It makes him efficient, but it also makes him predictable."

That elicited a stark laugh from Zaina. "To this point, Williams has done a lot of things, has been a lot of things, but I wouldn't say he's predictable."

"That's because you're not a shooter or a spook," Cockayne said. "Once you get to know one, you'll know them all. Try to get to know Ben, if he lets you in, and the next time you see a soldier out of uniform, you'll spot him and you will just know."

Zaina turned to face Cockayne. "You said that he wouldn't allow me to divulge your identity. What makes you so sure?"

Cockayne let out a deep breath. "Ben Williams is a lot of things that I can't stand, but one of his redeeming qualities is loyalty. I've never seen him screw people over that didn't have it coming. He would never leave me hanging out to dry."

"Sounds like there's some history there," Zaina probed.

"I see what you're doing there," Cockayne said, with a smile. "You'll have to get that story from him. My lips are sealed."

"Fair enough," Zaina said. She waited a beat and asked, "You don't seem to think our chances are good, do you?"

"The whole country's hunting you *and* the embassy's disowned you? Yeah, I wouldn't be sanguine about your chances. But your situation isn't one hundred percent dire."

"How so?"

"You make it to the dock, my boat driver will get you to international waters. Once you're in the clear, you're smooth sailing all the way to Cyprus. Mubarak doesn't have the juice in Cyprus to have you extradited. He also doesn't have the balls to come after you once you're outside his jurisdiction."

"But the hard part will be getting to the dock."

Cockayne nodded. "Every pair of eyes toting a badge and a piece will be looking for you two. Ben's gonna have to bring his A-game to get you where you need to go."

Williams came back inside and stood with his hands on his hips. "Your car's ready to go."

"Then what are we waiting for?" Cockayne asked. She wandered over to where Abdul-Rahim had fallen asleep on the floor and grabbed him by the shoulders. In Arabic, she said, "Time to take a little trip."

"C'mon," Williams said, motioning for Zaina to follow him. They walked down the stairs and back to the black Fiat. He opened her door for her. Before she got in, Williams reached in the back, retrieving an olive drab *hijab* and a red-and-white checkered *keffiyeh*. He handed the *hijab* to Zaina.

"Put that on," he said. "We need to hide your face as best as possible."

"You've got it," Zaina said. She took the *hijab* from him, sat down, and fastened her seatbelt. Williams closed the door and walked around the front of the car. As he walked, he folded the *keffiyeh* into a triangle and began wrapping it around his head.

Cockayne dragged Abdul-Rahim down the stairs and guided him to her new car. She threw him across the backseat, closed one door, and then went to her shotgun seat. In the seat was a small kit, where she removed a hypodermic needle and a clear vial. Cockayne plunged the needle into the vial and filled the syringe halfway. She opened the other rear passenger door, held Abdul-Rahim's head off to other side, and stuck the needle in his neck. His screams were muted by the duct tape over his mouth, and he went still a few moments later.

"Slip him a Mickey Finn?" Williams asked. He tied the final knot in his head wrap.

"Rohypnol," Cockayne confirmed. "Should keep him knocked out until I get to the airport. I'm sure you appreciate the irony."

Williams raised his eyebrows. "Yeah." He looked to Cockayne. "Look, I didn't mean to crash your op like that."

"It's whatever," Cockayne said. "We'll download him in Romania."

"Yeah." Williams nodded and turned to his car.

"Ben?"

He looked back, and for a second, he thought he saw a hint of concern on her face. It was gone as quickly as it came.

"Keep your head on a swivel."

"Always do," Williams answered as he got behind the wheel. He closed his door and looked over to Zaina. Her *hijab* was in place, and all that was visible were her eyes. He nodded in approval, buckled his seatbelt, and started the ignition.

* * *

Ten miles southeast of Damanhour, Egypt
25 July 2006
17:32 hours Eastern European Time (15:32 hours Zulu)

THE DRIVE HAD BEEN silent. Williams required it from the onset to concentrate on keeping an eye out for law enforcement. Leaving Cairo had been the most difficult part. There had been a couple of municipal squad cars he spotted from a distance, but he had maneuvered around them without much trouble. Once Williams reached the highway, he settled into a steady cruise speed and loosened the *keffiyeh*. Zaina loosened her *hijab* as well, but kept her face concealed.

Zaina tried to get some sleep when they reached the highway, but found she was too wired. Instead, she got as comfortable as she could and sipped on a bottle of water that she had grabbed from the back. As they reached the last third of the journey, Zaina looked to Williams for a few moments, debating whether or not to initiate a conversation.

"I can feel your eyes on me," he said. His eyes continued their scan pattern as he spoke. "What is it?"

"Karen…she said a lot of things about you."

Williams scoffed. "I'm sure she did."

"You sure you she isn't your ex?"

"I'm sure."

Zaina shrugged. "Because she sure sounded like an ex—"

"I'm *sure*. She's also got a lot of nerve, trying to act like the scorned party."

"How's that?"

Williams took a deep breath. He was not keen on recounting the story, but he figured that satisfying her curiosity would make for an easier drive. "I met her when I was still working for the government. I was tasked to find an arms dealer and she was working for him. Turns out, she was working undercover, one of the 'good guys.'" His words were soaked in bitterness. "She screwed me and my guys over to solidify her cover. Got one of my men killed. When she tried to make amends, I told her what she could do with her apology."

"Sounds like you got screwed," Zaina observed.

"Oh, that's an understatement," Williams said. "Trust me: take anything Karen Cockayne says with a grain of salt."

"She also said that you were loyal to a fault. Said that if I decided to make a book deal of the whole affair, you'd make sure that her name stayed out of it."

Williams shrugged. "Yeah, well, she wasn't lying about that. You've got to keep her out of it. That goes for me, too."

"Why protect a woman who almost got you killed?"

"I don't burn people. Despite her total disregard for everyone, she's done a lot of good work for the war. A lot of bad guys are out of business due to her work."

"But you said it yourself: you're not a soldier anymore. You're here to do a job. Nothing more."

Williams glanced over at her. "Just because I took off my uniform doesn't mean my oath's invalid."

Zaina smiled. "She may know you better than you care to admit."

"What do you mean?"

"She said you were a soldier at heart."

He let out a sigh. "So, what about you? What made you become a teacher?"

"It was my passion ever since I was a little girl," Zaina said. "Both of my parents were professors. They were my heroes. They taught me of the importance of an education early on, and I knew that was what I was destined to do." She turned in her seat and gestured with her hands. "Think of the world's major ails. I count four: poverty, hunger, illness, and war. You can collapse hunger and illness into poverty, which leaves you with two: poverty and war. How do you stamp out poverty?"

"Educate the populace," Williams said.

Zaina nodded and continued, "A more educated populace means more people working and less people starving or sick. You'll have more doctors, and more people who can afford health care. Now, how do you prevent a war?"

"I know where you're going with this. I hate to be the party pooper, but war's here to stay. It will change. The focus will shift, the tactics will improve, the weapons will grow deadlier, but war is here to stay."

"Who do you take me for?" Zaina asked. "I'm

pragmatic. Eliminating war is for the idealists. What I aim to do is eliminate *unnecessary* war through education. Instead of soldiers that follow orders blindly, you have soldiers who think, who question what they're doing and why they're doing it."

"That's exactly why the top brass don't want those people as foot soldiers. The last thing they need is for somebody to question the morality of war halfway through a deployment, and in fairness, they have a semi-legitimate point."

"And what do you mean by that, exactly?"

"When you go downrange, you've got a job to do. It's not just your life on the line. Your buddies are counting on you, too. You decide war is wrong overnight, and everything is perfect, you're still screwing your buddies because now they've lost one rifle on the line. Most times, that's not going to happen, and you'll have a distracted soldier out of sync with the team."

"So, are you saying it's better to have idiots in uniform, carrying automatic weapons and having to work amongst built-up civilian populations?"

"Not at all. Focus on their education pre-military so they know what they're getting into when they sign up. If people are against war, then that's their prerogative. The moment you make hard contact with the enemy is *not* the time to be second-guessing yourself. I'm all for an intelligent military, full of critical thinkers. What I'm not for is a soldier getting his buddies killed because he started thinking about himself."

Zaina pondered that point for a moment. "That kind of altruism seems to be the opposite of the celebrated Western individuality."

"That's for civilians," Williams said immediately. "When you're working with a team, you must move and act as one. Your focus must be on protecting your buddies and your faith must be in your buddy's ability to protect you. That's all there is."

"I suppose you have a point," Zaina said. She rubbed her temples beneath her *hijab*. "I had meant to ask Ferran his opinion about that, but he was always working...before..."

Williams looked at Zaina for a moment. Reluctantly, with his eyes back on the road, he reached out with his right hand and squeezed Zaina's shoulder gingerly. He could hear her crying, though she kept it quiet and fought to get herself under control. His hand remained in place until he could hear her tears come to an end.

"I'm sorry," Zaina said. "I hate being such a little girl."

"No," Williams said. "You had a free moment, your thoughts returned to him. It's natural. You need time to grieve, and you'll have it. We just need to get to that boat first."

"What I need is to blow this whole thing wide open so Ferran's death has purpose," Zaina said.

"Once we get out of the country, his death gains purpose," Williams said. "Anything extra is icing on the cake."

Zaina took a deep breath. "Yeah. Let's get to the docks."

* * *

"C'MON, AYOOB," GAMAL HUSAM Ihsan Ishaq said as he drummed his finger on the squad car's dashboard. "Our shift is over."

"Not for another twenty minutes," Ayoob Mansur Qutb told his partner. Mansur had been on the Damanhour municipal force two years longer than Ihsan, but the two men were comparable in age. Their real difference was how they approached their police work. Ihsan liked clocking in a little late and leaving as soon as he could, whereas Mansur believed in thoroughness of work, and did not mind working overtime as long as the job was done well.

"It'll take us twenty minutes to get back to the station," Ihsan complained. "I'd kind of like to get off the clock at a reasonable time. Unlike you, I have a social life."

"Oh, really?" Mansur said dispassionately. "Do tell."

"I've got a date with Kalila," Ihsan said, emphasizing the woman's name with sensual pronunciation.

"That girl you've been talking to at the market?"

"The same. I'm taking her to that new nightclub. I can't wait to see how she cleans up." Ihsan said the last part with a lewd grin.

"Well, you're forgetting something."

"Yeah?"

"You're a cop. Your duty is to this city, not to chasing whores and testing your liver's alcohol threshold."

"Yeah, yeah, yeah." Ihsan rolled his eyes. "You

know, this isn't Saudi Arabia. You can be a Muslim and still enjoy the finer things in life."

"Yeah, well, then I would be a hypocrite. That might be acceptable in your eyes, but it wouldn't be acceptable in mine, and more important, it wouldn't be acceptable in the eyes of God."

"I worry about you sometimes, Ayoob."

"What's that?" Mansur brought the squad car to a halt alongside the curb.

"Hmm?"

"Hold on." He reached for the binoculars from between the seats and held them up to his eyes. The woman wore a *hijab*, whereas the man had wrapped a *keffiyeh* around his head. The man surveyed the area as he drove, almost mechanically. Mansur's eyes narrowed as he studied the oncoming vehicle.

"Gamal, take down this license plate," Mansur said as he rattled an alphanumeric sequence. "Read it back to me."

Ihsan repeated the sequence, then asked, "What is it?"

"Remember that BOLO that was put out a few hours ago by the CSF?"

"Vaguely. What about it?"

"We're supposed to be looking for a man and a woman driving a black Fiat. The man's driving around with a *keffiyeh* on his head to hide his features."

Ihsan shrugged. "That's not incriminating. And that's surprising, coming from somebody as devout as you."

Mansur lowered the binoculars and gave Ihsan a look. "It is suspicious. Call it in to Central."

"*Great.*" Ihsan stretched the word out as he dropped his head. "We'll probably have to file paperwork when we get back. I'll be late for my date."

"That's the job."

"I'll never get another shot with her after this."

"Should have thought about that before becoming a cop, Gamal."

"Yeah, yeah, yeah," Ihsan repeated as he reached for the handset.

CHAPTER FOURTEEN

Izbat an Nakhl, Cairo, Egypt
25 July 2006
18:00 hours Eastern European Time (16:00 hours Zulu)

THE LONGER AGHA SPENT on the Hip, the more agitated he grew. From his vantage point above the suburb, he could see the Cairo police cars combing the neighborhood, but the net was full of nothing but all-clear reports. With every passed moment, Agha felt that justice for the CSF troopers and his own *Mukhabarat* personnel was slipping further and further away. His face was glued to the window, peering down as if he could spot Williams. Every few seconds, he would force himself to breathe deeply to keep his pulse down and his wits about him. Thankfully, the rotorthrob drowned the sounds of his breathing and subsequently kept all eyes diverted elsewhere.

He adjusted his headset and keyed up. "All points, this is Colonel Agha. Give me a situation report."

"Colonel Agha, there is nothing to report here," Sergeant Mufeed said. "We are about forty-five percent accounted for, but so far, all owners of a black Fiat have checked out as legitimate."

"You need to search harder!" Agha insisted. "He is somewhere down there. Find him!"

"Yes, sir," Mufeed said evenly.

The sun slipped beneath the horizon, staining the indigo sky with vibrant streaks of orange. Sporadic clouds captured some of the sun and reflected it to create a picturesque sunset. However, as Agha stared off into the sky, his mind was not focused on aesthetics. Instead, he replayed the mental image from the crime scene—meeting Williams's eyes, drawing his pistol, and feeling it rock in his hands as the lead projectiles ripped through his enemy's body. Agha could see himself marching forward as Williams struggled, gasping for air and completely at his mercy. Agha would stand over Williams, raise his pistol, and squeeze the trigger until the slide locked back. Then, he would step back and watch Williams's blood stain the streets.

"Colonel?" The pilot's voice cut through his reverie. "Colonel Agha?"

"Yes, what?" Agha asked irritably.

"You have a Captain Darzi on the net asking for you. Should I patch you in?"

"Yes, go ahead."

"Colonel, there's something you may want to hear," Darzi said a moment later.

"What is it?" Agha asked.

"Damanhour Municipal Police report a black Fiat headed north a few minutes ago," Darzi said. "They did not report spotting Williams or Anwar, but the passengers were described as, quote, 'A man hiding his face with a *keffiyeh* and a woman wearing a *hijab*. The man seemed unusually alert, but not criminally so.' They did not have enough evidence to make a stop, but they did get down the license plate."

Agha bit his tongue. He wanted to lash out at the police officers for not stopping the car anyway, but he also knew Williams would have more than likely killed them anyway. The officers' initiative in taking down the license plate also helped to keep his temper in check. He took a deep breath, analyzed Williams's actions, and concluded, "He's headed to Alexandria. They're headed for international waters."

"That is the theory we're working with," Darzi said. "We have prepared an updated BOLO that lists the two of them as 'shoot on sight.'"

"No," Agha said immediately. "No. Follow at a distance, but do not apprehend. We need to wait until he's at the docks, when he is at his least mobile. Scramble the CSF chopper and get them to Alexandria immediately."

"Yes, sir."

"And prepare another chopper. I want to be underway to Alexandria immediately."

"Yes, sir."

Agha switched channels to address the police officers. "All points, this is Agha. Stand down. Return to your regular patrols." Before Sergeant Mufeed could respond, Agha switched to the Hip's internal frequency. "You need to RTB immediately. Break station now."

"Yes, sir," the pilot said, banking the helicopter toward the west. "Returning to base, time now."

* * *

Al Attarin, Alexandria, Egypt
25 July 2006
19:35 hours Eastern European Time (17:35 hours Zulu)

214

WILLIAMS BROUGHT THE FIAT to a halt several blocks from the docks. He took a few moments to take in the surroundings. For the moment, they were invisible. Dusk had fallen and streetlights had flickered to life. The buildings were concrete and drab, as were the people that traveled the streets. Williams wore a frown on his face as they continued down the street.

"Is there trouble?" Zaina asked.

"Not yet," Williams said. "Just a little bummed to see Alexandria like this."

"How so?"

"Alexandria used to be a lively place, a place where culture met. Most of the minority groups have been driven from here, so now it's not much different from the rest of the country. It's not as strict as, say, Tehran or Riyadh, but you won't see many drunken sailors and street walkers on the streets. Like the rest of the nation, it's considered fairly moderate for the region, despite its restrictions."

"Which is the justification that the US government uses to keep Mubarak in power," Zaina said, with a hint of bitterness in her voice.

"'The enemy of my enemy is my friend," Williams said as he continued to scan. "Popular foreign policy."

"Brought you the Taliban," Zaina pointed out.

"I know," Williams said. "I was there."

"I meant during the eighties."

Williams directed his gaze toward her. "So did I." He scanned a moment longer and said, "I think we're clear. We've got five blocks to the boat. It's called the

Parabellum."

"'For war?'"

"Karen has a thing for that quote," Williams explained. "Point is, five blocks and then we're on the boat. Let me do all the talking." He loosened his *keffiyeh* to expose his mouth and chin, but kept his neck, head, and most of his bruises hidden. "Loosen up your *hijab* enough to show your face. We're going to take it at a casual pace. Too slow or too fast, we'll draw attention."

"What if we run into any law enforcement?" Zaina asked.

"Well, I'd like to avoid lethal force, if possible," Williams said. "These are guys just doing their jobs. My beef isn't with them, aside from the fact that they're slinging hot lead in our general direction."

"Fourth Nuremberg Principle," Zaina countered. "They have it coming."

"Only applies if you know your orders are illicit," Williams said. "Why do you think the brass likes to keep the grunts in the dark? Teach them Nuremberg and then distort the full picture so they get the idea they're helping out when they're really being played to an end." He shook his head. "No, these guys aren't bad guys. They're just on the wrong end of a two-way shooting range."

"So, what are we going to do if we run into them?"

"Hopefully walk right past them without a second word. If they get suspicious, I'll figure out something from there."

"So, we're going to wing it," Zaina said.

"That's sort of been the game plan for a while now," Williams said. "C'mon."

Williams got out first, reached in, and grabbed the duffel bag that held the M4. The SIG-Sauer was tucked into the back of his waistband, with the Glock from the Muslim Brotherhood tucked cross-draw on his left hip. Williams slung the duffel across his chest and shut the door. He glanced over to Zaina, who exited the car and shut her door. They shared a brief nod, and Williams went to her side. He looked over to her and let out a sigh.

"Hold my hand," he said to her in French. "We're on a date. Don't look so nervous."

Surprise lined her gaze. "I had no idea you spoke French," she replied in the same language.

"Your accent is Swiss," Williams pointed out. "Mine's an attempt at Parisian, but it doesn't quite get there. It confuses native speakers all the time."

Zaina giggled and took Williams's hand in hers. Her eyes remained peeled for any sign of the law, but from a distance, they passed for a couple. His eyes continued to scan, but every few seconds, they would lock on her for a moment before returning to the search pattern.

"It is a lovely night out," Zaina said to break the silence.

"I'm sure it'll be much lovelier when we're twelve miles into the Mediterranean," Williams said.

Zaina sighed. "True enough."

They were only a couple blocks out. The ships were in view, and sailors could be seen heading to and from their vessels. Williams could see three sailors sitting on the bow of their ship, each of them drinking silently from flasks. There were a few other couples and a few singletons walking about, most of them speaking in quiet Arabic.

Williams's eyes spotted something. He continued to walk, but Zaina felt him tense up.

Zaina waited for a beat. "What? What is it?"

"Don't look," Williams said, his eyes glancing over the man sporting the dark uniform and the MISR assault rifle. "CSF trooper, two clock, he's got eyes on us." Williams locked his gaze straight ahead and continued to watch the man through his peripherals. The trooper's body posture shifted from relaxed to perplexed, and predictably, a moment later, he stepped off from his post and made his way in their general direction.

"He's headed to us," Zaina said, unusually calm.

"Laugh quietly," Williams murmured. Zaina waited a moment and then did so. By that time, Williams had found his choke point. "We're moving right. Follow my lead. When I make my play, clear out but stay close."

"You're the shot caller," Zaina said, forcing a smile that did little to ease her hammering pulse.

* * *

BOULOS HAZIM LUT HADDAD had served with the Central Security Forces for eleven years, five of those as a sub-officer in the Special Operations section. Most of the Central Security Forces personnel did not make a career out of it unless they came in as a sub-officer or a ranking officer from a police institute or academy, respectively. They did their conscript time, then returned to the civilian world and found work elsewhere. The native of the 6th of October City had quickly found his calling in paramilitary law enforcement, and made every connection he could with the hopes of attending the Police Academy. In the end, he settled for the Institute and was made a sub-officer, which gave him authority over the uneducated soldiers but made him middle management to the officers. Haddad quickly made his way to Special Operations, where he distinguished himself on several high-risk operations. This included joint missions with the *Mukhabarat*, where his team would act as the muscle to the intelligence types. The counterintelligence types were the creepiest to work around, always evaluating those around them as potential security risks.

This mission marked the first time he had ever worked directly beneath the lauded spy catcher, Abdullah Agha, and from what he heard on the radio, his reputation and his actual persona did not match up. The man who had contacted them when they arrived on-site a short while earlier brimmed with high levels of tension. He certainly was not the calculating chess master that outthought his opponents by four moves. Word around the campfire had it that Agha had lost a couple of friends to the suspect. Haddad could understand the notion of wanting vengeance, but Agha's borderline instability still worried him.

Still, it was not Haddad's place to question orders. Williams and his companion, Zaina Anwar, were to be taken into custody and held until the *Mukhabarat* could take custody. With that, Haddad had taken his post on a corner near the docks, his MISR at the low ready as he casually observed the sailors, merchants, and street walkers. He had never been to Alexandria, and he found the environment to be charming, if a little run down. The smell of the crisp ocean air was intoxicating and invigorating all at once, and it became a challenge to focus on the people rather than take in the scenery.

That was when he spotted them. A man and a woman, the former sporting a *keffiyeh* and the woman with a *hijab*. They walked with their arms around each other, like lovers, but something seemed off. After a moment, Haddad met eyes with the man, and he matched the BOLO photo enough to raise suspicion. The man paid Haddad no mind and talked with his lady. She gave him a knowing giggle, and the two of them made their way into an alley.

Haddad reached for his radio hand mic clipped to his tactical vest. "All points, this is Haddad. I have a possible visual on Williams. Stand by for confirmation."

With a deep breath, Haddad sauntered towards the alley. As he closed in, he saw the woman pressed against the wall and the man pressed against her. The duffel bag he had been carrying was on the ground beside them, and their arms were wrapped around each other as their lips and tongues danced. For a moment, Haddad considered leaving the lovers be, but again, something struck him as off.

Instead, he took a step forward and cleared his throat. This elicited no response, so he took another step and coughed loudly. The couple continued at it, completely oblivious to his presence. Finally he let out a sigh and said, "Excuse me."

The man broke off from the kiss long enough to spit out in exasperated breaths, *"Nous sommes occupés à l'heure actuelle. Merci."* Without waiting for further approval, the man resumed exploring his lady's mouth.

Haddad was taken aback by the abrupt disregard for the law. Most foreigners tended to listen to a man wearing fatigues and toting an automatic rifle, even with the language barrier. He quickly regained his authoritative composure and brought his rifle to an aggressive low ready.

"You need to separate right now or I'll have the both of you arrested." The couple kept going, and Haddad raised his rifle as he moved forward. "I mean it!" He got within inches of the couple and shouted, *"Hey—"*

Haddad and the man locked eyes at the last second, and he realized a couple of things too late: the man *was* Williams, and he had been drawn into a trap.

Williams broke his lip-lock with Zaina and his hands shot out, the left hand gripping the muzzle and the right wrapping around the banana magazine. He yanked and took a crescent step backwards with his left foot. The movement ripped the rifle clean out of Haddad's hands. Zaina had taken three steps back to clear the battlespace and watched as Williams drove the rifle stock into Haddad's abdomen. Williams mechanically unloaded the MISR, tossed the magazine down the alley, cleared the chamber, and tossed the rifle to the ground. The Glock came from beneath his shirt, and Williams picked up Haddad by the scruff of his neck. He slammed the CSF trooper against the wall and dug the Glock beneath his chin.

"Did you call it in?" Williams rasped in Arabic. Haddad said nothing, and Williams dug the barrel in deeper. "I keep the gun buried in your chin, and I pull this trigger, it'll mute the gunshot enough that I'll clear out before anybody thinks twice. *Did you call it in?*"

"Yes," Haddad said through clenched teeth.

"All right. Call them up. Tell them you've got a visual on me. I'm headed westbound, toward the end of the docks, and all of your men need to converge on the west side." With his left hand, he plucked the hand mic from Haddad's uniform and held it in front of his face. "You try to be slick and call in some kind of duress code, and I'll kill you where you stand. Are we on the same page?"

"We're on the same page," Haddad agreed reluctantly.

"Go ahead." Williams depressed the transmitter and held the mic close to Haddad's lips.

"All points, all points, this is Haddad. Be advised, I have positive identification on the target. He is moving due west. Need immediate reinforcements. Subject is armed and dangerous. I repeat, all points, move due west and box the subject in."

"Acknowledged," a voice returned. "All units moving west, time now."

Williams clipped the radio back on Haddad's uniform. "See? That wasn't so hard now—"

Haddad swept his arms upward and broke the contact between the Glock and his chin, then drove his knee hard into Williams's groin. As Williams gasped and doubled over, Haddad scrambled to key up his radio, but Williams cut him off, lunging forward and wrapping up his midsection. Haddad brought hammerfists and elbows down on Williams's back. He snarled through gritted teeth as he suppressed the urge to shriek. Williams blasted from a squatted stance and stood upright, simultaneously throwing his hips and dragging Haddad along with him. Haddad hit the ground first, and Williams landed on top of him. As soon as he made contact, Williams scrambled forward and brutally slammed the pistol's butt into Haddad's head several times. The body went limp. Williams rose to his feet and kicked Haddad in the jaw once more for good measure.

Zaina looked on, horrified. "I thought you didn't want to kill any cops."

Williams pressed two fingers to Haddad's throat. The pulse was still there, but it was weak. "He'll live," he said. "Might not return to duty." He then unclipped the hand mic and removed the radio from its pouch on Haddad's tactical belt. He tucked the radio in his cargo pocket, clipped the mic to his shirt, and turned down the volume. "Grab the bag and let's get out of here before he comes to."

* * *

MAKSIM BORISSOVICH PUDOVKIN LAZILY sipped bourbon from a flask, a smoldering cigar between his right index and middle fingers as he surveyed the port. He appreciated his break from stereotype by drinking the caramel-colored spirit. The truth of the matter was, Pudovkin could not stand the taste or smell of vodka. He actually preferred beer to anything else, but he had always had a fancy for Jim Beam, which he had first tasted as a boy of sixteen, working at a hotel as a bellhop. A drunk American entrepreneur had given him a bottle in lieu of a cash tip, which had upset the young Pudovkin at first. After his first taste, he immediately thanked the man in absentia by downing the whole bottle and taking the rest of the day off.

As he brought the Honduran cigar to his lips, Pudovkin heard shouting and the sound of pounding footsteps. On cue, a group of fifteen paramilitaries congregated and sprinted past, their rifles at the low ready. He watched dispassionately, but as the last of them passed up his vessel without a second look, he let out a sigh of relief. His vessel *was* full of illicit cargo, enough that every law enforcement agency in the world would want a crack at him if they found out who he was and what he had access to. However, it was not the first time Pudovkin had risked being arrested, and over the years, he had learned that nobody pays attention to a cool customer, so long as they were not too cool or trying too hard.

A few moments later, a man and a woman jogged towards the Handysize cargo ship. Pudovkin looked to one of his men and nodded. The man ran from his position by Pudovkin and jogged down the ramp, positioning himself at the base just as the pair arrived.

"State your business," the man said in heavily accented English.

"Tell your boss that the Tin Man sent us," Williams said, slightly winded.

The man retrieved a walkie-talkie from his belt and held it to his lips. He rattled off a series of words in Russian, and immediately received a response. The man nodded in affirmation, and then waved Williams and Zaina towards the ship. "Come. Come."

Zaina and Williams were guided to the bow of the ship, where they found the sinewy, black-bearded Pudovkin finishing the last of his cigar. He flicked the stogie towards the dock, faced the newcomers, and nodded in acknowledgement. With a sip from his flask, he said, "Karen told me to expect you. Glad to see you made it, despite what challenges she may have added to your journey."

"Yeah, well, I'll remember this next time she needs me to bail her out of a jam," Williams grunted.

Pudovkin chortled. "Yes, she can be a bit of a bitch. But you are here now."

Williams nodded and offered a mock salute. "Permission to go below deck and get settled in."

With a smile, Pudovkin returned the gesture and said, "My men will get you settled into your quarters. We'll be in Cyprus in a half day."

"Also, we need a medic," Zaina spoke up. "I think with all of the wear and tear we've both endured over the past few days, we could use a checkout."

Williams gave Zaina a look, which she returned with a glare that warned him not to contradict her. Pudovkin nodded and gave orders to his men in their native tongue, then reverted to English. "Sergey studied at the University of Chicago's Medical School and is a licensed doctor, both in America and Russia. He will check you both out."

"All right." Williams turned to leave, then

remembered the object in his pocket. He removed the radio he'd plucked from Haddad and said, "Well, suppose I won't need this anymore." Williams cocked back, took two stutter steps, and hurled the radio over the bow, watching it land and crack open on the dock, clear of any bystanders.

"Get this ship underway!" Pudovkin shouted in Russian. With that order, he took one last sip, pocketed his flask, and made his way to the bridge.

* * *

COLONEL AGHA LITERALLY BOUNCED in his seat as he waited for the Hip to touch down. His breathing had grown shallow, and he was on the verge of seeing red. After an eternity, Agha felt the impact, and he literally threw the door open, hit the ground, and sprinted towards the mobile command center. It was a series of hastily erected tents and some government SUVs on the perimeter. Agha barged through the door and went straight for the main communications hub.

"Do we have him?"

The CSF tactical commander, Major Sufyan, took a deep breath and stood at parade rest. He did not want to break the news, but he also would rather incur the colonel's wrath rather than allow his subordinates to suffer. "We don't have him. It seems our ground element leader encountered him and attempted to apprehend him, but suffered several contusions, a severe concussion, and broken bones throughout the face. We're still looking for him."

Agha locked eyes with Sufyan, his jaw trembling as his hands slowly balled into fists. "So what you're telling me..." He took a deep breath. "...is that he's evaded the net."

Sufyan nodded slowly. "It would appear so, sir."

Agha said nothing for a moment. The CSF troops sensed what came next and slowly backed away. Agha's head suddenly snapped right and locked on a laptop computer. He lunged for it, picked it up, and smashed it on the table repeatedly, a savage howl filling the air as he crushed the computer beyond repair. Agha tossed the laptop shell aside, grabbed another, and hurled it across the tent, narrowly missing two CSF personnel. He grabbed the table itself and with a deafening scream, he flipped it over. As all of the technology crashed to the ground, Agha locked his arms at his side, looked skyward, and screamed the only word his mind could process.

"NO! NO! NO!"

Silence loomed in the tent. The entire command center watched Agha slowly hang his head and let out a tired sigh. The confidence that had lined his posture only moments earlier had been replaced with defeat. He cleared his throat and blinked rapidly in an attempt to regain his composure. His mouth opened as he struggled to find the words.

"I...I..."

"Command post, command post, anybody, come in," a voice said. "This is Hakim. Come in."

Major Sufyan picked up the radio and answered it. "Hakim, this is Sufyan, send it in."

"Sir, we found Haddad's radio. It's directly across

227

from an empty dock, broken, almost like somebody threw it."

Agha stood a little straighter as he listened in. Sufyan said, "Have you identified what ship was docked there?"

There was a pause, and then Hakim came back on the line. "*Parabellum,* flying Cyprus colors, headed that direction as of forty-five minutes ago."

Agha stood ramrod straight. He had found his sense of pride again. He walked to Sufyan and said, "My behavior just now was completely unbecoming, and I apologize." He removed a business card from his pocket and extended it towards the commander. "Consider myself in your debt."

"Uhm…thank you, sir," Sufyan managed to stammer out.

With that, Agha walked out of the tent, reached into his pocket, and removed his cell phone. After hitting the speed dial, he held it to his ear, and a moment later, the other party answered.

"Captain Darzi."

"It's Colonel Agha. Scramble a Unit 777 maritime troop for immediate deployment. Have them meet me in Alexandria."

"Yes, sir."

CHAPTER FIFTEEN

Al Attarin, Alexandria, Egypt
25 July 2006
21:00 hours Eastern European Time (19:00 hours Zulu)

AGHA STOOD ON THE makeshift helipad as he watched the trio of Sikorsky S-70-21 Black Hawk helicopters make their descent, each of them carrying fourteen shooters. Each shooter was clad in olive drab Nomex flight suits, black gloves and combat boots, Kevlar helmets, and balaclavas. Their assault vests were full of kit and spare magazines for their weapons. Most of the men had a carbine in their hands or slung across their chest and a handgun holstered on their thigh. A few sported sniper rifles, which distinguished them as the designated marksmen. As soon as the choppers touched down, the operators dismounted the bird and walked briskly toward Agha. Their leader, the only one who had taken off his Kevlar and balaclava, walked directly to Agha, his rifle off to the side and his right hand extended.

"Major Malik Hamzah," the Unit 777 officer said. He possessed a swimmer's physique, which was fitting, given that he commanded a maritime operations troop. Hamzah's jet black hair was kept short and his beard well-groomed, an essential for undercover operations. He carried himself with the unmistakable swagger of a special operator.

Agha shook hands Hamzah. "What have you been told?"

"Just the basics, sir," Hamzah said. "High value target has fled the country and is in international waters. I had my men prep for a VBSS operation."

"Very good," Agha said. "Were you informed that I would be accompanying your team?"

Hamzah's professional mask faltered. "Sir, with all due respect, this is my operation. I need to have total control over my men. A divided command will prevent my men from accomplishing their task at capacity."

"I am not taking command of your operation, Major," Agha said. "I will be shadowing the lead operator. I want to get on the ship and personally confirm the killing or capture of the high value targets."

"Sir, that's not necessary—"

"It is, and that's the end of discussion," Agha said. "Who is your lead operator?"

Major Hamzah took a deep breath. "I lead from the front, sir. If you want to go in with us, that's fine, but the minute you try to contradict one of my orders, we'll leave you behind. You may have brought the mission to us, but once my shooters are boots on the ground, Unit 777 runs the operation, *not* the *Mukhabarat*. I hope I have made myself clear, sir."

Agha locked eyes with Hamzah. He had stated his point politely but firmly. The troop commander would not disrespect the colonel, but he would not budge, either. "That's fair enough," Agha said. "Follow me. Let's get this briefing started."

The two officers approached the briefing tent, side by side. By the time they entered, the men had found their seats and had doffed their helmets and balaclavas. Their faces were an assortment of young and old, but all men. All sported facial hair and most wore beards. Agha could pick out who had seen a lot of action and who was relatively new to the unit, but all had some sort of prior military service before being accepted to the unit. They were the very best that Egypt had to offer.

Hamzah took the front and commanded the attention of his men without saying a word. "Gentlemen, I know we were in a rest rotation, but we've got a job. So, without ado, I'll turn this briefing over to Colonel Agha. He's head of the counterintelligence section at the *Mukhabarat*."

Agha took the spotlight, and Hamzah stepped off to the side. He triggered a slide projector and the visages of his two targets filled the screen, complete with known particulars. From his pocket, Agha removed a laser pointer and highlighted the face on the left.

"This woman is Zaina Anwar," he said. "She is American. Attended college at Temple. She lectured at the American University in Cairo, then returned to Temple for her doctorate. Since then, she's been a respected educator until a few weeks ago, when we captured her during a raid to take down a dissident group engaged in terrorist activity against the government. She's more of a political philosopher than a shooter, preferring to do battle with her words than with a weapon."

Agha let out a measured breath as he shifted the laser to the other face. "This is Benjamin Williams, former US Army Special Forces and CIA paramilitary. Some of the older individuals in the room may recognize this man. During his time with Special Forces, he cross-trained with members of this unit during the Bright Star exercises. He has since gone into the private sector, where members of this dissident group hired him to break Anwar out of prison and escort her and her cousin, deceased First Sergeant Ferran Anwar, to the United States. Over the course of the past few days, Williams has been responsible for the deaths of two prisoners, nine members of the Muslim Brotherhood, and twenty-three members of the Egyptian government, including three members of my own staff. Eighteen of those civil servants have been killed in the past twenty-four hours alone."

He allowed those facts to sink in for a minute. The younger shooters were the first to have their eyes glaze over in calm hatred. It was the older operators, the ones that had worked with Williams before, that refused to believe it at first, but when presented with the stark facts, their eyes slowly gained the calm of a man who had sentenced another to death. Once he saw that all of the shooters were onboard with the mission, Agha cleared his throat and continued.

"This is a Visit, Board, Search, and Seizure mission, targeted on the Cyprus flag ship *Parabellum*, with two primary objectives. The first is to locate and detain Zaina Anwar so that she may stand trial for her crimes against the government. The second objective is to find and eliminate Ben Williams. Standing orders on all combatants is to open fire if under the threat of direct engagement, with exception to Williams. He has proven time and time again that he can and will exploit the slightest hesitation and turn the situation to his advantage. When you make positive identification on Williams, you kill him on sight. Weapons free. I repeat, on Williams, weapons free." He looked back to Major Hamzah. "Major?"

Hamzah resumed center stage. "All right, guys. This is not an ideal situation, but that is the name of the game. *In extremis* VBSS. You've got one hour to come up with primary, secondary, and tertiary attack plans and brief them back to me." Hamzah pointed to a table placed to the left of the projector screen. "Here are several blueprints on the type of cargo ship that *Parabellum* is. Study these. The ship's layout will be very similar, but keep flexible regardless." Hamzah clapped his hands. "Let's get to work."

As the several teams broke off to discuss their respective portions of the plan, Hamzah approached Agha. "Colonel, if you're coming in with us, you'll need to kit up."

Agha nodded. "Yes. Lead the way."

* * *

Parabellum, *eighty-five miles north-northeast of Alexandria, Egypt*
26 July 2006
01:15 hours Eastern European Time (25 July 23:15 hours Zulu)

ZAINA SAT IN HER bunk, a glass of water on the bedside table as she chronicled the past twenty-four hours. Her pulse picked up a notch as she recounted the prison break, and tears rolled from her eyes as she elaborated on finding Ferran's lifeless body. She took care not to mention Williams or Cockayne by name, nor did she reveal any pieces of background information that could lead an astute reader to conclude their identity. She also left out the part of the lover subterfuge for reasons she could not quite ascertain. That aside, Zaina described Williams's actions to paint a picture of what kind of a man he was.

I hope I have accurately painted a picture of the man who whisked me away to safety, she wrote. *If I haven't done so, then allow me to put forth my blunt assessment—this man is a sheer elemental force. When his mind is set on an objective, he allows no-one and nothing to stand in his way. Sleep deprivation, lack of nutrition, and a series of injuries that would have crippled an ordinary man were all thrown to the wayside to accomplish his mission. I knew from the moment I first laid eyes on him that there was nothing he would not do to bring me home.*

Some may find this endorsement odd in the wake of Ferran's passing. A few may even go so far as to say that Ferran's passing is a direct result of his lack of efficiency. I know I thought that when I saw Ferran's body. I've had some time to think it through, and at the end of the day, the man did all that he could. He is not to blame. The counterintelligence colonel, Agha, is the one who delayed the plan, and he and his men are the sole proprietors of Ferran's demise.

Zaina took a minute to wipe her eyes and cheeks. Once she had reached her bunk five hours earlier, she had closed the door and spent the next hour sobbing as silently as she could. After she reached a pause in her grieving, she showered, changed into clothes provided by the crew, fetched a glass of water, and started writing. Every time Ferran came to mind, the tears returned, but she was able to hold them back and push forward. Zaina was now focused on *her* mission: document every detail of her final days in Egypt while they were still fresh in her mind. She took another sip of water and pressed forward.

This is not to say that the man is a robot, by any means. He is empathetic, if just at a decreased level necessary to do his job. He is also a highly intelligent man, capable of intellectual conversation, perhaps not of an academic caliber but erudite nonetheless. I may disagree with his cynical world outlook, but to deny his mental capacity is to do him a disservice. I don't know much about his personality, and I'm sure that was intentional on his part. That is one thing I did pick up about him—he is cautious by nature. Everything he says and does is guarded, carefully controlled.

Being a pacifist, I regret that there must be men like him in this world, men who are incredibly proficient in the taking of life, but I cannot deny that without men like him, men capable of violence but grounded by a fundamental sense of right and wrong, I would not be alive right now. Regardless, I still regret that blood had to be spilled, and pray that when the people have decided they are done with Mubarak's oppression, the revolution will be bloodless. For my part, through this work and through my words, my civil disobedience, I will do what I can to bring about the revolution.

Zaina put the pen back in the journal and set it on the bed. She drifted from her room and into the hallway. It was dimly lit by bulbs hanging overhead, and there were small pools of water on the floor, which partially accounted for the rust on the floors and walls. It was not a luxury cruise ship, but there was not another place she would rather be. To her, the rusted cargo ship was *freedom*, something she would never again take for granted.

Catty-corner from her room was where she had seen Williams last. Zaina walked to the door and rapped her knuckles against it thrice.

"Enter."

She opened the door and found Williams sitting on his bunk. He wore a pair of jeans, combat boots, and a black rigger's belt. He had not put on a shirt yet, and Zaina could see that the bandages had been replaced. It was clear that he was still hurting, but he was doing his best to operate around it. He grabbed two more Percocets and dumped them in his mouth. A swig of water chased the pills down, and he shook his head briskly.

Zaina leaned in the doorway and folded her arms. "How are you feeling?"

"Better," Williams said. "A few weeks of R&R and I'll be as good as new."

"That's good," Zaina said. She eyed the ground for a moment. "Look, I just want to thank—"

"No need," he said. He stood up and pulled his shirt over his head. "I told you that I'd get you out. You're out."

Zaina held her mouth open for a moment, then

slowly nodded her head. "I also wanted to let you know…I don't blame you for what happened to Ferran."

Now it was Williams's turn to pause. "I appreciate the sentiment, but I should have been quicker about breaking loose. That's on me."

Zaina shook her head. "No, it isn't, and you're gonna have to let go of that." Her words were lost on him, so she decided to switch tact. "Let me ask you a question."

"Sure," Williams said. He grabbed his duffel bag and opened it up.

"Am I just a job to you?"

Williams took a breath and started to answer, but paused for a moment. His eyes met Zaina's as he considered his answer. After a moment, he hung his head and chuckled, despite himself, then turned his attention back to sorting through the duffel.

"You were, at first. Just a package to be delivered, nothing more. I can't say I agree with all of your convictions, all of your stances, but I respect that you've got your convictions, and I respect you were willing to go to jail for them. I respect that you were willing to die for them. You're a strong woman, and I admire that."

A smile dawned on Zaina's face. "You know, for a second, I thought you were gonna say you changed your mind in the alley."

Williams chuckled. "You trying to give me ideas, Ms. Anwar?"

Zaina shrugged as she stepped into the hallway. "None that you couldn't have devised on your own, Mr. Williams."

Williams grinned and shook his head. A moment later, Maks's voice sounded off through the wall-mounted intercom.

"Mr. Williams, please report to the bridge. Mr. Williams, please report to the bridge."

The request perplexed Williams, but he knew better than to contradict the ship's captain. He grabbed the SIG-Sauer from the bag, checked it was loaded, tucked it into his waistband, and made his way to the bridge.

* * *

AFTER THE FIRST FEW minutes, the Black Hawk's rotorthrob faded into the background, due in large part to the large radio headset that Agha wore. He was dressed in the same kit as the other Unit 777 operators. A M4A1 carbine was slung across his chest and dangled between his legs, barrel down. Through the AN/PVS-7 night observation device mounted to his Kevlar, he could make out the ship just beneath the horizon as it trudged its way to Cyprus. He could feel his veins pulsating and he took a deep breath to keep himself level. His hands flexed around the carbine's heat shield and pistol grip. The thought crossed his mind that if he squeezed any harder, he might snap either polymer component.

"Five minutes out," the pilot said.

Agha looked to his right and saw the third chopper flying a parallel path. The lead helicopter was ahead of both of them to form a vee formation. He then turned to the operators inside of his helicopter. The sniper rifles he had noticed earlier were M21s, an American rifle and derivative of the M14 battle rifle. Each helicopter would leave behind two men to provide precise covering fire as a balance to the door gunners, who wielded FN MAG machine guns on coaxial mounts. The gunners and snipers would provide cover while the assaulters touched down and fanned out. Start to finish, the operation was planned to take no longer than thirty minutes.

"Four minutes."

He eyed the thick abseil rope, curled in a pile between him and the man in front of him. The top of the rope rose from the pile and was secured to a steel bar. Seeing the rope, Agha remembered to check that his fast rope gloves were clipped to a string loop on his regular gloves and were ready to be donned. That was critical: it would be a seventy-foot descent to the deck, and without the leather to cover the Nomex, his hands would either be severely burned, or he would let go and fall to the metal deck.

"Three minutes!"

The ship was large enough to make out some of its features, but not large enough to distinguish any of the crew patrolling the deck. Agha's eyes narrowed as he revisited the vision from the crime scene at Izbat an Nakhl. Williams would be in his sights, the weapon would kick in his hands, and the American would die at his feet, by his hand. Agha refused to shelve the thought. At that point, it was the only thing that kept him going.

* * *

WILLIAMS ENTERED THE BRIDGE and walked directly to Maks, who was at the helm. The captain stood over his radar operator, who observed his screen with a worried look. Williams's brow furrowed as he approached the captain.

"What's going on?"

"We've got blips on the radar," Maks said. "Marko, show him."

Marko leaned his chair back and pointed at three white spots. "They're helicopters. They're flying close and they're headed straight for us."

Williams's face darkened. "Neither one of you has a military background, do you?"

"No, but I do have a pretty good gut instinct," Maks said. "I just needed a military mind to confirm it."

"Ain't no doubt about it," Williams said. "Those choppers are flying in a vee formation." He looked to Maks. "We've got company. Sound the alarm and get men on the deck. Every gun you can get, and grab some RPGs if you've got them. Don't stand in the open. Get to hard points. They're going to have machine guns at the minimum, maybe snipers."

"How do you know all of this?" Maks asked.

"I've trained with the guys they'd send to do this kind of mission." Williams took off running back to his quarters. "Get your men ready!"

Maks reached for his intercom microphone and held it to his mouth. "All hands, we are about to come under attack from Egyptian military forces. I say

240

again, we are about to be attacked. Grab your rifles and take defensive positions on the deck. This is not a drill. I say again, this is *not* a drill."

CHAPTER SIXTEEN

Parabellum, *eighty-five miles north-northeast of Alexandria, Egypt*
26 July 2006
01:24 hours Eastern European Time (25 July 23:24 hours Zulu)

"THIRTY SECONDS."

THE SIDE doors slid open and the Black Hawks broke formation. The lead chopper took a position by the stern, while the right chopper swooped to port and prepared to deposit its shooters. Agha's chopper took an overwatch position off the starboard quarter. The door gunner racked his bolt to the rear, rode the charging handle forward, and rest his thumbs on the butterfly triggers. On the opposite side of the door, the sniper team settled in and shouted to each other. They were on the team internal net, which meant Agha could not hear them over the headset. He had worked with enough operators to know the procedure. The snipers were judging distance, elevation, and wind, and were making the necessary adjustments to their optics. After a few moments, the spotter clapped the sniper on his shoulder, a sign that they were dialed in and ready to fire.

"We've got hostiles emerging from aft and moving forward," the chopper pilot announced. "Flanking aft and starboard."

Major Hamzah adjusted his microphone. "All points, this is Hamzah. Execute, I say again, execute."

Even through the headset and the rotorthrob, Agha heard the MAG speak as it spewed 7.62x51mm

NATO rounds downrange in six-round bursts. His eyes were on the sniper team as they picked up targets and engaged them rhythmically. After every hit, the spotter would tap the shooter and call out the next target. He directed his vision to the deck. Through his NODs, he saw bright green dots fall one by one, either chopped down by the wall of machine gun fire or through precision fire. Most of the crew sought cover behind a myriad of containers, and the covering fire kept them hidden. When the occasional defender stuck his head out to search for a target, the sniper would drill a bullet through his head.

While the third chopper provided overwatch, the other two dropped their coiled ropes out the side. With resistance suppressed, the operators slipped on their fast rope gloves, gripped the rope, and descended, one after another, using their hands and feet to control their rate of descent. As they hit the deck, the shooters fanned out and pull security for their comrades. Once the last man was on the deck, one of the crew members unclipped the rope from the steel bar. As the ropes hit the ground, the chalk leaders flashed a thumbs-up to the chopper pilots, who saw it through their NODs.

"All points, this is Bird One, Chalk One is on deck," one pilot said. "I say again, Chalk One is on the deck."

Another radioed in immediately, "This is Bird Two. Chalk Two is on deck. Chalk Two *is* on deck."

"Bird Two, this is Bird Three. Withdraw to an overwatch position. We're moving to insert our chalk."

"Roger," Bird Two's pilot acknowledged. "Moving

to overwatch position, time now."

As the second helicopter cleared out, the third's sniper team pulled back from the door and braced themselves for movement. Bird Three banked left and maneuvered to the port side deck. Agha slipped on his fast rope gloves and flipped up his NODs. He removed his Kevlar long enough to remove the chopper headset, then donned the personal headset that had been on his lap and put his Kevlar back on. His boot was tapping uncontrollably against the chopper floor in anxiety and anticipation.

Major Hamzah waved the operators toward the door. One by one, a few seconds part, each man grabbed the rope and descended upon the *Parabellum*. Agha moved to the door. He looked back to Hamzah, who motioned for him to move forward. Agha took a seat on the edge of the Black Hawk, grabbed the rope, and pushed off. He immediately pressed his feet against the rope to slow his descent. Despite the thick leather gloves atop their Nomex counterparts, Agha could feel the friction build. Before the pain grew too unbearable, Agha felt his boots touch the deck, and he pushed the rope away. In one fluid motion, he doffed his rope gloves and brought his M4 to the ready. A moment later, he felt a hand on his shoulder. Major Hamzah had joined them on the deck.

"You good, sir?" Hamzah asked.

"I'm good," Agha replied.

Hamzah turned to the chopper and flashed them a thumbs up. In turn, Bird Three peeled off and took up an overwatch position. Every square inch of the deck was covered, which left the operators to clear the inside.

"Status," Hamzah said into his mic.

"Chalk One's up."

"Chalk Two's up."

"Roger, all elements are up. Move out." Hamzah motioned aft with his off-hand.

* * *

WILLIAMS TOOK THE STEPS three at a time and leapt when he was five steps from the ground. Five seconds later, he was in his room, breathless as he dug into his kit duffel. He found the Blackhawk SERPA holster for the SIG-Sauer, removed the pistol from his belt line, and slipped it into the holster. The paddle went on the inside of his pants to mount the pistol on his right hip. Next, he grabbed a lightweight coyote brown MOLLE plate carrier, slipped it over his head, and clipped it in place. Williams winced as he cinched down the carrier. Finally, the M4A1 came out of the bag and was slung around his neck and under his left shoulder. He removed a magazine from his plate carrier, slapped it into the magazine well, and chambered a round.

Zaina burst into the room, her own SIG-Sauer in her hand. "Williams, what the fuck is going on?"

"Get in the corner and stay down," Williams ordered. "Anything comes through that door that isn't me, you kill it. Got it?"

Zaina nodded. She was not the type to be bossed about, but she also knew that Williams would not give her orders unless the situation was dire. "Be careful," she said with a nod. She moved to the corner and pulled the hammer back on the SIG-Sauer.

"You too," he said.

Williams closed the door behind him as he entered the hallway. He saw two of Maks's men, both armed with AK-103 rifles. He approached them and cut straight to the point. "What's the situation up top?"

"It's bad," one of the men, a blond with a boyish face and baby blue eyes, said in decent English. "They're cutting us down with machine guns and snipers."

"Then they go first," Williams said. "Where do you keep your RPGs?"

As the blond replied, Williams heard the tell-tale sound of metal clanging against metal rhythmically. He saw the steel sphere as it rolled down the stairs, and training took over.

"*Grenade!*" Williams shouted. He took two steps back and dove into his doorway. As soon as he hit the ground, the M67 fragmentation grenade exploded, sprayed shrapnel in all directions, and incinerated both of Maks's riflemen. Williams felt the ground tremor beneath him and heard shrapnel whizz past him. He shook his head and moaned as he climbed back to his feet and braced himself against the corner. On cue, he could hear boots pressing against the stairwell, and as the first shooter reached the bottom, he heard a faint *splash*.

That was when Williams moved from cover. He flicked his selector switch from SAFE to SEMI, and picked up his first target over the top of his ACOG. He stroked the trigger twice, and both rounds struck center mass, which only caused the target to stumble backwards. Williams automatically transitioned to the head and his finger twitched. The 5.56x45mm round struck the operator in the head, beneath his Kevlar, and exited out the back. The bullet's decreased momentum allowed for the Kevlar to ricochet the round back into the skull to do more damage. Pink slosh fell from beneath the Kevlar as the shooter's body went limp.

Lead filled the corridor as the enemy operators laid down suppressive fire and took up defense positions. Williams ducked behind cover and waited for the lull in the fire. That pause came much faster than expected, a testament to their fire discipline. He dropped to a knee, turned the corner, flicked the selector to AUTO and held down the trigger as he backpedaled. Bullets whizzed over his head for a moment before the operators took cover, which gave Williams the time he needed. He took up his hard point as his carbine locked empty. Mechanically, he dropped the box from the weapon, slammed a fresh one home, and slapped the bolt release.

Williams overheard hushed Arabic. "Bound forward!" the section leader told one of his subordinates. From a knee, Williams exposed a sliver of his head and the barrel of his carbine. He put the tip of the chevron just beneath where the nose would be and stroked the trigger. As that enemy hit the ground, Williams picked up his second target and killed him. Both men hit the ground within a second and a half, just in time for Williams to duck behind cover. The enemy returned fire and elicited a curse from Williams. He took deep breaths in through his nose and out of his mouth, and sweat trickled down his face. Once he heard the lull, Williams rounded the corner and reentered the fight.

* * *

SERGEANT FARID ADAN WAS the Chalk Two leader. Like most operators cut from the same cloth, Adan was trained to lead from the front, so once they had secured their landing zone, he moved to the front of the stack and led the eleven operators past the containers and up the stairs toward the bridge. It had taken them more than a few minutes to battle back the opposition, but with gunship and sniper support, a path was cleared.

They made their way up the stairs and halted outside of the bridge entrance. Adan halted his element and signaled for his breach man. While the third man in the stack broke formation and moved to the door, Adan removed a Deftech No. 25 flashbang from his tactical vest, pulled the pin, and held the spoon down. Adan and his breach man made eye contact, exchanged mutual nods, and the latter yanked the door open. The former leaned to the left of the stack and tossed his flashbang toward the open door, the spoon separating from the cylinder as soon as he released it. As expected, it went off a second and a half later.

What Adan did not expect was for somebody on the other side of the door to bat the flashbang back onto the stairwell, especially given its short fuse.

The stun grenade expended its blend of magnesium and ammonium percholate, which blinded and deafened the entire team. In their daze, they failed to spot Maks step out of the door with his AK-103, turn left, and put a single round between the eyes of the breach man. He then leveled his rifle barrel with the stack and held down the trigger until his rifle clicked empty. Maks grabbed a spare magazine, used it to trigger the magazine release and eject the empty box in one motion, rocked the spare into the well, reach over the rifle, and worked the charging handle. Maks then walked up to each operator and placed one round in each of their heads.

Machine gun chatter reached Maks's ears, and he sprinted up the stairs and inside the bridge before the rounds closed in. He slammed the door, locked it, then looked to Marko. The radar operator had taken up a position beneath the window, peeping up with a pair of binoculars to observe the battle.

"How's it looking?" Maks asked in Russian.

"Eh, not good, boss," Marko replied. "The men in those choppers know what they're doing. They're ripping our guys to shreds."

"Son of a bitch," Maks spat.

"Can you get down to the RPGs yourself?"

"That'll leave you up here by yourself if they try another attack," Maks said. He shook his head. "I've got to stay here."

Marko looked back. "Boss, it won't matter if those choppers stay in the air. They'll just swoop in and light us up. You heard Williams. We gotta shoot them down."

"What if he's already dead?" Maks asked.

"That's a risk you gotta take." Marko set down the binos and picked up his own AK. "I'll be fine. Go help Williams."

Maks looked to the door to the lower levels and then back to Marko, who had been a loyal companion on the ship from the very beginning, even before Karen Cockayne entered his life. He could see the answer in his friend's eyes. Reluctantly, Maks shouldered his rifle and turned to the door. He looked over his shoulder once more, only to receive an encouraging nod from Marko.

"I'll be back," Maks said before he disappeared into the stairwell.

* * *

"MOTHERFUCKER," WILLIAMS SNARLED AS he lunged behind cover. He ripped the empty magazine free and loaded a full one in its place. His eyes glanced down at his vest and found two remaining magazines. He released the bolt and peeked from behind cover just long enough to get an updated body count. Williams had managed to take out two more assaulters, which left him with seven more targets. The enemy had found their battle rhythm and were talking and shooting as one. His training and experience had kept him alive to that point, but that would not be the case if he went black on ammunition.

Williams stood, took a preparatory breath, and sprung from cover. His carbine spat three- and four-round bursts as he moved laterally. He reached cover, flicked his selector switch from AUTO to SEMI, and leaned around the corner after a beat. Through his ACOG, he came eye-to-eye with an operator who had drawn down on him. He was faster on the trigger, and a lone 5.56mm round tore through the man's face. Incoming bullets whizzed past him as he ducked behind cover. His face and clothing were drenched with perspiration, and he could feel every minute of abuse he had endured throughout the ordeal. Williams knew the pain would intensify once the adrenaline wore off. He also knew that if he did not keep focused, there would not be a later.

Footsteps echoed in the corridor, and Williams reentered the fray on a knee. His carbine kicked against his shoulder as he loosed rounds on the pair of inbound operators. Each of them dove for cover and cheated death for a moment longer. That was when he heard metal clang against metal again. Instinctively, he huddled up and waited for the shockwave, but instead of a ground shaking explosion, a thunderous *bang* engulfed the hallway.

Flashbang? Williams thought. He peered around the corner. Operators clutched their ears and stumbled, their equilibrium shattered by the stun grenade. A lone figure emerged from the stairwell, and the AK in his hands chattered as he sprayed 7.62mm Soviet rounds towards the pair of operators providing overwatch. The remaining two that found cover further along the hallway staggered into the clear, which gave Williams a clear shot. He dropped the shooter to his right and the stairwell figure killed the second one.

A chilling silence fell over the hallway. Williams kept his carbine trained toward the stairwell. "Friendlies?" he called out in English.

"Williams, it's Maks!"

Williams kept his carbine at the ready until Maks came into view, alone. He jogged towards the *Parabellum*'s captain. "I owe you one, man."

"I'm cashing in now," Maks said. "It's a bloodbath upstairs."

"Lead the way," Williams said.

* * *

AGHA DUCKED BEHIND A container as the defenders let loose a stream of blind-fire. The overwatch choppers had done a fantastic job of taking out the more gung-ho amongst the enemy riflemen. The disadvantage was, now only the smarter enemies remained, and they had maximized their cover in a textbook fashion. He peeked around the corner and saw an adversary moving up. Agha lined up the red dot of his Aimpoint M68 Close Combat Optic and squeezed the trigger twice. The carbine spoke, and his target fell to the deck, a pair of neat, tiny holes punched through his sternum.

Next to him, Major Hamzah keyed his radio and spoke with volume but without panic. "Chalk One, Chalk One, this is Chalk Three, give me your SITREP, over." A few seconds passed. "Chalk One, this is Chalk Three, come in, over?"

Agha looked over his shoulder. "They're dead. We

need to press forward."

"Now's not the time, colonel," Hamzah said evenly. "Chalk Two, this is Chalk Three, come in, over?" He waited a beat and said, "Chalk Two, this is Chalk Three, give me your SITREP."

"He's murdered your men," Agha said gravely. "If we don't press forward, he'll murder you, too."

"He's just one man," Hamzah said pointedly. "Give my men the benefit of the doubt, sir."

"He's one man who managed to escape from a maximum security prison and evaded a national dragnet," Agha countered. "He's one man that knows your tactical protocols, one man who turned a simple board and seizure mission into a massacre. If you want to survive, it would behoove you to take the son of a bitch a little more seriously."

"I *am* taking the son of a bitch seriously," Hamzah shot back. "You're the one with the bloodlust. You are *not* thinking rationally. This is my operation, and I'm not going to endanger my men for your revenge. Now, unless you have something tactically relevant to impart, then with all due respect, shut the hell up."

Agha stared at Hamzah, his expression cold. After a moment, Hamzah resumed his attempts to establish communications. Agha bit back a curse, and leaned around the corner once more, teeth bared as he fired his carbine and searched for people to kill.

* * *

THE DOOR SWUNG OPEN, and Marko raised his

rifle, finger on the trigger. He relented at the last second, when he saw Maks and Williams emerge from the stairwell, each of them toting an old-school RPG-7 and a satchel of rockets on each of their backs. In his left hand, Williams carried a PKM machine gun with two hundred and fifty rounds of 7.62x54mmR attached in a metal container. Marko sighed and lowered his rifle.

"What happened?" Marko asked.

"They went below deck first," Williams explained. "They were probably told to clear the bottom two floors and look for me and Zaina. Did you have another team try to breach the bridge?"

"How did you know?" Marko asked.

"That's what they're trained to do," Williams said. "A simultaneous assault is harder to repel."

"That means we've killed two-thirds of their people," Marko said. Hope seeped into his tone.

"Yeah, well, don't get happy yet." Williams handed him the PKM. "You're on diversionary detail. You need to draw the helicopter's fire and engage any remaining hostiles on deck. Create a window for Maks and me to start dropping the choppers."

"You've got it," Marko said. He grabbed the machine gun but Williams held fast.

"I'm going to be straight with you," Williams said. "All that fire focused on you? There's a good chance you won't make it. I hate to saddle you with this, but I don't see another option."

"If it saves the rest of my friends, then I don't care."

A look of understanding was shared between the two, and Williams relinquished control of the machine gun. He looked to Maks. "You ready?"

"Of course," Maks said. He grabbed a rocket from his satchel and loaded it into the breach.

Williams nodded, grabbed a rocket of his own, and loaded it. "Let's do it."

Marko slung the PKM, opened the feed tray cover, laid the belt on the feed tray, slammed the cover shut, and worked the charging handle. He took a deep breath and approached the port-side door. The young man looked at Maks and Williams, and the latter gave him an encouraging nod. He took a deep breath and smiled. As he opened the door, his face twisted into an expression of absolute hatred.

"*GET SOME, YOU MOTHERFUCKERS!*" Marko shrieked in Russian. He stepped out on the stairwell, shouldered the PKM, took up aim with the first Black Hawk, and let loose with a ten-round stream that whizzed past. Marko sprinted around the bodies of the fallen enemy chalk as the door gunner turned his attention to him. NATO machine gun rounds nipped at his feet as he ran. Once he reached the bottom of the staircase, he raced starboard, his PKM roaring in his hands as he reached cover.

Maks stepped out from the bridge, his RPG shouldered. He checked his backblast area and centered his sights at the top of the Black Hawk, just beneath where the rotors met the hull. At the bottom of his optic, he saw the snipers as they scrambled for a shot, but their efforts fell short. Maks squeezed the trigger, and the rocket-propelled grenade exploded from the launcher. A second later, the grenade hit the rotor and detonated, tearing it to shreds. The Black Hawk fell from the sky and plunged into the sea.

With a wry grin, Maks stepped into the bridge to reload.

Marko took a deep breath and sprinted to the other end of the container. He leaned out and laid down a flurry of machine gun fire towards the operators making their way aft. After two extended bursts, Marko faced the Black Hawk positioned starboard. He held down the trigger as he strafed port to avoid the incoming fire. On cue, Williams emerged from the bridge, took aim, and scored a direct hit on the Black Hawk's main rotor. The chopper made one half-spin before it made impact, killing everyone aboard as the hull slipped beneath the surface.

"*Fuck yeah!*" Marko screamed in his native tongue. "*You want to mess with us? GET SOME!*"

Marko rounded the corner and unexpectedly came face-to-face with the last Black Hawk. The door gunner held down his butterfly triggers and cut Marko off at the knees. As his screams filled the air, the sniper team zeroed in on him and ended him with a lone 7.62x51mm round between the eyes.

Maks rounded the corner, his RPG at the ready. He centered his sights on the rotor and opened fire. The 85mm grenade howled as it left the launcher and thundered on impact. Gravity ripped the Black Hawk from the sky and pulled it into the sea. A satisfied feeling started to spread through his body until he found Marko's body beside the PKM, blood pouring from his wounds. Every inch of his body went cold, and his mind immediately assaulted him with the knowledge that he had condemned his friend.

"Maks!" Williams called. He jogged to Maks. "You up?"

"I'm up," Maks said stoically. He dropped the RPG and the satchel, and brought his AK to the forefront. "Let's go hunting."

* * *

"SHIT!" HAMZAH HISSED. HE switched frequencies to the higher command net. "Any station, any station, this is Vulture Six Actual! Request immediate air support, over!" There was no response. He tried the alternate command frequency. "Any station on this net, this is Vulture Six Actual! Request immediate air support, *over!*"

"You're out of range," Agha said.

"No fucking shit," Hamzah spat. He switched back to the internal frequency. "All points, listen up. All three of our helos have been shot down, no survivors. It is probable that Chalks One and Two have been taken out. All survivors, you need to reach the bridge and radio for air support. Chalk Three elements, we are going to push forward to the bridge. Do you copy?" The surviving operators of Chalk Three radioed their acknowledgement. With that, Hamzah took a deep breath, exchanged his partially spent magazine for a full one, and looked to Agha. "You ready?"

"I was ready ten minutes ago," Agha said through clenched teeth. "Let's go, already."

Hamzah glared at Agha, then spoke into his headset. "All points, converge on the bridge. I repeat, converge on the bridge." Hamzah stepped out from cover, with Agha on his left and one of his men crossing over to his right. They walked on line, their weapons at the ready. One of the defenders leaned out from behind cover and killed the man to Hamzah's right with a headshot. Hamzah and Agha picked up their pace and increased their rate of fire.

To his left, Hamzah heard footsteps, and he spun around. Agha had mysteriously disappeared, and he was face-to-face with a Russian rifleman, murder etched into his face. Time slowed down as Hamzah started to squeeze the trigger. The enemy beat him to the punch, and a round caught Hamzah in his throat. A follow-up shot ripped through his jaw. Hamzah choked on his own blood, and he tried to stand but his body refused. All he could do was watch the rifleman approach him, look at him with pity, and then raise his rifle. The muzzle flash was the last thing that Hamzah saw.

* * *

FROM HIS PERIPHERALS, WILLIAMS watched the remainder of Maks's men make short work of the Unit 777 boarding party. His focus was on his search for any more assaulters. He took his time, pied every corner and scanned every inch of his sector. Every muscle in his body ached, and as the adrenaline wore off, his back's protests grew more violent. Williams clenched his teeth and continued to put one foot in front of the other.

An operator stumbled into his field of vision, and

Williams put two in his chest and one between the eyes. His barrel followed his eyes to the ground for potential follow-up service, and then returned to eye level. On instinct, he deviated from his path parallel the starboard guardrail and turned to port. His breathing was level and silent to better hear any incoming threats. He continued to traverse, his finger alongside the trigger well.

A sound redirected his aim to the corner, and a moment later, a wounded operator tripped around the corner, his SIG-Sauer extended in front of him. Williams pumped two rounds in the threat's head. Once the body hit the ground, he moved forward. As he walked, he tipped his carbine to the left and saw that the bolt was locked to the rear. Automatically, he dropped the spent mag and reached for a fresh replacement.

An assailant struck Williams from behind and thrust him against the container. The attacker grabbed the M4's sling, wrapped it around his neck, and cinched it tight. Williams fought to dig his fingers between the sling and his neck, and his vision grew blurry. The attacker leaned in close and murmured in Williams's ear.

"I didn't quite imagine it this way, but this is more satisfying. You've got a lot to answer for, you piece of shit." Colonel Agha's voice had taken an obsessed, maniacal tone that had been absent in Istiqbal-Tora. Agha's strength was surprising for a man of his build, no doubt fueled by the rage that coursed through his veins.

Williams threw his head back, caught Agha in the jaw, and gave himself just enough space to slip his fingers into the makeshift noose. He balled his hands, squatted, and yanked the sling up and forward as he hunched over. Agha refused to relinquish his hold, and paid for it with his collision with the Connex. Williams removed the sling from around his neck and dropped the carbine to the ground. He went for the SIG-Sauer on his hip, but Agha sprung forward and speared Williams into the Connex. Connecting with the steel container sent the pistol flying out of Williams's reach. Agha struck Williams twice in the jaw, but when he went for a third, Williams grabbed Agha's fist with his left hand and the throat with his right. Williams spun Agha around and hurled him into the Connex. As Agha stumbled forward, Williams feigned a right kick and lunged forward to connect with a right straight to the cheek.

Agha stumbled, and Williams followed him to the ground. He dug his knees into Agha's ribs and rained fists on his face. After the third blow, Agha leaned his head left at the perfect moment, and Williams slammed his fist into the metal deck at full force. He howled as the pain shot through his wrist and up through his arm. Agha took that opportunity to trap Williams's leg, roll him over, pick him up by the plate carrier, and slam him into the deck repeatedly.

When Agha lifted him again, Williams grabbed a fistful of Agha's hair and held tight as he was thrown to the ground. Agha's hands moved to his head instinctively, which allowed Williams to unwrap his legs from around Agha's midsection, cock back, and plant both boots into Agha's chest, which propelled him several feet back. Williams leaned back, eyes squeezed shut and teeth bared, and kipped up. He assumed his fighting stance—squared off with the target, hands held slightly in front of him and closed in loose fists. His right hand throbbed from the contact with the deck, but Williams shook his head and kept his focus. Agha adopted a similar posture and closed in slowly.

"You killed my friends," Agha rasped. "Good men, men who died defending their country!"

"They picked up a gun," Williams said coldly. "They knew the risks."

"*Bastard!*" Agha shrieked as he launched himself forward. Williams underestimated Agha's speed and caught a solid right cross to the jaw, followed by a left uppercut. Agha wrapped his hands around Williams's head and drove it into his knee, which broke cartilage and blood vessels. As Williams reeled back, Agha grabbed him by the shoulders and rammed him into the Connex, face first. His hands deftly unclipped the plate carrier, and he tossed it aside. Blood had stained through the shirt, which drove Agha into a frenzy.

Agha grunted as he drove his fists into Williams's back. Williams shouted with every blow and fell to his knees. Agha took a step back and lashed out with snap-kicks in cadence. Williams's arms went limp at his side, and his neck and head went slack. Agha hunched over and looked Williams in the eye.

"*C'mon!*" he shouted. "*Stand up! FIGHT ME!*"

When Williams made no attempt to stand, Agha grabbed him by the arm and head, lifted him to his feet, and slammed his head into the Connex. Agha's eyes grew crazed as he repeated the move. The vision had come true, and it was even more glorious than he had imagined. It was justice in the most visceral sense, fantastically gruesome, the kind of death fitting of a person who murdered without compunction.

Agha threw Williams to the ground and stood over him. He drew his SIG-Sauer and leveled it at Williams's face. "See you in Hell, Williams," he snarled as he thumbed back the hammer.

Williams's eyes flared wide open. He drove his boot vertically and caught Agha in the testicles. The next kick caught him in the side of the knee, which forced him to kneel. Williams scrambled forward and tackled Agha to regain the high mount. He tucked his knees deep into Agha's armpits and used his left hand to choke Agha. With an animalistic glint in his eye, Williams brought his fist down on Agha's face. He breathed through his mouth and could taste his own blood dripping from his broken nose as he struck Agha in cadence, alternating hands throughout.

The more his fists crashed into Agha's head, the greater his rage grew, and for the first time in weeks, Williams allowed that rage to consume him. His fists came down harder and faster, and with every blow, he remembered every civil servant he'd had to kill. He remembered Zaina's imprisonment at Agha's hands. He remembered Ferran's lifeless body inside the safe house. And, as his bruised ribs and the burns on his chest reminded him with every punch, there was his treatment at Istiqbal-Tora that Agha had to answer for.

When he finished, Williams stood, his hands covered in Agha's blood and gray matter. His fists trembled as he looked at the mess he had created. Williams looked to the nocturnal skyline with its dazzling stars, and took a deep breath of the crisp ocean air.

Maks walked into the passageway and stopped when he saw Williams standing over Agha. A shiver crawled through his body. He swallowed and asked, "You okay, Williams?"

Williams opened his mouth to speak, but it all caught up with him at once. He tried to walk forward, but his legs gave out and he fell on his face. The last thing he heard as he blacked out was Maks screaming his name, punctuated by rapid commands in Russian.

CHAPTER SEVENTEEN

United States Embassy
Garden City, Cairo, Egypt
1 August 2006
09:00 hours Eastern European Time (07:00 hours Zulu)

LANA BOUTON FIDDLED WITH the ballpoint pen as she and the Ambassador awaited the arrival of their guests. For the past week, Bouton took fire from two sides. Her superiors in Langley wanted to know why one of their former employees was being accused of slaughtering Egyptian government personnel and why she knew nothing about it. Foggy Bottom—which had a tenuous relationship with Langley, at best—took it a step further and accused her of arranging the whole affair.

The writing was on the wall. Even if she managed to pull out all the stops and use every favor she had banked over the past eighteen years, all she could hope to do was hit twenty and retire. That was more of bragging rights deal than anything that would effect her retirement: unlike the military or federal law enforcement, case officers could retire before twenty years with full benefits due to the nature of their work. Bouton had stayed longer than most, and she could definitely cash in and go private sector, or go into politics. That had been her original plan before she was recruited.

Bouton set the pen down, reached into her pocket, and pulled out the worn business card. It bore the Cato Institute's emblem, as well as the name and number of a classmate that had been a fellow College Republican who had become a senior fellow with the Institute. She looked at the card and smiled as her thumb slid across the paper.

"What are you smiling at?"

Bouton looked up and to her left. Delilah Lantos frowned at Bouton's expression. Bouton quickly wiped the smile from her face, put the card back in her wallet, and slipped it back in her jacket pocket. "Nothing, ma'am."

Lantos studied Bouton for a moment before she resumed her staring contest with the wall across the room. She was four years older than Bouton at forty-four, and was one of the most renowned names in the American Diplomatic Corps. The daughter of a Marine colonel, Lantos had rebelled against her father by joining the Red Cross to stem the effects of war rather than enable them. Her first experience was in Honduras and El Salvador, where she saw first hand the atrocities committed by both sides. That compelled her to finish her studies and enter the State Department as a policy analyst. Somehow, she found herself in the Bureau of Intelligence and Research during most of the 1990s. In 1999, she was appointed the *charge d'affaires* for the Ambassador to Saudi Arabia. In 2005, she was appointed by President Davis to be the Ambassador to Egypt.

Anyone who said Delilah Lantos was a beautiful woman was prone to understatement. Her Magyar roots blessed her with flawless olive skin, high cheekbones, warm brown eyes, and a curvaceous model's physique, accentuated by her black pantsuit. Her shoulder length black hair was worn in a bun, and square glasses rest high on the bridge of her nose. Early on in her career, Lantos ignored her looks and even went out of her way to downplay and masculinize her appearance. As she got older, Lantos came to embrace her femininity as a source of strength, particularly after witnessing the state of women in the Middle East. While she did not weaponize it like others she knew, she refused to hide it anymore.

The door behind Bouton and Lantos opened, and both women turned and stood as the two men entered the room. Ahmed Aboul Gheit was the first man in the room. He stood just shy of six feet tall and held a regal air about him. His gray hair was balding, but his brown eyes emanated sharp intellect. Gheit's coal gray suit was crisply pressed, and he wore a black polka dot tie.

Behind him was Omar Suleiman, the head of the *Mukhabarat*. Soviet trained, Suleiman had worked in intelligence for most of his forty-two year government service. He was appointed to his current posting by President Mubarak thirteen years earlier. A man of average build, Suleiman's bald head and thin moustache gave him the appearance of a kindly grandfather. Bouton saw right through that mirage. She knew that Suleiman had to be ruthless in order to survive in the intelligence world as long as he had. Bouton and Suleiman exchanged polite nods as the Egyptians moved to the opposite side of the table and took their seats.

"Mr. Minister," Lantos said. "Director Suleiman. Good morning."

"Good morning, Madam Ambassador," Gheit said.

"Thank you for seeing us on such short notice."

"Of course," Lantos said. She gestured to Bouton. "This is Lana Bouton, my cultural attaché."

Suleiman raised his hand to speak. "Forgive my interjection, Madam Ambassador, but I would prefer we speak frankly. We know that Ms. Bouton is the chief of your CIA station here in Cairo. We also have reason to believe that she was either complicit in last week's events, which included the death of an entire section of our maritime counterterrorism unit, or that she had knowledge and that she chose to turn a blind eye. I would like to hear what Ms. Bouton has to say for herself."

Lantos looked to Bouton and said nothing. Bouton suppressed a smile. She knew Ambassador Lantos would hang her to dry, which was fine. She had her own game plan up her sleeve. Bouton interlaced her fingers, rest her hands on the table, and leaned forward. When she spoke, her voice was even and neutral.

"Mr. Director, I would love nothing more than to speak frankly. The fact of the matter is that you detained an American citizen. Rather than adhering to long-established political etiquette and deporting her, you imprisoned her in one of your most notorious prisons."

"Ms. Anwar holds dual citizenship and is thus accountable to our laws," Suleiman said.

"Laws which nearly got her raped during her incarceration," Bouton said. "I've been in contact with Ms. Anwar since her return to the United States. I have the full story of how you treated her, how you brutally tortured and killed cousin—"

"That is an internal security matter," Suleiman interjected.

"—how you tortured Mr. Williams, who has also since returned to the States," Bouton continued, raising her voice. "How your Colonel Agha chased both Ms. Anwar and Mr. Williams into international waters and attempted to assassinate them. We have all of it." Bouton leaned in closer, her voice barely above a whisper. "Mr. Director, don't think for one second that if you elect to make this a public issue, I won't make sure Ms. Anwar's side of the story plays on CNN, on loop, for the next four weeks, because believe me...I will."

"This is an outrage," Suleiman said, looking to Gheit. "You have the audacity to defend two of your citizens that have killed over one hundred of our countrymen? Nations have gone to war for less."

Bouton smiled as she looked between Suleiman and Gheit. "I may not be a diplomat, but I'm sure of two things: the United States is the last nation on Earth that you want war with, and that Ambassador Lantos and Minister Gheit won't allow it to come to that point."

"Mr. Minister," Suleiman said in exasperation.

Gheit held his hand up to silence Suleiman, and looked to Ambassador Lantos. "Madam Ambassador, I do not appreciate Ms. Bouton's insolence."

"Neither do I, Mr. Minister," Lantos said. "I can assure you that this will be reported to her superiors and she will be disciplined."

"I'm sure," Gheit said. "However, her insolence does not make her words any less true. We could certainly file a complaint with the United Nations, but you could just as easily do likewise, and we will both have, as you say, egg on our face. I propose an agreement that will allow us to sweep all of this under the rug."

Lantos nodded slowly. "You have my undivided attention. Mr. Minister."

"Director Suleiman tells me that during the course of these events, Ms. Anwar and Mr. Williams interrupted a meeting hosted by Jafar Abdul-Rahim, Muslim Brotherhood cell leader and financier. He has since vanished and we have not been able to locate whom he was meeting with, though we know it was a woman. Our intelligence analysts were perplexed as to why he would divert from his escape and evasion plan to attack the Muslim Brotherhood."

Lantos's brow furrowed. "I'm not quite sure where you're going with this." Bouton locked eyes with Suleiman and fought to maintain a passive expression.

"Ms. Anwar and Mr. Williams departed aboard the *Parabellum,* flying Cyprus colors. An Ekaterina Korovina entered the country aboard the *Parabellum*, and yet, there's no record of her departing the country aboard it. There was no record of Ms. Anwar and Mr. Williams boarding it, either. It was through sheer eyewitness reports that Colonel Agha was able to ascertain they were smuggled board."

"With all due respect, Mr. Minister, what is your point?" Lantos asked.

"Our *point,* Madam Ambassador, is that we have reason to believe that Ms. Korovina is known to your intelligence community some way. Perhaps she is a case officer, or perhaps she is an asset. Either way, it is obvious that Ms. Anwar and Mr. Williams struck an arrangement with Ms. Korovina for safe passage from the country. We also believe that Ms. Korovina has slipped out of the country with Mr. Abdul-Rahim in tow."

An intelligence officer's worst fear was being discovered, and it was all that Bouton could do not to have a meltdown. A legitimate operation had been compromised due to her desire to act on behalf of a fellow countryman against an oppressive government. Suleiman read her expression and a small smile crossed his lips.

Gheit continued. "We're willing to slide all of this under the rug. We'll even help you spin it in your favor and blame the dead Egyptian soldiers and law enforcement personnel on the Egyptian Brotherhood. Colonel Agha exceeded his mandate. It will be relatively easy to make all of this go away."

"What do you want in exchange?" Lantos asked.

"I want the full results of your interrogation with Mr. Abdul-Rahim passed along to Director Suleiman. Abdul-Rahim was on our radar for some time. He knows the inner workings of the Muslim Brotherhood. His compatriots will certainly change their protocols once they figure out that he's been captured, but he knows enough to give us leads to follow internally. You give us that in a written agreement and we will make this entire incident disappear."

Bouton opened her mouth to object, but Lantos spoke first. "Deal. You'll have that written deal by the end of the day." Lantos rose and extended her hand across the table. "I'm glad that we could quickly reach an agreement that benefits all parties."

"As am I," Gheit said. He took Lantos's hand and shook it. Suleiman also shook Lantos's hand. Neither one offered the gesture to Bouton, who sat in her chair, arms folded, a cross look on her face. Gheit nodded and said, "We look forward to hearing from you later today."

"Of course," Lantos said.

Gheit and Suleiman left the room. Once the doors were closed behind them, Bouton leapt to her feet and squared off with Lantos. "What the hell have you done?" she half-shouted.

"I've cleaned up your mess," Lantos said. "I know you traveled back to the States and recruited Williams for this goddamn debacle. Out of all the people you had to recruit, you approached Ben fucking Williams. Are you out of your fucking mind?"

"You're going to give intelligence on an ongoing operation to the *Mukhabarat*," Bouton said. "The same organization that every report presents strong evidence of infiltration by the Brotherhood and other jihadist groups. You've just as good burned our asset."

"*You* did that," Lantos hissed. She took a step closer to Bouton. "You couldn't leave well enough alone. Anwar would have done a year, two tops, in an Egyptian prison, and then she would have been deported, but that wasn't good enough for you. You just *had* to spring her now."

"Zaina Anwar is a goddamned *person*," Bouton yelled. "Does that not register to you? Or are you so concern with kissing foreign ass that you stopped giving a fuck about our own citizens?"

"One hundred dead citizens," Lantos shouted. "Are they not people because they're Egyptian? Or just because you happen to find their particular brand of government unsavory, it's okay to kill them? That'd be something you and the Muslim Brotherhood share in common."

"Fuck you, bitch," Bouton hissed. "If you think this is how this ends, you're dead wrong." She turned and marched for the door.

"Thinking of leaking the information?" Lantos said. "I wouldn't do that if I were you." Bouton turned back around to face Lantos as she continued. "Just because the Egyptians buried this doesn't mean I have to bury it between us. I find out that you've leaked this agreement, or if you refuse to pass the information, or if you warn your asset or Ben Williams, and I'll have enough to lock your ass up in Supermax as a traitor."

Bouton did not respond. She knew that Lantos spoke the truth. All she could do was glare and ball her hands into fists.

"You keep your silence, then you can leave the Agency on a high note," Lantos said. "You talk, and not only will I call in every favor I have with the FBI to bury you under the jailhouse, I'll go after Williams too. You want to protect him? Shut your mouth."

Bouton put her hands on her hips. "This isn't just about diplomacy versus intelligence. You've got an axe to grind with Williams."

"Over the years, Ben Williams and his actions have constantly obstructed peace attempts. The man is a wrecking ball. I've had to clean his messes for the better part of twenty years and I'm sick of it. It's time for him *and* you to learn that actions have consequences."

A scowl seized Bouton's face as she forced an audible exhale out of her nose. "Fine. You've got my silence. I won't say a word to Williams."

"Good."

"*But*, if this comes back and gets one of Williams's friends killed, and he figures out I had something to do with this, I'm not going to lie to him." Bouton paused. "If it gets Williams killed, then you're going to need every single one of those favors to keep me from ruining you."

"I own your ass," Lantos said. "You want to crash and burn with me?"

"If it comes down to that? Yes."

Without another room, Bouton threw the door open and stormed out of the conference room.

Lantos reached to the untouched water pitcher on the table, poured herself a glass of lemon ice water, and sipped it quietly as she processed the events of the past few minutes. She knew Bouton was harmless, and there was nothing she could dig up. Lantos's ascension to the ambassadorial stage was as clean as they came in the business. Williams, on the other hand...

Goddamn it, Williams. She took another sip. *Goddamn it.*

* * *

University of Bern

Bern, Switzerland
4 December 2006
14:35 hours Eastern European Time (13:35 hours Zulu)

"THAT IS THE FUNDAMENTAL conflict between the Egyptian people and the government," Zaina Anwar said in French, her hands placed on either side of the podium. Her hair was tied in a bun, and she wore a white button-up blouse, a gray blazer, a matching skirt that cut off just beneath her knees, and black heels. Square glasses covered her eyes and completed her academic look. Behind her was a poster board that featured a burning Egyptian flag and the visage of Hosni Mubarak, with the word "Exodus" emblazoned across the top and her name at the bottom. The gathering of fifty students was far more relaxed than some of the venues she had been invited to for discussion regarding the background and events of her novel.

"How do you think that will be addressed?" a student asked from the crowd.

"It's just like any other revolution," Zaina said. "The people will reach a threshold where they can no longer endure the government's abuse of power, and they will resist."

"So, are you advocating an insurgency?" another student inquired.

"Absolutely!" Zaina said. "But an insurgency of ideals. To effect true change, the cause must maintain the moral high ground. Allow the other side to show its hand and reveal its oppressive nature, and what little popular support it holds will be lost. This is not a new concept. Civil disobedience and non-violent protests have worked to great effect in the movement for Indian independence from the British, as well as the American labor rights and civil rights movements.

"In comparison, violent insurgencies last longer, achieve much less, and leave lingering animosity between the participating groups upon the conclusion of hostilities. A prime example of this is South Africa. The African National Congress took to armed conflict, and it took them over forty years to achieve the repeal of apartheid. Even today, there are smoldering embers between the native Africans, who have in effect become the ruling class, and the Boers, some of whom are genuinely resentful regarding the fall of apartheid and others who feel that they are being punished for the sins of their fathers. That friction can be exploited to reignite the violence. Civil disobedience and non-violence greatly reduce the chances of such enmities developing to those levels."

"You resorted to violence," a student pointed out. "You say so in your book: you killed a man and you assisted the mercenary in killing many others. How can you advocate a non-violent approach when you have violated your own principles?"

Zaina looked at the student, a young man with combed brown hair and a natural swagger about him that belied both intelligence and overconfidence. She took a deep breath, eyed the podium for a moment, then met his eyes again. "You're right. I have killed. And let me tell you, it is the emptiest feeling in the world. It is not a feeling I wish to revisit, nor would I wish upon somebody who couldn't handle it. The circumstances were extreme. The mercenary's life

275

was in danger, and by extension, *my* life was in danger. I did what I had to in order to save the mercenary's life. Was there an element of self-preservation? Absolutely. But further more, I knew that my dialogue on the government needed to reach the light of day, and that would never happen as a political prisoner.

"And as for how I can preach non-violence, having committed the ultimate act of violence? It's simple. I can attest first hand that violence only begets more of the same. For true, lasting change, civil disobedience is the only answer. You don't have to take my word for it, and in fact, I would prefer that you didn't. Research the examples I have provided and draw your own conclusions. After all, that's the only way we learn, isn't it?"

A pretty blonde student cleared her throat and spoke up. "What would you say to the allegations that an Egyptian revolution would share parallels with the Iranian revolution? The latter gave rise to the ayatollahs. Egypt has been in gridlock with the Muslim Brotherhood for decades. Who's to say that the Mubarak regime isn't the only thing keeping Egypt from becoming an Islamist nation?"

Zaina smiled. "In times of strife, people turn to religion. It happens. I think there are far more secular elements in Egypt than there were in Iran, and while it's possible that the Muslim Brotherhood may take seats in a new government, so long as there is consent of the governed and transparency of state, Egypt won't go the same route."

A man at the back of the classroom caught her eye, clad in a black button-up shirt, a leather jacket and jeans. She squinted to discern his features, but once recognition was achieved, she could not help but smile. Zaina cleared her throat and said, "We've had a very lively discussion thus far. Let's take a fifteen minute break, stretch our legs, and I'll answer any other questions you have."

Zaina waited for the students to vacate the classroom before she left the podium. She fetched her overcoat, walked off stage, and made her way down the aisle. When she reached the man, she folded her arms and looked up at him. "How long have you been standing there?" she asked.

Ben Williams shrugged. "Non-violence is the key to a lasting peaceful coexistence. Take your cues from Ghandi, King, and Chavez. Otherwise, you'll have a lingering animosity."

"You're a good student," Zaina praised.

Williams smiled, and motioned to the door. "Care for a smoke?"

"I'd love to," Zaina said. "Follow me."

Zaina led the way to the front of the building and to the designated smoking area. Light snow fell from gray clouds overhead, but with no wind to alter their direction of travel, they fell straight to the ground. It was chilly enough to merit the outerwear, but pleasant enough for the two smokers.

She removed a cigarette case from her pocket and retrieved a single Newport menthol. Williams fetched a beaten soft pack of Marlboro Reds from his right jacket pocket, along with a Zippo lighter emblazoned with a teal arrowhead with a golden sword and three lightning bolts across it. He flicked the flame to life, touched it to the tip of the cancer stick, then proffered it to Zaina. Once she was lit, Williams flicked the lighter closed and replaced it in his pocket.

"You dropped off the grid for a while," Zaina said. "I was a little worried, given the state I last saw you in."

"Took about a month off to heal," Williams said. "Got back to one hundred percent and I've been working ever since. I was in the neighborhood, heard you were giving a lecture, and figured I'd stop by, check in on you."

Zaina took a pull off of her cigarette. "Well, I honored our agreement. I only provided the necessary details to get across your personality."

"I know," Williams said. "Bought the book upon release, finished it the same day."

"What'd you think of it?"

"Your passion is admirable," Williams said. "I'm not sure if things will turn out the way you predict. I honestly think you're underestimating the Muslim Brotherhood's influence. But who knows? Maybe I'm wrong. I'm no politician."

"There is a possibility," Zaina allowed. "But until that point, I still have hope. Precautions can be taken. It's entirely possible that Egypt can replace Mubarak with a government of the people."

Williams shrugged. "Regardless, that book's been a cash cow for you. Number one spot on the New York Times Bestseller's List, international acclaim, pissed off a lot of politicians and diplomats, here and abroad. Both the Egyptian and American governments are clammed up on the whole affair. I'd say the book has had an impact."

Zaina laughed. "You know...I never thought of

myself as a political figure. Work behind the scenes, effect change where I can, do my part to make a difference. But now, I'm in the spotlight, and it's all a bit shocking, to be completely honest."

"It's an opportunity. Run with it. What's something you've always wanted to do?"

That gave Zaina pause for thought. She took another drag of the cigarette and blew the smoke skyward. "I want to represent women. I want to show every woman that she has power within, and she can harness it to great effect. Bringing about democracy to Egypt will always be a passion of mine, but female empowerment has always been near and dear to me."

"Then who better to promote that than a woman who has endured adverse conditions and lived to tell about it?" Williams smiled.

"Yeah," Zaina said. She returned the smile. "I've saved up most of my royalties. I've just been deciding what to do with it. Now, I think I know."

Williams smiled as he finished his cigarette. He dropped the butt and ground it into the pavement with his boot. "You'll do great."

Zaina nodded, then paused a beat. After a moment, she said, "I have the evening free if you'd like to grab something to eat, kill some time."

"Lovely proposal, terrible timing," Williams said. "I've got work to do. I just wanted to stop by and see how you were doing." He looked at her for a second and said, "Rain check?"

"I'd like that," Zaina said.

Williams reached into his cigarette pocket and removed a business card. It was blank, aside from a ten-digit phone number. "Call that number when you find a good time. Call it if you get into trouble. Call it if you need to talk. I'll do my best to help you where I can, but I'm not the government. Don't expect any miracles."

"If our incident wasn't a miracle, then I can only wonder what you can do with government backing."

Williams shrugged and removed a can of Red Bull from his left jacket pocket. He cracked the can open and sipped on the liquid. Zaina shot him a confused look.

"Energy drinks?"

"Yep," Williams said.

"Never figured you for the type. Isn't it a bit cold out for that?"

"I don't drink coffee after noon."

Without another word, Williams turned and walked down the street, his free hand in his pocket. Zaina took a moment to look at the card. She did not recognize the area code. When she glanced up, Williams was nowhere to be seen. Zaina chuckled, then tucked the business card into her jacket pocket, next to the cigarette case. She disposed of her cigarette and returned to the classroom with a smile on her face.

ACKNOWLEDGMENTS

This is the third time I have published this book. It started off as a novella and my first published work, albeit electronically, and while the first product received some solid reviews, I felt that I could do better. So, bearing that in mind, I pulled the original from the market and set out to make some changes. What started off as a simple edit grew into a full-blown rewrite, and a novel-sized one at that. But, I rushed to publish it and missed some things. So, I went back and fixed some of the most grievous errors, as well as changed a couple of background items for future works.

I wouldn't be here without several people. First and foremost, I would like to thank **Zayne Amer** for her friendship, as well as her first-hand accounts of Arab Spring, which served as an inspiration for the story. There is a lot of her in the female protagonist, Zaina, and there is a reason I picked that name. This is a work of fiction, but I wanted the female lead to exemplify the kind of strength and intelligence that Zayne does.

Kevin Granzow of Kevin Granzow Design & Multimedia deserves special recognition for his redesign of the cover. He has never let me down and I see us creating many more books together, with me providing the words and Kev providing the graphics.

Dellani Oakes also deserves recognition for her

friendship and for putting me on her blog talk radio show, which allowed me to promote my work even further. It was a new experience, and one that I thoroughly enjoyed. She's an author, as well, so if you're looking for another book to pick up after this, you have another starting point.

Tub-Bee Louis deserves thanks for his mentorship, both in character dynamics and in how to be a man. He is an incredible man with a kind soul, but he does not suffer fools lightly…or as he would say, "I'm done with you!"

Thanks to **Jack Murphy** for tips on tactics, mercenaries, and publishing, and to the entire crew of **SOFREP** for providing me an education into the special operations community.

Special thanks to **Peter Nealen** for his friendship and his pointers. Most of them were directed towards my second work, but his input also had an impact on the second edition of my work.

Benjamin Cheah, **Nate Granzow**, and **Stephen England** have been some of my staunchest friends and colleagues in the writer game. I do not think I will ever be able to pay off the debt I owe them, both on a writing basis and on a personal basis. The same goes for **Jack Blakely**, who has always enthusiastically promoted my books, and **Phillip Smyth**, who not only promoted my books but called me out on inaccuracies in the Alexandria scene in the original run of this book.

Speaking of the writer I am today, thanks to **Douglas P. Wojtowicz**, who saw potential in a thirteen-year-old kid, took him under his wing, and taught him more about writing than he ever learned in school. It is because of Doug that I have any type of literary aptitude.

Ryann Costlow deserves recognition, as she pushed me to broaden the scope of the novel even more than I had initially planned. I also lost a bet to her—I bet that I would wait three months before I published the Kindle edition, which is not really going to happen, so I owe her $2. C'est la vie!

Finally, thanks to **YOU**, the reader, for all of your support, especially if you have been following my blog, Facebook, or Twitter! Without you guys, I would not be where I am at today. I hope I've done you proud with this work and that I've got you looking forward to the next book!

If you liked The First Bayonet, *turn the page for other exciting and thrilling works, coming soon or available now...*

From New York Times Bestselling author and Special Operations veteran Jack Murphy comes a new military thriller about what happens when America's best go bad.

The right man in the wrong place.

They call themselves Liquid Sky. A group of rogue SEAL Team Six operators turned soldiers of fortune. They've got the training and combat experience to pull off the impossible as their client hires them to stoke the flames of the Arab Spring in certain Middle Eastern countries...and suppress it in others.

Deckard faces the most challenging mission of his career when he comes across intel that puts him hot on the trail of Liquid Sky's latest assassination in Pakistan, a mission that targets a pro-democracy advocate.

Failing to stop the rogue cell, Deckard shoots from the hip and drops his name in the running to be Liquid Sky's newest member, replacing the one he just killed. It is a mission unlike any other that Deckard has ever faced. As they strike their targets in the Philippines, Afghanistan, Egypt, and beyond, Deckard has to maintain his cover while sabotaging their operations.

If he can hold out just a little longer, he might be able to find out who Liquid Sky is taking their marching orders from. But the missions are only getting dirtier, and Deckard's hands are far from clean. When the time comes, not even Deckard knows if he will be able to do all that is necessary to take down Liquid Sky.

AVAILABLE NOW ON AMAZON.COM

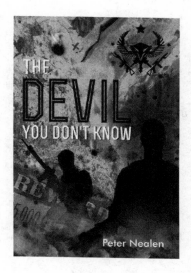

He is called "El Duque."

No one knows his real name. Only vague descriptions and fuzzy photos of him exist. What is known about him is that he is the up-and-coming power in the converging underworlds of guerrilla warfare, spies, terrorists, and organized crime. He is known to have ties with Islamist extremists, Communist guerrillas, drug cartels, gun runners…if it is involved in global chaos, he has a hand in it.

Now Praetorian Security has been contracted to hunt him down. Jeff Stone and his team pick up the scent in northern Mexico. But the closer they get, the more elusive El Duque seems to become.

Jeff and his compatriots have long since learned that in the shadowy world of modern conflict, little is ever exactly what it seems. But as the manhunt leads them into some of the darkest, most lawless corners of the Western Hemisphere, they come upon an explosive revelation that changes everything.

No one is coming out the other side of this mission the same.

The Special Operations contractors of Praetorian Security go to the darkest corners of the world, to face the worst that the underworld of modern conflict has to offer.

AVAILABLE NOW ON AMAZON PRINT, CREATESPACE, SMASHWORDS, AND THE AMAZON KINDLE STORE

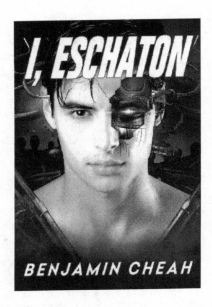

Master Sergeant Christopher Miller has returned home from war, but war has come to find him.

The Sons of America are targeting the Wilshaw Foundation, and Miller's lover, Sarah Grey, is at the top of their hit list. To survive, Miller must go underground with Sarah. But to prevail, they must ally themselves with the enigmatic artificial intelligence that calls itself Eschaton.

An extension of the smart networks that underpin the Republic of Cascadia, the AI offers contacts, resources and the full power of the national security apparatus. But at what price?

AVAILABLE NOW ON THE AMAZON KINDLE STORE AND SMASHWORDS

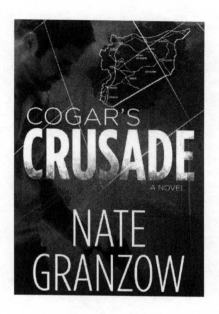

My name is Grant Cogar.
The world thinks I'm dead.
I'm not sure they're wrong.

July 2013. Foreign correspondent Grant Cogar has gone missing
and is presumed dead. His last known whereabouts: Aleppo,
Syria. Another casualty lost to a brutal civil war already
responsible for claiming over 100,000 lives. But when an
anonymous message reaches Cogar's editor with news of the
reporter's survival, his old friend and mentor decides to retrieve
him.

Only, Cogar doesn't want to be saved.

**AVAILABLE NOW ON AMAZON PRINT,
CREATESPACE, AND THE AMAZON KINDLE STORE**

Turn the page for a preview of The Sovereigns,
the next thrilling entry in the Ben Williams series…

THE COMPOUND WAS THREE square acres, or a little more than a football field's length per side, and surrounded by an electrified barbed wire fence. Most of that area was on a steep hill, with a main cottage and a series of small barns converted into living quarters. It was designed to house three hundred occupants. Crude but effective guard towers stood at each corner of the property, as well as one at each side's midpoint, for a total of eight towers. An unimproved road circled the compound and led from the main housing areas, to each of the towers, and back to the front. There were also two smaller roads, one that led to a known-distance range and another to an obstacle course.

Over fifteen years had gone into building the compound, and just as long was invested in keeping it off the radar. Favors were called in and palms were greased. Even during the Clinton years, when the focus was on supposed "terrorist hate groups," the compound remained under the radar. Part of that was due to the recruiting process. Other groups with an axe to grind with the government were proactive with their recruitment, and were often ran by people deficient in intellect. That left them wide open to investigation and infiltration by federal agents. On the other hand, the compound's proprietor had gone out of his way to maintain legitimate appearances, and had an early warning system if any of the various federal agencies took an interest. When their agents arrived, they were treated well, shown the facilities, offered training and prices, and then were sent on their way. Each report came back the same: while the occupants were a bit funny, there was no impropriety or cause to investigate further. Taxes were paid and illicit materials and substances were disallowed on the premises. The compound and their inhabitants were bulletproof.

At least, that was the case up until three months prior.

Mark Matsuda was a woodsman and a man accustomed to long waits. Growing up ethnic Japanese in Tennessee, Matsuda was used to being the odd man out and finding his own way. What he truly loved about nature was that it cared not about his skin color. It only cared that you had the skills and wherewithal to survive. Its harshness was the purest equality. It was in that austerity that Matsuda was forged into a hunter, guided by his father. When he was eighteen, he was further tempered in the hottest fires the United States Navy had to offer: Basic Underwater Demolition/SEAL Training. His eight years with SEAL Team Two saw combat in Panama and Kuwait.

After he left the Navy, Matsuda tried to occupy himself with college, but he missed the thrill of hunting men. That led him to abandon pursuit of his master's degree and to the Federal Bureau of Investigation. Long hours of surveillance had Matsuda eating far too much junk food and bored to tears. The Hostage Rescue Team was the answer he sought. He proved himself for four years as a Red Team assaulter, then attended the Marine Scout Sniper Course to learn the tradecraft of the stalk.

That was what brought Matsuda to his current position. Watch duty was a four-hour chore to the tower guards, and Matsuda and his partner, Al Testaverde, were nothing more to them than tall grass in the distance. The ghillie suit smelled like a mix of horse manure and white thorn, which respectively concealed their natural body odor and acted as a snake repellent. They had started five kilometers out from the compound perimeter, outside of visual distance, and low-crawled at a pace of roughly two hundred and forty meters per hour. It took them nearly a day to reach the final firing position. They ate very little and drank small mouthfuls of water during the crawl, as the order of the day was minimal motion.

Once they were in position, Matsuda and Testaverde made sure to stay hydrated. While Texas had not hit the peak of its summer heat, the combination of direct sunlight beating down on them and the caffeine pills they popped every few hours to stay awake stole water from their bodies. Conversation was kept to a bare minimum. To pick up where the caffeine pills left off, they played mental games, imagining how their targets would react or guessing what they would do next. The tough part of that exercise was to remain objective. Whether they came from law enforcement, the military, or the intelligence services, long-distance marksmen were psychologically screened for their ability to take the shot and not to take the shot. Sniping was an extremely intimate experience, a sort of voyeurism that ended in death. While the ability to end the experience on command was important, equally important was the ability to walk away without taking the shot.

Matsuda chewed on a piece of venison jerky. The bag in his chest pocket was part of the kill he made last season in Beaverhead-Deerlodge National Forest, an eight-point monarch bull elk he stalked for hours and then shot at five hundred meters. The head was mounted in his den back home in Virginia, and the meat had been turned into steaks, burgers, and jerky. Matsuda had perfected his jerky recipe over the years, a blend of teriyaki sauce, garlic, paprika, and black pepper. Testaverde, who loathed long stakeouts and hide sites, loved being partnered with Matsuda for the sole reason that he always brought an extra bag of homemade jerky just for him.

The voice of the Red Team leader, Supervisory Special Agent Walt McKinney, filled both Matsuda's and Testaverde's low-profile earpieces. "Red Six to all OPs. Genevieve. I say again, Genevieve."

Were they part of the assault element, Matsuda and Testaverde would have exchanged looks and perhaps even shared a fist bump. Genevieve was the end of their wait, the sign that things were coming to a head. Genevieve was the mission go-code, and the sign that they had passed the threshold for the situation to be resolved peacefully. Genevieve was the government's blessing to take lives, the grace for state-sanctioned killing. It would not be the first time either man had taken a life in the service of their country.

"Red Six to all OPs, I have control. Execute on my mark. Stand by."

Normally, one member of the two-man team would be on a spotting scope while the other serviced targets. With two men per guard tower and the necessity to kill all of the perimeter guards simultaneously, the Red Team snipers were forced to alter their *modus operandi*. Both Matsuda and Testaverde were behind modified Remington 700 rifles, chambered in .308 Winchester, with suppressors affixed to the barrels. The supersonic rounds would still be very audible, but those in the living area would only hear the shots aimed at the towers closest to them, and those were far enough away that they would not be readily recognizable as firearm reports. That was also contingent on each man scoring a kill shot on the first go, cold zero. Each sniper was a professional, but that did not make them immune to mistakes or bad luck.

Matsuda smiled. *A couple of inches make the difference between a clean raid and Waco Part II.*

McKinney's voice put him on alert. "Five…"

"I've got Dopey," Matsuda murmured to Testaverde. "You take Grumpy."

"Four…" McKinney said over the net.

As Matsuda set the Leupold mil-dot crosshairs on his target, a thin blond man with a cowlick and thick circular glasses, Testaverde said, "Next time, I pick the nickname scheme."

"Three…"

Matsuda said, "We could always pick the

Aristocats. My daughter loves that movie, too."

"Two…"

"I prefer snakes," Testaverde said. "Call 'em 'Cobra' or 'Cottonmouth' or something cool."

"One…execute."

Matsuda and Testaverde squeezed their triggers at the same time. The Remingtons bucked against their shoulders. Bullets launched through barrels and sound suppressors. Neither target in the tower heard the shots that killed them. The rounds found their targets and tore jagged passages through bone and gray matter before tumbling out of the back. Both men fell out of sight. They waited a moment and scanned their surroundings, and the echo of the other suppressed gunshots lingered in the air. There were no shouts, no cries of alarm. Silence once again reigned over the compound.

"All OPs, status," McKinney said.

Without removing his eye from glass, Matsuda said, "Dude, you don't want to give the people you're going to kill cool nicknames. Give them something stupid so you don't feel so bad about killing them afterward."

"That's not how that works," Testaverde insisted. "You give them cool nicknames as a final favor before you kill them. Come on, now."

Matsuda shook his head slightly as his free hand reached up for his throat mic. He heard the OP two stations down call in. Once he heard the closest one confirm their status, Matsuda said, "OP-5, both tangoes down."

"We're going to have a talk about this later,"

Testaverde said with faux-disappointment.

"Oh, I'm sure," Matsuda said.

Once the final OP checked in, McKinney said, "All other OPs, hold position. OP-5, move to your secondary position."

"Roger that," Matsuda said. "Oscar Mike." He retracted his Remington's bipod legs, slung the precision rifle over his shoulder, and grabbed his patrolling rifle, an M4 SOPMOD Duracoated in a desert camouflage pattern, equipped with a Knights Armament sound suppressor and a Trijicon Advanced Combat Optical Gunsight. Matsuda took a knee and waited on Testaverde. After a moment, he glanced over his shoulder and said, "Now would be good, Al."

"Bitch, bitch, bitch," Testaverde said. "That's all you ever do." He finished slinging his rifle and shouldered his patrol rifle. "All right. Lead us out."

* * *

BRAD PERRY AND SCOTT Burton were hard at work. Perry would shred the paperwork, then hand the shreds to Burton to be tossed into the fireplace. While this was a tedious task, it was far more pleasant and less physically and mentally draining than the duty that led to the clean-up. They knew every task was important, and while their duty was not as dangerous as that of those who had moved on past the compound, it was no less critical that the task be done to thorough completion.

Perry was an average-looking yet strapping young man, three inches shy of six feet with dirty-blond shaggy hair, a thick beard, and tanned skin encompassing a sinewy physique. Burton was a big man, a full half-foot taller than Perry, with fair skin, red hair, and a handlebar moustache. Perry had done time in the Marine Corps, while Burton was a former star football player at Texas A&M. Both had walked a philosophical path that led them to this compound, and for a while, both had proven themselves to be amongst the top candidates for the end game.

Then, like any other sports team or military unit, both Perry and Burton suffered injury. Burton's had come from taking a wrong step during a hike and twisting his ankle. Perry's knee had blown out during a sprint. Both would heal, given time, but they would be liabilities if they were allowed to accompany the main group. Originally, their duty was to maintain appearances that all was normal and to supervise the rotation of work and the guard shifts. It was when they learned of the security breach that their roles expanded in weight.

"How are we looking?" Burton asked.

"We're on the last box," Perry said. His nose wrinkled, and he looked to the refuse in the corner of the room. "Just wish we could get rid of that stench."

"For all we know, the pigs have eyes on us," Burton said. "We do anything out of the ordinary now, they'll move on us and have us dead to rights. We get rid of this paperwork first, then we can see about cleaning up in here."

"Right." Perry sighed as he fed another document

into the shredder. "Nasty work."

"Revolution often is," Burton said. "The occupational government didn't grow so massive overnight or without considerable bloodshed. It won't be taken down overnight or without considerable bloodshed."

"I know," Perry said. "The fuckers aggressed upon us with their wars-for-profit and their police state. I don't feel bad about killing them. I just wish there was a cleaner way. I don't like war, man."

"That's what separates us from them," Burton said. "We don't crave war or bloodshed. We only do it when there is no other choice, and honestly, we have been long overdue for an insurrection."

"Yeah," Perry said. "Just wish we were there with Rothbard."

"I know," Burton said. "Trust me. I know. But we can help him here." He tossed another bucket of shredded documents into the fireplace, grabbed a bottle of lighter fluid, and squirted it into the fire to feed it. "Almost done?"

"Half a box more," Perry said. His eyes glanced over the paper as it disappeared into the shredder. It was a bank account statement. What he found as he shredded the documents was that none of them on their own posed any sort of significant threat to their organization, but when pieced together, they formed a clear picture that law enforcement could use to oppress them and others like them. There was no telling what law enforcement knew, how badly their organization had been compromised.

Perry looked across the room to the source of the

compromise. "Statist piece of shit," he grunted.

"Yeah, fuck that asshole," Burton agreed. "C'mon. Step it up, brother."

* * *

CLIVE HERMAN WAS NO stranger to high-risk warrant service. The Chicago native was always something of an adrenaline junkie, opting to drop out of college after earning his associate's and join the Chicago Police Department. Long nights on patrol and longer days in college to finish his degree paid off, and earned him the bachelor's degree he needed to join the FBI. Four years in North Dakota made Herman question his decision, but his ASAC talked him into trying out for HRT. He worked his way up the chain and was now an assault team leader.

It was rare that HRT was authorized to revert to its old *modus operandi* of kill first and investigate later, but the CIRG team leader had signed off on it from the start. Eight suspects were dead, killed with laser precision, and as Herman led his team to the front door of the main cabin, he registered in the back of his head that there would be an uproar from the anti-law enforcement types.

The thought left as quickly as it came. Herman's focus was on the lime green world provided by his AN/PVS-14 night observation device attached to his Modular Integrated Communication Helmet. He peered through the EOTech 552 attached to his 10.5" barreled M4 carbine. Through his NODs, he could clearly see the EOTech's circular reticule.

Herman and his team reached the back door of the main house. He and the man behind him, Rawlings, took the left side of the door, while the last two men, Jameson and Banner, set up on the right side of the door. Windows on both sides of the door prevented them from remaining in a single stack, but thousands of hours in the kill house conditioned them to adapt to their surroundings without conscious thought.

Herman heard voices through the door, but he could not make out what they said.. He also smelled smoke and heard the cackle of a fire. He raised his support hand to his throat mic and keyed up. "Red Six, this is Two-Six. In position. You've got at least two tangoes on the other side of the door and there's something burning. How copy?"

"Solid copy," McKinney said. "Stand by."

Another voice said, "Red Six, One-Six. In position."

"Roger."

"Red Six, Three-Six. In position."

"Roger."

"Red Six, Four-Six. In position."

There was another pause. "Roger, solid copy."

"Red Six, this is OP-1," Matsuda said. "We are on-site at Position Bravo. We've got eyes on all points."

The announcement quickened Herman's pulse. He gripped his carbine a little tighter as he waited on McKinney. Four seconds later, he heard the words.

"All points, this is Red Six. I have control. Stand by. Five…"

Herman tapped his helmet three times with a closed fist. Rawlings moved from behind Herman and removed a roll of explosive tape from his vest. The first bit of adhesive was already exposed. Rawlings put the tip of the roll at the top of the door and unfurled the charge from top to bottom. Once the charge was in place, he tossed away the paper strip that preserved the adhesive, then placed a radio-controlled blasting cap in the center of the charge. Rawlings then returned to the stack, detonator primed and in hand. By this time, Herman and Jameson had both removed the pins on their stun grenades and held them tight in their fists.

"Two…"

Rawlings triggered the clacker, and the walls shook as the breaching charge tore through the wooden door. As the door's remains fell, Herman and Jameson threw their flash-bangs inside. Each only had a fuse of about one and a half seconds. The room's occupants started to open their mouths to sound an alarm, but the flash-bang's package of magnesium and ammonium nitrate detonated and produced a stunning flash and a thunderous *boom*.

McKinney's voice filled the unit's ears via their headsets. "*Execute, execute, execute!*"

Herman was the first through the door. He traveled a diagonal path, with Jameson moving immediately after him and taking the opposite direction. Herman found two men about fifteen feet away from him, and both of them held Glocks in their hands. As he closed in, his thumb moved the carbine's selector switch from SAFE to SEMI and his finger moved from along the trigger well to inside it.

"*Police! Police! Get on the ground!*" Herman shouted.

"*Fuck you, statist pig!*" the bigger of the pair retorted. "*Light 'em up!*"

The big man raised his Glock. As much as Herman wanted to take them alive, both for the investigative value and for the satisfaction of giving them their day in court before being thrown into a dark hole to rot, it was not worth his life or the lives of any of his men. Herman had already lined up the EOTech's reticule on the big man's chest. The moment his arm was forty-five degrees away from being parallel to the ground, Herman's finger twitched twice. The carbine spoke, and the pair of 5.56mm hollowpoint rounds tore massive holes through the suspect's chest. The suspect did not fall, so Herman transitioned his point of aim to the head. One final round tore through the suspect's forehead, and he finally fell. Herman turned to address the second threat, but found that Rawlings already killed the man. Both of them fanned out to clear the rest of the room.

"Clear!" Banner called from across the room.

"Clear!" Rawlings called.

"Boss…" The voice was Jameson's. "You might want to come take a look at this."

Herman looked to Rawlings and Banner. "Go relieve Alpha Team in the front of the house. We'll hold down the fort."

Rawlings nodded, then moved to the connecting doorway. "Friendlies coming through!"

"Come through!" the operators in the front room said.

Herman turned off his NODs, reached for the nearest light switch, and flipped it on. The room was some sort of study, with plenty of animal heads and a fireplace. The two dead suspects lay atop of a pile of mostly shredded paperwork, their facial expressions blank. Just past them, the fireplace roared, fueled by destroyed evidence. Herman was not concerned with that. The CIRG guys would sift through that and develop anything actionable from it. It was Jameson's tone that concerned him. When he turned around and made his way across the room, he saw why.

The man was in his forties. Long, frizzy, orange hair, not unlike Herman's, was pulled into a ponytail. The man's goatee was thick and chest-length. His shirt had been torn from his body. "Thoroughbred" and "Irish Stock" were tattooed in a circle in Old English print. Several cigarette burns were seared into his sinewy torso, as well as bruising to the face and ribs. Like Herman, Jameson had been a beat cop prior to joining the Bureau. Jameson had been calloused to more mundane violence through hundreds of service calls for assault and domestic violence. A dead brother in arms was every lawman's worst nightmare, but that did not account for Jameson's ghostly facial expression.

Jameson read the inquisitive look on Herman's face and answered, "Check his hands."

Herman stepped to the man's side and found the hands zip cuffed behind his back. Each of the finger and thumb tips had been removed, and then crudely cauterized to prevent bleed-out. Herman's throat dropped into his stomach, and for a split second, he allowed himself to feel gratitude that he had killed the suspect. They deserved much worse, but better they die than take the off-chance a competent lawyer would get them a light sentence.

"He's dead," Jameson said. "I already checked his pulse. Looks like shock."

Herman believed his partner, but he needed to know for himself. He removed his Nomex glove and pressed two fingers to the man's carotid artery. All he felt was cold skin. As his ear filled with the sound of all points announcing "all clear" to McKinney, Herman took a knee and looked at the man bound to the chair. Ten men were dead tonight, and it was all for naught. Knowing the man's killers were dead satisfied Herman's sense of justice, but it would not bring his brother lawman back.

After a moment, Herman cleared his throat and keyed up. "Red Six, Red Two-Six. Blowfish is down. I say again, Blowfish is DOA."

* * *

MICHAEL IRELAND WAS NOT a man given to emotional outbursts. He did his suffering in private and maintained a stiff upper lip, qualities that separated him from the kinder, gentler man of the Millennial Generation. Part of that was being calloused to the ills of the world. He knew intimately the sort of heinous acts man regularly visited upon one another. Ireland had spent the better part of nineteen years hunting bank robbers, jihadists, pedophiles, fugitive murderers, sex slavers, and every other depraved criminal he could think of.

Seeing Bart Gannon dead in the chair, tortured in his final moments, was absolutely chilling. He fought to maintain his composure. In his nearly two-decade career, Ireland had never buried a partner. Thirty-five special agents had been murdered in the line of duty since the Bureau's inception. Gannon made thirty-six, and was the first time Ireland had sent somebody out or had been tasked with bringing somebody home and failed.

Gannon had been Ireland's friend. The two men had served together several times, first on a Joint Terrorism Task Force in Baltimore in the early 1990s, then again at the Counterterrorism Division's International Terrorism Operations Section I. Their final pairing was when both had done a two-year stint at the FBI Academy in Quantico as instructors. Gannon taught interrogations and field interviews, while Ireland was an investigations instructor.

The two men were inseparable. Both were God-fearing sons of preaching men and active in politically conservative circles. About the only difference between the two was that Gannon saw nothing wrong with the occasional beer or tattoo, neither of which placed any doubt in Ireland's mind regarding Gannon's commitment to God. The consolation that Gannon was in a better place was not much consolation at all, especially when Ireland took into consideration that the group Gannon had infiltrated was still at large.

Ireland rubbed his jawline slowly. If his gun, badge, and FBI windbreaker were taken from him, he would look more like a professor or an accountant than a federal agent. While his appearance did not scream "law enforcement," it certainly also did not scream "scumbag," which was why his career's focus had been entirely investigatory. That was not a bad thing: Ireland's intellect and work ethic arguably made him the Bureau's foremost terrorism investigator. Yet, he still was not quick or smart enough to save his friend.

He placed his hands on his hips and glanced to the sky. *Our Lord in heaven, please watch over my friend, my brother, as he takes leave of this world and is returned to You. Grant me the patience and the knowledge to bring those responsible for his murder to justice. In Jesus's name, I pray, Amen.*

"You okay, boss?"

Ireland looked over his shoulder. Jaden Wilson had served with Ireland, on and off, for the past five years. Where Ireland had no prior civil service experience to the Bureau, Wilson was a former Reconnaissance Marine who saw combat in the first Gulf War. He joined the Bureau in 1996 after earning his bachelor's degree in Middle Eastern studies with a minor in Arabic. Three years later, he found his way to the Counterterrorism Division, working underneath Ireland in ITOS-I. When Ireland switched to the CIRG, Wilson followed. The two worked very well as a team, and Ireland had no doubt that Wilson had a bright future with the Bureau.

Ireland shook his head. "I'm not okay," he said. "Bart was a good man." Before Wilson could pry, Ireland said, "Get anything we can use?"

"All that's left is a series of emails," Wilson said. "They detailed what we already knew. The Liberty Brigade was making nice with cartel weapons traffickers to get their hands on Semtex. They literally shredded everything else. We have nothing on this 'Colonel Rothbard' or where the rest of them went. Everybody at the compound who knew anything is dead."

Ireland nodded once. There was no use in getting angry at the Hostage Rescue operators. He knew them to be competent and professional enough that if they took the shot, there was no other solution.

"What do we do now?" Wilson said.

Ireland shrugged. "We get Bart cleaned up, gather what we can, and we start heading home."

"And then?" Wilson pressed.

Ireland met Wilson's gaze. "They've gone to ground. Our inside man is dead, and we've got no other leads. All we can do now is wait."

Made in the USA
Lexington, KY
07 August 2017